Human
Shadow

Also by Michael D. Graves

THE PETE STONE SERIES

To Leave a Shadow
2016 Kansas Notable Book

Shadow of Death

All Hallows' Shadows
2021 Kansas Notable Book
Midwest Book Award Finalist
J. Donald Coffin Memorial Book Award

Shadows and Sorrows

————

Green Bike, a group novel
with Kevin Rabas and Tracy Million Simmons

Human Shadow

by Michael D. Graves

Meadowlark
PRESS
Emporia, Kansas, USA

Meadowlark Press, LLC
PO BOX 333, Emporia, KS 66801
Meadowlark-books.com

Cover photo by Dave Leiker
daveleikerphotography.com

FICTION / Mystery & Detective / Private Investigators
FICTION / Mystery & Detective / Historical
FICTION / Crime

Library of Congress Control Number: 2023939117

ISBN: 978-1-956578-40-9

In loving memory of Mom, who read the stories to me that opened the doors.

"Art is nothing more
than the shadow of humanity."

Henry James

Monday

July 4, 1938

1

"He didn't do it. I'm sure of it."

Ethan Alexander lowered his shaggy head and stared at his feet. I stared at Ethan and said nothing.

"He couldn't have. He couldn't. I know the man. I've known him for years."

I picked up the newspaper, Sunday's edition of the *Wichita Eagle,* and read the headline. The words MURDER and FIERY BLAZE blared in all caps. I'd read the story the day before. The police had issued all points bulletins to neighboring counties. They'd mounted a city-wide manhunt.

"He isn't capable of something like this," Ethan said.

My friend vented. I waited. I didn't agree or disagree. I listened and fought to ignore the pain and the heat. A streetcar jangled its bell and rumbled through my brain. Salty beads mustered across my brow. An unseen hand twisted the blade in my skull.

The bourbon, that bottled temptress, had wooed me the night before and turned traitor at the break of day. A rivulet of sweat ran down my back. A ceiling fan worked in tandem with an open window to stir stale air in a losing battle against summer heat.

"A man is dead," I said when Ethan paused for a breath. "A corpse is lying in the morgue. A witness ID'd the suspects."

He gave me a look I didn't care for.

"You look like hell, Pete," he said.

"Thanks," I said. "I'd hate to feel this bad and not have it show."

He grunted and spun his wheelchair to the icebox behind him. He retrieved a couple of bottles of Coors beer, uncapped them both, and slid one over the table toward me. We hoisted them in unison, a brief salute, and took long pulls on the stubby bottles. It was just what the doctor ordered. Mother's milk. Ethan loaded tobacco into a pipe and struck a wooden kitchen match. I lit a Chesterfield.

I'd first met Ethan Alexander years before when he mentored my son through graduate studies at the Municipal University of Wichita. Professor Alexander taught history. He possessed a vast knowledge of past events and stayed abreast of current news. On more than one occasion, he'd shared that knowledge with me, knowledge that helped me solve a case. He'd been a valuable ally in my work as a private investigator, but on this day I had not come to him seeking his help. On this day he needed me. Ethan Alexander needed a private eye, and when he called, I came. He was more than an ally. I considered him my friend.

We usually huddled at his desk in his campus office amid piles of papers, books, and assorted clutter, but the university was closed that day. It was the nation's birthday, its 162nd for those keeping score, so we sat at his kitchen table in the rooms he rented on the edge of campus. My original plans for the holiday included cracking a fresh pack of Chesterfields and nursing the hangover I'd earned making love to a bottle of Kentucky's finest. The hangover arrived on schedule. Nursing it would have to wait.

"Let's go over what we know," I said.

My tone suggested we stick to the facts and set emotions aside. I didn't belabor the point. Ethan understood. We went over what every citizen who read the newspapers already knew. On Saturday night, two men allegedly broke into the art studio behind the home of Terrance Hightower near Bluff and English in the

College Hill District. Hightower had been in his study listening to music on his Victrola, Mozart's forty-first and final symphony, Jupiter, according to the report. Hightower was interrupted by noises from behind his home, loud voices followed by screams. He called for his assistant, and when he got no response he left his study to investigate.

As the elderly man reached the back door, he heard loud pops. By the time he stepped out of the house, his art studio was in flames, and his assistant lay on the walkway with a gun on the ground nearby. Two men scurried off into the shadows. One man appeared to be wounded. The second man supported him with one arm. He carried an object under his other arm.

Hightower heard one man say, "Hurry, Dunlap!" They moved into the alley and disappeared behind a hedge. Hightower leaned on his cane and knelt to check on his assistant. The man was dead, shot in the chest. An engine in the alley roared to life. Tires squealed. The taillights of a pickup truck disappeared into the night.

Firemen doused the flames in the studio. Most of its contents were destroyed, several paintings and other works of art. A valuable antique vase was missing. Hightower speculated that it was the vase the fugitive was carrying.

Newspapers stated that the suspects were known to Hightower, laborers his assistant had hired to work at Hightower's art gallery in the Riverside District. Hightower had little interaction with the men known as Earl and Dunlap. Their descriptions were generic, each of medium height and build. Earl was a Caucasian, Dunlap a Negro. Hightower had once noticed a distinguishing tattoo on Earl's arm. It spelled his name in capital letters, EARL, situated over the profile of a head with two faces, one face looking left, the other looking right.

"When I read the description of that tattoo, I knew right away who the man was," Ethan said. "I know the man who wears that tattoo."

"If you know the man, you shouldn't be talking to me. You should be talking to the police."

Ethan agreed.

"Yes, I know, and I knew you'd say that. I called the police yesterday right after I read the newspaper. They've been here. I've talked to them. They questioned me. I gave them my answers."

The way he said, "I gave them my answers," made me pause. I wouldn't expect Ethan Alexander to lie, but I wondered what he'd held back from the police. Our beer bottles were empty.

Ethan held his up. "Another?"

I shook my head, not because I didn't want another beer but because another beer was exactly what I did want. I wanted another beer and another one after that. It had been that way recently. It had been that way for too long. It was time for me to stop hitting the bottle and get back into the game. What I wanted was a drink. What I needed was a clear head. The day was warm, but I needed caffeine delivered hot and strong.

"Let's have a cup of joe," I said.

Ethan mulled that for a beat.

"Okay, coffee," he said. "How about something to eat?"

Ethan's telephone call woke me early that morning. All I'd ingested since then was the bottle of Coors and several Chesterfields.

"Yeah, I could use a couple of aspirin," I said.

The coffee hit the spot. The heat stoked my insides and left me bleeding bourbon, but it brought me around. The aspirin dampened the clanging bell in my head, so I went back for seconds and swallowed a couple more.

"Tell me about the police," I said. "Tell me what you told them."

"They came here. We sat at this table. I told them what I told you. I told them I know the man, Earl. I also told them he didn't do it. They seemed unimpressed by my statement."

"Ethan, the police have a witness. The police have a body.

They have a dragnet running through the city looking for Earl and Dunlap. They'll find them. You need to get your mind around that."

I was repeating myself, but Ethan didn't seem to hear my words.

"Go ahead," I said. "What else did you talk about?"

"They asked if I knew Earl's whereabouts," he said. "I told them I didn't know where he was. I haven't seen him recently. I have an address that I gave them. They asked about the other man, Dunlap. I've never met him, and I told them that."

"They'll pick them up soon," I said, "especially if one of them is wounded."

"How can you be sure?" he said. "They may not find them. There are places to hide."

"Not for long," I said, "not in the city. What do you know about other friends, maybe a woman?"

Ethan shook his head.

"I wish I knew," he said. "We were close years ago, but our lives don't cross paths often these days. I don't know a thing about his social life or his love life. We live worlds apart. Wichita is a big town."

"Wichita isn't a big town," I said. "Wichita is a small town with a lot of people. People talk. There's a body in the morgue and art gone missing. There'll be a reward. I expect this Hightower to put up some dough. Murder and money loosen lips. Somebody will talk."

Ethan puffed on his pipe. He looked discouraged.

"Find him for me, Pete, before the police do. That's why I called you. I'll get him to surrender himself, but I have to be with him when he does. I have to talk to him first, before the cops get to him. He'll need a good lawyer. You can help with that. He's my friend, Pete. I have to help him before it's too late, if it's not too late already. I have to try."

He took a deep breath.

"You should understand that," he said. "I have to try."

My coffee cup was halfway to my lips. It didn't make it the rest of the way. I froze, then lowered it back to the saucer. Yes, I understood. I'd lost a friend, a friend who'd been framed and murdered. Ethan Alexander knew that. He knew that I understood how he felt.

"What else did you discuss?" I said.

He furrowed his brow.

"They asked how and when did we meet? How well did I know him? Why would he do something like this? There were two of them. One asked the questions. The other scratched in his book."

"What were their names?"

"I have their cards here somewhere," he said and sifted through some papers and envelopes on the table. "The senior officer asked the questions. The other man took notes."

"Uniforms or civvies?" I said.

"Coats and ties. I invited them to take off their coats, but they declined. I spotted leather straps over their shirts. Shoulder holsters?"

"Sounds right," I said.

He found their cards and handed them to me. I read names I didn't recognize.

"A guy downtown is a homicide detective, Lieutenant McCormick," I said. "He'll be involved in the investigation."

"One of them mentioned Mac."

"He'll want to talk to you," I said and rubbed my fingers across my brow. "Let's go over everything first."

He looked at me. His face brightened.

"That means you're willing to help?"

"I think we're wasting our time, but you're right, Ethan. I do understand. Even if we come up dry, we have to try. What's time to a couple of bums like you and me? No one is clamoring for a history professor in the middle of the summer. It's time you got off your butt. It's time I got my head out of mine."

There was no doubt in my mind that Earl and Dunlap were guilty, but Ethan was my friend. I would help a friend.

"Okay, we'll go over everything," Ethan said, "but I'm starved. Beer and coffee don't cut it. I need solid sustenance. Let me scrape together some chow."

"We'll eat. Then we'll talk," I said. "You're going to tell me two things."

"Two things," he said. "Go ahead."

"First, you'll tell me again what you told the police, this time with all the details."

"That's one thing," he said. "What then?"

"Then, you'll tell me everything you didn't tell the police."

2

The rooms Ethan occupied were part of a large frame house owned by a young couple. The forward thinking pair planned to fill the house with little ones over time. Their first child arrived a year earlier, so they had a small toddler, a big house, and spare rooms to rent. The husband was a carpenter by trade. The kitchen he crafted had a lowered sink and countertop to accommodate a man in a wheelchair.

Ethan placed food on the countertop and went to work. While he put together our meal, I moved down the hall. In the bathroom, I discovered further adaptations, a lowered sink and medicine cabinet along with strategically placed bars and handles to allow Ethan to use the bathtub and toilet unassisted. The floors, including those in the bedroom and study, were bare hardwood or tile. Bare floors gave the place a Spartan look. Ethan preferred floors free of carpets that might snag or drag on the chair's wheels.

Back in the kitchen, Ethan prepared cold roast beef sandwiches, thin, tender slices of meat piled atop fresh bread slathered with mustard and horseradish. A dill pickle spear topped off each sandwich. The food looked and tasted delicious. We dug in. He offered another beer, but I stayed with coffee, and he did the same.

I wasn't a drunk, but sometimes a drink helped me forget.

Sometimes it took more than one drink. A pal of mine had died some months before in a plane crash. Thoughts of his death nagged me. Dark thoughts lingered in the shadows. When ghosts haunted, I chased them with spirits, one drink after another. It was lousy therapy, and it didn't work. I needed something the booze couldn't give. I needed a reason to crawl out of the shadows.

"Go back to the beginning," I said. "You say you've known Earl for a long time."

Ethan swallowed his last bite of sandwich, wiped the corner of his mouth with a napkin, and dropped the napkin over the crumbs on his plate.

"I've known him for a long time, yes. We met in the Army, Camp Funston, a couple of eager beavers anxious to stick it to the Huns and return home heroes with medals pinned to our chests. Stupid kids."

He shook his head and drummed his fingers on the table.

"His name's not Earl," he said.

I raised my brows.

"His name is Lopez, Bobby Lopez. His father's people come from Mexico. That's part of his story. His mother's ancestors are Swedish. He favors his mother in complexion. Folks are surprised when they hear his full name. He wears that tattoo, EARL. People see that and mistake it for his name. They call him Earl, and he doesn't correct them. I even call him Earl from time to time. Don't worry. The police know all of this. I told them."

Ethan had emptied his pipe of tobacco before we ate. He set it aside and picked up an empty one lying nearby. He gathered his thoughts while he packed the pipe with tobacco. I remained silent and waited.

"Stupid kids," he said again. "We shipped out of Funston in the spring, 1918. That was twenty years ago. We thought we were two of the luckiest guys on the planet. Can you believe it? That was the time of the epidemic. We got out of camp just ahead of the flu. Many of our comrades weren't so lucky. They came down with it, but not us. We took that as a sign. We were kissed by the gods, destined for great and wonderful things.

"At first being a soldier was great and wonderful. At least it wasn't bad. We arrived in France and served as a reserve unit. Our division trained and maintained readiness, but we didn't come under heavy fire, not right away. We found time to savor a glass of *vin* with the locals and snuggle with the occasional *jeune fille*. That was high adventure for a couple of Kansas lads.

"Then that fall, the 89th Middle West Division was ordered into action. We were part of the Meuse-Argonne campaign, forty-seven days of grueling battles. We encountered incessant barrages, bullets, and bombs, all serenaded by the screams of wounded and dying men. To top it off, the flu caught up with us. We had sick soldiers, wounded soldiers, and then there were those who were silenced forever."

He paused and stared at visions only he could see.

"Meuse-Argonne. It sounds beautiful in French, doesn't it? It wasn't. It was a slice of manmade hell. That campaign brought an end to that dreaded war."

Ethan's memories took a toll on him, the dredged up nightmares rarely discussed. He went silent. I lit a cigarette and smoke curled toward the ceiling fan. As if on cue, a blast echoed in the distance. A reveler with a firecracker kicked off the nation's birthday celebration. The coffee pot had gone dry. Ethan spun his wheelchair and brought down a pair of drinking glasses from the cabinet. He grabbed an icepick and opened the top of the icebox. He used the pick to chip slivers of ice from the block and dropped the slivers into the glasses. Then, he opened the lower door of the icebox and removed a pitcher of tea. He filled the glasses and passed one over.

"Sugar? Lemon?" he said.

"This is fine, thanks," I said.

We sipped the cool beverages.

"I tried to explain my story to the cops. I wanted them to understand Bobby, but they weren't interested. 'Stick to the facts,' they said, 'stick to the facts.' You'll have to bear with me while I get this out, Pete. It's important that you understand a few things before we discuss what happened the other night."

"We have the time," I said. "Go ahead."

Another firecracker echoed, then another.

"Fighting was hell for everyone," he said. "We all suffered. I bought the blast that took my legs, at least my use of them."

He slapped his hands down on the arms of his wheelchair.

"The Army awarded me this throne for my efforts. After that campaign, the fighting ceased. We were shipped home and discharged. Bobby was released right away, but I spent time at Walter Reed before the Army cut me loose. I came home in a wheelchair. Bobby Lopez came home unscathed. That's what I thought. I was angry and frustrated. I felt sorry for myself. Why me? Why did I deserve this? I searched for answers in a bottle. Does that sound familiar? The bottle held no answers. Over time I reached an acceptance. This was the hand that fate dealt me. Moaning and cursing wouldn't change the cards. I made it home. Others did not. My remains weren't buried under French soil.

"Through it all, Bobby stayed by my side. He didn't leave. He hung around the hospital in D.C. until I was released. Then, he followed me to Wichita. He stayed close for a time, but he felt adrift. I sensed it. When I enrolled at the university, Bobby enrolled, too. He never finished a class. His head wasn't in the game, as you like to say. He was wasting his time, and I told him so. I thought he was hanging around because he felt sorry for me. That angered me. I wanted him to move on, live his own life."

Ethan stopped and held another match to his pipe. The sky was dark. Fireworks blasted in the distance. A realization hit me.

"Bobby Lopez is the reason you're in that wheelchair," I said.

Ethan pursed his lips.

"The Germans called their weapon stielhandgranate," he said.

"In English it means stick hand grenade. We called it potato masher. One of those devil toys sailed into our trench. It plopped into the mud behind a soldier who never saw it coming. All I saw was a potato masher and a pair of legs. I leapt forward and body blocked the guy into next week. We tumbled into the mud, me on top, him underneath. I caught enough of the blast to put me in this chair. The other soldier was uninjured. That soldier was Bobby Lopez.

"Bobby fell under me and didn't get a scratch. I no longer walked. *C'est la guerre.* They awarded me the Distinguished Service Cross and a Wound Chevron. Those are nice honors, but every grunt in those trenches deserved as much."

"That was a real act of bravery," I said. My words sounded anemic. "I'm sure Lopez was grateful."

"Yes, he was grateful, too grateful I thought. I mistook his gratitude for pity. I didn't want pity, his or anyone else's. I was wrong, though, about Bobby Lopez. He had other problems.

"When we got back to the states, I wanted to let go of the war. I wanted to carry on with my life. It took time, but I came to my senses. I quit feeling sorry for myself. I put what happened in France behind me. When I expected Lopez to do the same, I discovered that he couldn't. That war changed Bobby Lopez—up here."

Ethan tapped his temple with his forefinger.

"He was wasting his time in Wichita, so he returned home to Lindsborg. He enrolled at Bethany College and struggled there, too. He finally opened up to me. He told me about the ringing in his ears, about how he often forgot little things, how he couldn't concentrate or hold a thought. He had trouble reading. No wonder he struggled in the classroom. He couldn't sleep. The man was nervous, anxious, and he jumped at the slightest noise."

Another barrage of fireworks went off.

"Even now, all these years later, he still dreads the Fourth of July. He hates fireworks. He can't abide the noise. I can't walk, but

I do sleep at night. I don't flinch when I hear a firecracker blast. My injuries are visible. You can't see Bobby's. No matter. His injuries are every bit as real as mine."

"What did he do?" I said.

"He visited a doctor. Fat lot of good that did. The doc prescribed pills to help Bobby relax, let him sleep. That was all he did for him. Bobby wasn't alone with his affliction. Other soldiers returned after the war with similar symptoms, both here and across the pond. A British psychologist gave it a name, shell shock, and claimed it could be treated over time. Other doctors pooh-poohed the psychologist, especially in this country. They called it yellow fever—cowardice. Bobby Lopez was not a coward, not then, not now. Neither are those other men who struggled with shell shock. They carry no scars. They look unscathed, but they're not. They were wounded just as I was wounded, and not one of them was awarded a Chevron."

"What happened then?" I said.

"Bobby was ready to leave Bethany College. The bookwork was just too much for him. He couldn't concentrate. A counselor at the college recommended an art appreciation class. He sensed Bobby's intelligence and thought he might do well with visual studies, something that required less reading. It turned out that counselor was correct. He took the art class.

"Bobby loved art. He came alive and thrived. Art opened doors to other parts of Bobby's mind and closed doors to darker recesses. The occasional nightmare still calls but nothing like before."

I didn't discount Ethan's explanation of Bobby's behavior or the effects of shell shock, but nothing he said pointed to the innocence of the two suspects. Nothing Ethan told me was proof that Lopez and Dunlap hadn't committed a crime. I started to speak. Ethan raised a hand.

"One moment, Pete. It's important you know more about Bobby. Art became his love. It didn't cure his problems, but it helped him cope. Are you familiar with Birger Sandzén?"

"I've seen some of his work. He's an artist. Swedish isn't he?" I said.

"That's right. He teaches at Bethany College. His full name is Sven Birger Sandzén. He's highly respected both as an artist and an educator. His work is internationally admired. He instills in his students the importance of order and quality of life, fundamentals of great art, fundamentals missing in Bobby's life. Bobby thrived under the man's tutelage. I spoke to Sandzén by telephone years ago. He described Bobby's talent as raw and his passion as fiery.

"Bobby admired Sandzén's patience and calm demeanor. The artist's bold landscapes soothed Bobby's mind. Those were good years. Then he completed his studies in Lindsborg and needed to make a living. Art helped him cope, but it didn't pay the bills. He had no desire to work on the farm, so he came back to Wichita.

"He found work, odd jobs, and managed to survive. He continued to study art. He paints. He listens to music. Music brings peace. He doesn't make much money, but he gets by."

"This doesn't change what went down Saturday night," I said. "Someone fired a gun. You can't be sure it wasn't Bobby Lopez."

"I'm telling you that it couldn't have been Bobby Lopez. Bobby could not have fired a gun. He is not capable of firing a gun."

I was a lousy poker player. The doubt and disbelief showed on my face. I understood why the cops were unmoved by Ethan's account. He read my expression.

"The cops wouldn't listen to this," he said. "I tried to tell them."

"The cops wouldn't give two red cents for a word of it," I said. "Your story proves nothing of Lopez's innocence."

"There's something else," he said. "In France, during the lulls in fighting, soldiers swapped stories in the trenches, stories about our lives back home. Bobby loved to hunt. I was a hunter, too. We reminisced about those crisp dawns back home, stomping through cornrows, a retriever on the scent, coming upon a pheasant rooster or a covey of quail. We looked forward to returning to those times. We planned to swap our rifles for shotguns and bag some birds together.

"That never happened. After the war, Bobby swore off firearms. He declared he would never fire a gun again. He said he couldn't be around guns. He made a promise twenty years ago, a vow I know he's kept."

"Maybe he did make that promise," I said. "That was twenty years ago. People change. Also, he wasn't alone. Dunlap could have been armed. Maybe he fired the gun."

Ethan wouldn't buy it.

"No, Bobby would have known if his partner had a gun," he said. "He wouldn't have allowed it. They worked together before, remember. Bobby would have known if Dunlap was armed."

"Someone shot that man," I said. "An eye-witness fingered the pair."

"Yes, someone shot that man," he said.

We sipped tea. Ethan had more to say. I gave him time before he continued.

"Something else happened, something strange. A visitor called on me Saturday night."

"Why do I suppose you withheld this from the police?"

"It never came up," he said. "It was getting late. I was awake, sitting right at this table sipping a glass of tea as a matter of fact. There was a knock at the door."

Ethan indicated a door over his shoulder.

"I opened it. When I did, a man backed away. He stood in the porchlight, barely visible. He fidgeted in the shadows, hopping from foot to foot, dressed in tatters and dark as midnight."

"Dunlap?" I said.

"I don't think so. This man spoke in rhymes, doggerel."

A memory crept into mind. Hairs tingled on the back of my neck.

"Doggerel?"

"That's right. 'The man says give you a holler. The man says you give me a dollar. The man says he don't shoot. The man says don't want no loot.' Those were his exact words. I asked him to repeat them. He did, word for word."

It was my turn to stare at the table.

"Are you okay, Pete?" he said. "You look like you've seen a ghost."

"What happened then?" I said.

"Well, I was bewildered. Who was this strange man, and who told him to say those things? Remember, this was Saturday night, before the story was in the newspaper. I knew nothing about the shooting. I was in the dark. Like I said, he repeated his riddle exactly, just as I recited it. When he finished speaking he waited in the shadows."

"What did you do?"

"What could I do? I fished a dollar bill out of my pocket, and an arm reached forward. He wrapped a bony fist around the bill and took off. That was it. He disappeared into the shadows like a wisp of smoke."

Tuesday

July 5, 1938

3

I sat at my desk, alone in my office. It was early, and Agnes, my assistant, hadn't arrived yet. I sipped black coffee and mulled over my meeting with Ethan Alexander the day before. The cops hadn't wanted to hear details about Ethan's friendship with his war buddy. They wanted the facts, just the facts. That was no surprise. Ethan's judgment was clouded by his loyalty to his friend. I was convinced that the suspects were guilty.

I ran through the details of our conversation in my mind. I fought to stay focused. My mind drifted. The cops were on the lookout for suspects ID'd by a witness. They'd tighten their net over the city. In a matter of days, they'd haul in the fish. If the fish fought back, their execution would be swift. I hoped to prevent that.

Ethan had told me more than he'd told the cops. I wondered if he'd told me everything. I thought about that, but something else nagged at me, something that had nothing to do with the case. An itch in my brain told me I'd forgotten something. What was it?

I soon got my answer. A tap at the door interrupted my thoughts. Agnes stuck her head into my office.

"Well, good morning, stranger," she said. "I'm glad to see you're alive and well. I was beginning to worry."

"Why the worry?" I said. "Here I am, same as always."

"So, what happened yesterday?" she said.

"Yesterday? Why do you ask?"

"We missed you," she said. "I was concerned. I hoped you weren't a casualty of too much celebration."

I raised an eyebrow.

"You know, too much drinking," she said and dropped her head back. She mimed tipping a glass.

"Agnes, sweetheart, connect the dots for me," I said. "What are you talking about?"

"You forgot didn't you?" she said. "You and Lucille were supposed to meet us last night, remember? Percy and me at the stadium? We waited for you until it got dark. We finally gave up and went on in. Lucille called me at home this morning and said you never showed up at her place. I figured you'd had too much to drink and weren't able to answer the bell. Shame on you. You'd better give her a call. She's steamed."

I groaned and swore, "Dammit. It slipped my mind."

"So, you were drunk," she said.

I shook my head and felt stupid. Wichita service clubs, Rotarians, DAR, and others had sponsored a July 4th fireworks display held at Lawrence Stadium the previous evening. A large crowd was anticipated. The stadium boasted a recent expansion, and officials were eager to show off the accommodations.

When we left the office on the previous Friday, Agnes suggested that Lucille and I meet her and her husband, Percy, outside the stadium and attend the show together. Then, Ethan Alexander telephoned the morning of the fourth, and I ended up at his kitchen table listening to his story well into the night. My date with Lucille slipped my mind.

"Pete, are you okay?" she said. "I'm worried about you. Were you drinking yesterday?"

"No, kiddo, I wasn't drunk. I sipped iced tea with an old friend and lost track of time. As matter of fact, I was working on a case yesterday, but that's no excuse. I am sorry. Give my apologies to Percy, too. I completely forgot about our plans. You're right. I have to call Lucille."

"I doubt if a phone call will do the trick, Pete. She's really upset. I accept your apology, but you won't get off that easily with Lucille. You owe her more than that."

"Noted."

"Tell me about the case," she said. "Who's the old friend?"

We went over my visit with Ethan Alexander. I used the opportunity to review my notes. Ethan and I chatted through the early evening and into the night. He related more stories about his friend and turned to events after the war. We sipped tea until the pitcher ran dry, then we toasted our nation's birth with two fingers of bourbon, one drink each. When the sounds of fireworks abated, we called it a night.

"Shell shock. I've heard about shell shock," Agnes said.

"Ethan told me that Lopez had difficulties concentrating," I said. "He struggled to read. He enrolled in art classes after the war. His studies quieted his mind. Art led to music. Lopez turned to music for solace, classical music, jazz, the blues. He visited art museums. Eventually, he regained the ability to read. He read literature. He studied subjects that gave him pleasure. He read books and magazines on art and music.

"Appreciation of the arts brought a calm to Lopez that had eluded him since the war. Ethan thinks Lopez's interest in art led him to seek employment at Hightower's gallery. That may be true. It also may not be true. The police will speculate that getting a job at the gallery fell right into Lopez's plans. They'll figure he plotted the whole thing, first getting the job and then stealing the art, and ended up bungling the attempt."

I handed Agnes a photograph Ethan had given me, two soldiers in uniform mugging for the camera.

"That was taken in France," I said, "twenty years ago. That's Ethan on the left before his injury. The lad next to him is Bobby Lopez."

Agnes studied the photo and handed it back.

"They look so young, not more than boys," she said.

"There's something else," I said. "Ethan had a visitor Saturday night. A stranger knocked at the door, a man who lurked in the shadows and spoke in rhymes and riddles."

"Oh, Pete," she said. "Do you think Rum-Rum is involved in this?"

"He fits the description," I said.

The character in question, Rum-Rum, was an enigma. Little was known about the man. I'd met him on a prior occasion. Our encounter was brief. However, that encounter saved my life.

Rum-Rum lived on the streets. He haunted the cracks and the crevices of the city, an invisible entity who emerged without warning from the shadows and disappeared as quickly, like a wisp of smoke in Ethan's words. He made his home in alleyways, beneath porches, wherever he could find a quiet spot. He laid his head down where it suited his fancy. He shopped in dumpsters.

This mysterious man had once saved my skin. A cop killer had roamed the city. I got involved in the case. In the middle of a gun battle, when the killer drew a bead on me, a cry came from the shadows. That cry saved me from a bullet. Rum-Rum's alarm saved my life. Then, he disappeared. Since that dark, rainy night, I hadn't seen or heard of the man.

"I want to bring Ralph Waldo in on this," I said. "Give him a call and see if he's available."

"Will do," Agnes said. "You might call Lucille. It won't fix things, but it would be a start."

Agnes left my office. I reached for my telephone and took a breath. I dialed Lucille's number on my private line. The telephone rang a half-dozen times. No answer. Then, I remembered the date. On Tuesday mornings Lucille visited the beauty parlor.

I tapped the cradle with a finger and got a ringtone. I dialed the police station. A female voice told me that Lieutenant

McCormick was out of the building. She asked if I would like to leave a message. I declined. I didn't want to leave a message. I thanked her and cradled the receiver. Agnes returned to my office.

"I got no answer at Ralph's number," she said. "I tried it twice."

"I struck out, too," I said and glanced down at my feet. "Looks like I need a shoeshine."

My shine man kept his stand in the Hotel Eaton just down the block at the corner of Douglas and St. Francis. I left my office on the third floor of the Lawrence Block Building at Douglas and Emporia. It was a short walk.

The shine man had almost no formal education. He was also one of the most intelligent men I'd ever known. His parents were former slaves who moved north after the Civil War. His father never learned to read, but his mother taught herself. She learned by reading yellowed newspapers to her son.

The boy listened. As he grew, his thirst for the printed word grew with him. He recognized that reading opened doors to places he'd never reach otherwise. Before long, he read newspapers to his mother, then magazines and books and anything else he could find. When her hair turned gray and her eyesight failed, his mother rocked in her chair and listened to her son. He read poetry and prose alike, borrowed from the city library.

The shine man's name was Ellis Waldo. No one called him Ellis. He went by Waldo. His son, Ralph Waldo, was who Agnes tried to reach that morning. Like his father, Ralph Waldo had a quick mind. He also had a quick temper. He tangled with the law in his youth. When he matured and promised to go straight, I encouraged him to become a private investigator.

Ralph was reluctant to go into the business. He figured that a man with dark skin would face challenges as a detective. I assured him that he would face challenges. Doors would slam in his face. That came with the job. I also assured him he would pass through doors that slammed in my face. He thought that over. Sometimes

Negroes were shunned. Sometimes they were ignored, simply not noticed. Maybe he could turn that to his advantage.

Ralph began working for me, unlicensed at first. He hung out, listened, and gathered information, strictly on the Q.T. He observed, took notes, and remained silent, unnoticed. He listened and learned. Ralph Waldo, Ellis's son, invisible man. He took to the work. Before long, he got his license and opened his own agency.

I stepped through the door of the Hotel Eaton. The clamor of the street fell away. I passed through the lobby arrayed with plush sofas and over-stuffed chairs. Hushed voices replaced the squeals of brakes and horns. Only brick and glass separated pillars and carpet from concrete and asphalt, but pedestrians and motorists existed miles away.

Patrons in suits and dresses lounged beneath lazy ceiling fans that whisked away fumes from cigarettes, pipes, and Cuban cigars. Across the floor, the hotel dick caught my eye and gave me the high sign. I touched the brim of my fedora and walked on.

I passed the front desk and went down a hallway. A gentleman on my right made a purchase at the tobacco shop. A customer occupied the chair in the barbershop. The barber raised his clippers and grinned as I went by his window. Just beyond the shop, a man sat on a stool with his back to me. His gray head was tipped forward, his nose in a book. He sensed my presence, marked his place in his book, and turned to greet me.

"Well, Mr. Stone, how good to see you," he said. "I didn't expect to see you today."

His grin extended into his crinkled eyes.

"Hello, Waldo."

We shook hands, and I climbed into the chair.

"What's the book?" I said.

He reached for a brush and buffed dust from my shoes.

"It's a collection of short stories by William Sydney Porter," he said.

"O. Henry," I said.

"That's right."

He dipped the fingers of one hand into the polish and worked the polish into the leather.

"Reading passes the time between customers."

"The Gift of the Magi," I said. "One of my favorites."

"Yes, that's a good one," he said. "That one always gets me to thinking. The story is sad, you know. At the same time, it's funny and absurd. It saddens me and makes me laugh, too. That's life, I suppose. We never know, do we?"

"No we don't. Waldo, I've been trying to reach Ralph. No one answered his phone. Is he around?"

"Aha," he said.

"What's 'aha' mean?" I said.

Waldo looked up from his work and grinned.

"It's always good to see you, Mr. Stone," he said. "You know that, and I'm grateful for your business. But I put a shine on this leather just the other day. You usually wait a spell before you climb into my chair again. I figured something must be on your mind today, other than a shine, that is."

"I guess Ralph isn't the only detective in your family," I said.

Waldo chuckled.

"He'll have his legs under our dinner table this evening. He took a little trip up to Kansas City. He said he had a hankering for jazz and barbecue. That was his story, anyway."

"Kansas City, jazz, and barbecue. That sounds good," I said.

"Yes it does, but we have jazz and barbecue right here in Wichita," Waldo said. "No, there's something more. I suspect a lady is involved." He laughed and said, "I'll see him tonight. I'll tell him to give you a call."

"Thanks, Waldo."

"K.C.'s all right, I suppose," he said. "It's been a long time since I was there. The missus and I haven't left town for quite a spell. No reason to go out of town. We have all we need right here."

He wiped my shoes with his rag and grew thoughtful.

"It's funny getting old," he said. "The days roll by gently. The older I get the less I need. The more satisfied I am with what I have. Our family's grown. Money isn't the worry it once was. I finally have the wherewithal to go and do, but I lack the desire. I could afford to take time off, yet here I sit, day after day. It's funny, isn't it? Maybe a bit absurd?"

He popped his rag and chuckled.

"Not so funny," I said. "You like what you do, and it shows. You're good at what you do, Waldo."

"I have no complaints, no sir. My folks did what they could do for us. They provided for us all, brothers and sisters and me, until we were grown, then they nudged us out of the nest. They suffered plenty, but they laughed a lot, rest their souls."

"They came from Tennessee," I said.

"That they did. They never spoke about those days, though. They put those days behind them. They got their freedom, and they left that life. They buried those memories deep inside. They never spoke about their lives before Kansas. They never complained, either. Who'd listen if they did? They were young and full of hope, determined to marry and raise a family in a free state. That's what they did. They settled in Wichita and never left. Neither did this child.

"Other people came from the south and established communities, too. Some of those communities thrived. Others struggled and failed. Kansas is sprinkled with settlements founded by former slaves."

Waldo popped his rag one last time and leaned back. I admired his work. The leather gleamed.

"I'm just an ordinary Joe hustling to make a dollar," I said, "but your shine makes me feel like a million bucks. Thanks, Waldo."

We settled up. Waldo repeated his promise to have Ralph call. I moved away from his stand, and he reached for his copy of O. Henry stories. The tobacco shop was idle. A young lady waited at the counter. I touched the brim of my fedora and asked for a pack of Chesterfields. She handed over my cigarettes and flashed a smile that was the real McCoy.

I left the Hotel Eaton and stepped back into the city bustle, fortified by a shoeshine and a young lady's smile. One city block later, I entered the Lawrence Block Building, climbed three flights of stairs, and reached the door that read "Pete Stone Private Investigator" on pebbled glass.

I turned the knob, walked in, and froze. A blonde stood in front of Agnes's desk, her back to the door. The blonde turned and faced me.

"So, there you are," she said.

She fixed a cool glare on me.

"Hello, Lucille," I said.

Behind Lucille, Agnes waved her arms and pointed to her hair. Then, she pointed to Lucille.

"You look lovely," I said. "Your hair is beautiful."

"Thanks, Romeo," she said. She held her glare. "Thank you, too, Agnes."

Agnes rolled her eyes and shook her head.

"I'm sorry, sweetheart," I said. "I have no excuse. I forgot about our date. It slipped my mind. Mea culpa. I throw myself on the mercy of the court."

"Ha, mercy of the court. The jury is out on you, buster," she said. "Agnes just explained you were on a case. Fair enough, you had other things on your mind. That's still no reason not to call me. A simple telephone call. That would have been nice."

"You're right. Let me make it up to you," I said and glanced at the Seth Thomas banjo clock on the wall. "Let me take you to lunch. How about it?"

Her glare didn't soften.

"Thank you, no," she said. "I've had a better offer."

Agnes pulled her purse out of a drawer and stood up. She came around her desk. The two ladies moved toward the door, noses in the air. Each wore a smirk. I stepped aside. Agnes stepped through the door with Lucille on her heels.

The door closed behind them.

4

College Hill, a neighborhood located east of downtown, was christened when the Methodists proposed building a college there some years earlier. The Methodists ended up building their college in another town, but the name stuck. Real estate speculation prompted growth. The residential area was noted for tree-lined streets and upscale homes.

I headed east on Douglas with the top down on my Jones roadster. A flower shop near the intersection with Hillside caught my eye. I pulled over. I had some work to do to get back into Lucille's good graces.

A bell tinkled above the door, and a matronly lady with gray hair and gold rimmed spectacles came from the back carrying a fistful of daisies.

"Good morning," she said. "What's the occasion?"

"You get right to it," I said. "I admire that."

"You look like a man in a hurry," she said. "Birthday? Anniversary?"

"I need something for my gal," I said, "no occasion."

"Well, there's nothing like a red rose to say I love you," she said. "It's traditional, but it never goes out of style."

"I think I'm going to need more than a single rose," I said. "I stood her up on a date."

"Yes, I see your point," she said. "That wasn't very nice of you."

"I didn't intend to stand her up," I said. "I just forgot about our date."

"Oh, dear. That's even worse, forgetting about her. There's nothing worse than being forgotten," she said. "You'd better go with a dozen roses, and you'd better have them delivered this day. Don't worry. Leave it to me. I'll take care of everything."

The lady knew her business. I gave her Lucille's address, settled up, and left.

Bluff intersected English near the Wichita Country Club. Across the grassy expanse lay a pool and bathhouse built the year before with WPA funds. In the distance, portly gentlemen decked out in plus fours and tams gathered around a putting green. Caddies shouldered golf bags and hovered at their elbows.

My roadster rumbled over brick streets that led to a Tudor-style home nestled beneath towering oaks and maples. I pulled over in a shady spot along the curb. A circular driveway extended beneath a peaked porte-cochere at one end of the home. No automobile was in sight. The structure's design featured timber and stone, dark shingles, and enough windows to keep a cleaner in beans and bacon for days. I cut the engine on the roadster and left it parked in the shade. At the top of the driveway, I stepped beneath a smaller peak, a younger brother to the one over the porte-cochere, and rang the bell. My summons went unanswered. No automobile. No answer. No surprise.

I stepped onto the grass and strolled toward the back of the house, pausing to peep through a window. There were no signs of activity inside. The backyard was surrounded by a wrought iron fence. I entered through a gate. The charred remains of the art studio stood near a shrub hedge that ran along the back fence. The studio's stone walls matched those of the home before they were blackened with soot. A shard of shingled roof remained in one corner. A dark spot stained the walkway in front of the studio.

A dog barked from a neighboring yard. A female voice called out, "Lily!" I strolled over to the fence and looked down at a French poodle, a white specimen coiffed in all the right places. The little gal stuck her nose through the wrought iron spires and wagged a ball of fluff.

"*Bonjour*, Lily," I said.

Lily barked again. Her mommy arrived.

"Lily!" she said.

I tipped my fedora to the lady over the fence and repeated my greeting.

"*Bonjour.*"

The lady gave me a puzzled look.

"You look like a cop," she said. "Whatever you are, you certainly don't look French."

Her comment sounded like an insult. *C'est la vie.*

"I'm a private investigator," I said.

Lily barked again. The lady told her to hush.

"Neighbors get testy when they hear a dog bark. Actually, neighbors get testy when they hear most anything. This is a quiet neighborhood, emphasis on quiet," she said.

I raised an eyebrow and glanced over my shoulder toward the burnt hull of the studio and the stained walkway. Her gaze followed mine.

"Yes, that," she said. "Quiet except for that."

"I was hoping to meet Mr. Hightower," I said. "He seems to be away."

"He's probably at his gallery across town," she said. "Did you have an appointment?"

I ignored her question and asked my own.

"Did you see anything Saturday night?" I said. "Or did you hear anything? It must have been loud. Maybe you heard the commotion?"

"Yeah, I heard something, all right. I heard my mother-in-law complain about the pot roast I cooked. I also heard her ask me if I was putting on weight. Some nerve. I should've smacked her, but she's getting up there, you know. The old gal doesn't know any better. We weren't home Saturday night. Jim, that's my husband, Jim and I spent the evening with his folks. We took supper. Can you believe it? Night after night we sit at home and stare at the walls and listen to the radio and nothing happens. Then, the one night we go out, bam, we miss all the hullabaloo. The only one at home on Saturday night was Lily here."

Lily heard her name and barked.

"She may have heard something," the lady said. "My hubby and I didn't know a thing about your commotion until we read it in the Sunday newspaper."

"Have you talked to anyone, another neighbor perhaps, who saw or heard anything?"

"No, I haven't spoken to the neighbors. We aren't the chummiest group."

"Well, I appreciate your time," I said and touched the brim of my hat. *"Merci."*

"How about it, Frenchie?" she said. "Tell me. Do I look fat?"

That was a conversation I didn't want to have.

"Mais non, Madame!" I said.

"Good answer," she said.

"Au revoir," I said.

I walked to the house on the other side of Hightower's place. The door opened on the first ring. A woman in a white uniform read my card and shook her head when I asked my questions.

"Sorry, I'm a day nurse," she said. "I wasn't here Saturday night. Miss Devlin was home, but she didn't hear anything."

The nurse seemed sure of that.

"There was gunfire and shouting," I said. "There was quite a racket. I'd like to speak to Miss Devlin myself. May I see her?"

"You'd be wasting your time," she said.

"Time is all I have."

The woman deliberated for a moment, then chuckled.

"Why not?" she said and stepped back. "Come on in."

The nurse ushered me into a dimly lit parlor where a small woman sat in a large chair and nodded her white head. Summer heat in the room was oppressive, but the windows remained closed. A lap quilt covered the frail woman's legs. The nurse handed Miss Devlin my card. I extended my hand.

"Hello, Miss Devlin."

She rested a weightless hand in mine.

"I'm Pete Stone."

From beneath her quilt, Miss Devlin produced a brass ear trumpet. She placed the tapered end into her ear.

"Eh?"

I leaned over the cone and spoke.

"Pete Stone," I said.

She raised her eyebrows. I spoke into the cone again, loudly.

"Pete Stone!"

Her eyes widened.

"Tea and scones? No, thank you, dear. I just had lunch."

Over my shoulder, the nurse in white struggled to contain herself. She could have struggled harder. She lost the battle and burst out laughing. I thanked Miss Devlin for her time and left.

Back at Hightower's place, I stood in the yard and tried to visualize the scene that unfolded Saturday night. The suspects parked their pickup truck in the alley. They arrived and departed together in the one vehicle. They labored under the direction of Hightower's assistant. Those three men had a working relationship at the studio behind the house and at Hightower's art gallery located across town. Those men knew each other. What happened Saturday night? What led to the altercation?

Something on the side of the house caught my eye. A closer look revealed a hole in the wall outlined in chalk. I looked over my shoulder toward the alley and walked that direction. I followed the walkway past the charred remains and sidestepped the stain on the stone. A gate split the hedge. I went through the gate into the alley. I searched for a clue I didn't expect to find. A curtain fluttered in a window of the house across the alleyway. I kept my head down and paced the two-track stretch of ground.

The alley consisted of dirt and pebbles. Charred bits of paper littered one spot, remnants of fireworks left by neighborhood urchins celebrating the holiday. I strolled back and forth, then bent down and picked up a pebble. I held it up for inspection and pretended it was just what I was looking for. I put it into my pocket.

The door of the house sprang open. A male voice shouted, "What are you doing there?"

A man in wrinkled khakis and a soiled undershirt stepped out onto a porch. A patch covered one eye beneath a thatch of uncombed, gray hair. I waved at the man.

"Just looking," I said.

That didn't satisfy him. He strode toward the alley. A scowl covered a face that hadn't smiled since the Hoover administration.

"Who are you?" he said.

A scar ran from the corner of his mouth to the cleft in his chin. I offered a card. He snatched it from my hand but didn't look at it.

"Pete Stone, private investigator," I said. "Who are you?"

"None of your business," he said.

I didn't push. We wouldn't be exchanging Christmas cards.

"What're you doing snooping around here? You're not the police. I've seen you talking to my neighbors, folks too good natured to give you the bum's rush. What're you after?"

"Answers," I said. "Maybe you can help. You look like a concerned citizen. Did you see what happened here Saturday night? You must've heard gunshots."

"Yeah, sure, I heard gunshots. Lots of gunshots. One after the other. Bang, boom, bang, boom. Lots of gunshots."

That was a surprise. The newspaper reported only a few shots fired, not a barrage. That's what I told the man. The man uttered a laugh that wasn't a laugh.

"Bang, boom, bam, all night. I know what I heard, gumshoe. Could've been gunshots."

"I don't understand," I said.

"Firecrackers, moron. Little scamps blasting firecrackers. Could've been gunshots, too. I wouldn't know."

"Firecrackers? This took place Saturday night," I said, "two days before the Fourth of July."

"Don't be dense," he said. "Since when did a kid with a firecracker give a tinker's dam what day it was?"

He had me there.

"Run along, private eye," he said and waved my card under my nose. "I'm going to keep this."

"Oh, darn," I said. "I'm down to my last few hundred."

He turned on his heel and stormed off. I walked back to the house and paused at the hole in the wall outlined in chalk. I turned and looked again toward the alley and the house beyond. After a moment, I walked to the front of the house. I wasn't surprised to see an automobile parked under the porte-cochere. The one-eyed Paul Revere must have alerted Hightower to the stranger in his midst stirring up trouble. The car's engine ticked. Hightower had arrived moments before. The car was a beauty, a burgundy Cadillac convertible sporting whitewall tires and a load of polished chrome that outweighed a sumo wrestler. I paused to admire it.

"She's a runner, the only V-16 around here," a voice called out from over my shoulder.

An elderly gentleman dressed in pressed slacks and a smoking jacket leaned on a cane in an open doorway.

"You must be Mr. Hightower," I said.

"And you must be the pest who is hounding my neighbors," he said. "Who are you and what do you want?"

I walked over and handed him a card. He glanced at it. I introduced myself.

"Private, huh? Now who would hire a private dick to investigate a murder that took place in my back yard?"

"I'm not at liberty to say," I said. "I've been hired to locate one of the suspects."

He snorted.

"That means you're looking for that Earl character," he said.

"I didn't say which suspect I was looking for," I said.

"No, you didn't," he said. "I doubt anybody hired you to look for the Negro."

I didn't like his tone or his implication that only a Caucasian would hire a detective. He studied my card. I waited for him to tell me to get lost. He didn't. His brow furrowed, and his demeanor softened.

"Why don't you come inside? We'll have something cool to drink," he said.

Hightower led me into a great room and paused for me to admire the décor. So, I did. I scanned the vaulted ceiling and timber trusses and all those windows. Sunlight brightened open spaces. Shadows fell into corners and lent a sense of intimacy. Crystal chandeliers and ceiling fans dangled above. Tiffany lamps perched atop tables. Persian rugs covered the floor. Paintings lined the walls. A marble fireplace with sculpted curlicues lay dormant along one wall. Pearl-handled pistols, crossed and mounted, hung over the mantel. Hightower watched me. I pretended not to notice. Seeing that I was suitably impressed, he spoke.

"My father was raised in the states, in the south, but our ancestors hail from England. Father was proud of our heritage. After the war between the states, he left the south and came to Kansas to seek his fortune. He made money in cattle and later moved into oil, not far from this very spot. He built this home as a reminder of who we are and where we come from. This home was one of the first in this area. Enough of that. I promised you something cool to drink. I prefer lemonade at this time of day. Is that suitable?"

"Lemonade would be fine," I said.

Hightower leaned his cane against the wall and shuffled out of the room, abandoning me to its elegance. I roamed the great room and admired the paintings. A doorway led to a study. I remained in the great room and peeked through the door. Books lined the walls. An escritoire with its desktop unhinged held an open ledger book and a Burroughs adding machine. Strewn across the desk were pencils, envelopes, and paper clips. A pair of books lay atop a table near the door. The cover of one volume read, *The Rising Tide of Color Against White World-Supremacy,* by Lothrop Stoddard. Next to it was a copy of the Holy Bible.

I returned my attention to the paintings. I stopped before a depiction of the surrender ending the Civil War. Many artists had rendered that scene, but Hightower's was unusual. I studied the artwork. Hightower edged across the floor with a drinking glass in each hand. I stepped over and took the drinks while he retrieved his cane. He joined me in front of the painting, and I returned his glass of lemonade.

"My birthday," he said and gestured at the painting with the tip of his cane. "I hope this lemonade isn't too tart. Age has dwindled my sense of taste. Subtlety and nuance are wasted on my palate. Only sharp flavors will do. People my age don't die. We dwindle. We lose our smell, our taste, our eyesight, and our hearing. Everything goes in dribs and drabs."

I sipped the lemonade.

"Tart but tasty," I said.

I turned back to the painting.

"Your birthday?" I said.

"April 9, 1865, the day the doctor slapped my backside, and I announced my presence unto the world. The day General Lee surrendered to Grant at Appomattox. My father commissioned that painting and presented it to me on my twenty-first birthday. The artist never gained fame. No matter. My father admired his work. The man who painted it fought for the Confederacy. There are no prints. What you're looking at is the one and only."

Other paintings I'd seen depicted Lee and Grant standing or sitting or shaking hands, each wearing a somber expression. The scene on Hightower's wall was unusual. Lee stood in the foreground and towered over a smaller Grant who sat at a desk, arms crossed over his chest. Lee wore a haughty expression. Grant cowered.

"Let's sit," Hightower said and motioned toward chairs on either side of a low table.

An unlit cigar with a double band in gold, silver, and red lay next to an ashtray. Hightower picked it up and clipped off the end.

"I keep a supply in a humidor. Care for one?" he said.

I declined and lit a Chesterfield. Hightower reached for a gold lighter on the table with the letter 'H' embossed on its side. He held a flame to his cigar. He returned the lighter to the table, and I spotted the letter 'J' embossed on the other side.

"That's a beautiful lighter," I said.

He seemed irked by my comment and stammered a reply.

"The lighter, ah, yes," he said. "My father's. It belonged to my father, John Hightower."

He picked it up and stuffed it into a pocket. Then, he puffed on his cigar and blew smoke with a sigh.

"My doctor warned me off these," he said. "He told me to give them up. I enjoy one every day. Forbidden fruit is always the sweetest."

"I'd have to agree," I said.

"You can't buy this brand in America," he said. "A family in Cuba farms the tobacco and manufactures the cigars, a local production. I have a special arrangement with the family."

He rolled the ash to a point in the ashtray and leaned back in his chair.

"So, you're looking for one of the suspects?" he said. "That's it? That's all you've been hired to do?"

"That's all I've been hired to do," I said. "If they're together, I'll find both. If I'm successful, that is."

"Will you be successful?" he said.

"I often am. The police are looking for them, too."

"And yet someone hired you."

"And yet someone hired me. For the record, I tried to talk that someone out of it."

"If you do find them, you'll also find what they stole from me," he said. "Is there a chance you'll find those men before the police do?"

"There's always a chance. I wouldn't wager a fortune on it. The police have more men and more resources at their beck and call than a lowly gumshoe does. There's a strong possibility that they'll find them first. If they do, they do."

"Someone has faith in you. The person who hired you must have had a reason."

He waited for me to supply a reason. He'd keep waiting. I sipped lemonade.

"I suppose you're right," he said. "The police would have more resources than a lone bloodhound would."

"Why should that matter to you?" I said. "Either I'll find the men or the cops will. Either way, you should be happy."

"Not necessarily," he said.

"I didn't think so," I said. "Otherwise, I wouldn't be sitting here drinking your lemonade. Why don't you tell me what's on your mind, Mr. Hightower?"

"Those men took something that belongs to me," he said. "I want it back. I don't want it in police hands. The police will hold onto it. They'll claim it as evidence. It might get damaged in their possession, or worse yet, disappear. It's valuable. I want it returned to me."

Two suspects had been accused of murder and were on the loose. Hightower's associate lay dead. A fire destroyed Hightower's studio and the art inside. Yet, the item that earned top spot on his hit list was the return of a single piece of stolen art.

"Your assistant was murdered," I said. "The men suspected of that murder are on the lam. Shouldn't their capture be your first priority?"

Hightower didn't give me an answer. He grew defensive. His face turned red.

"Don't lecture me on my priorities, gumshoe! I can't bring that dead man back to life, nor can I replace what's been destroyed! What's done is done."

He paused for a moment to regain his composure. He scanned the walls. Then, he spoke in a normal tone.

"My art is all I have left," he said. "I'm alone with my art. I have no family. Few friends remain. People fall away. It happens. It all falls away. Art endures. Art sustains me. A valuable piece of artwork was stolen from me. I want it back."

He reached into a jacket pocket and retrieved some dough. He fanned five crisp bills and laid them on the table. Each bill bore a portrait of Benjamin Franklin.

"I wish to hire you. I want you to locate the object that was stolen from me. I want it returned," he said.

I glanced at the money and sipped my lemonade. Hightower was desperate. I was not.

"Tell me about your assistant," I said. "Who was he? The papers withheld details. They won't print anything until next of kin are notified."

"His name was Karl Weaver. I know little about him, nothing about his family or next of kin. He came from Kansas City. He was an artist, moderately successful, but his work as an artist didn't provide a living. I hired him to run my gallery. Those duties included minor restoration and cleaning as needed. He performed those tasks in the studio out back."

"Why work in the studio?" I said. "Wouldn't it be easier to do that at your art gallery?"

"That was once the case, but the gallery has flourished. We needed the floor space for showings, so we turned to the studio for other work. I built that studio myself, years ago when I dabbled in painting. I tried to paint, create my own work. My love of art did not translate into a talent for making it, however. The studio was idle, so Weaver worked there. He painted there, too, nothing of note."

"Reports say a gun was found lying next to Weaver. Did Weaver carry a gun?" I said.

"He kept a small caliber handgun on his person for security. It was found near the body. The police took it. I don't know what it was. I'm no authority on firearms. I don't own them, and I don't care for them."

I looked toward the pistols mounted on the wall.

"Those belonged to my father," he said, "Colt .45s purchased at auction, a fundraiser of some sort. Their provenance declares they were worn by Buffalo Bill Cody. The way my father told it, Cody was paid a handsome sum to attend the auction. He strapped on the pistols, twirled them once or twice to polite applause, then unstrapped them and took a bow. They've never been fired."

"What can you tell me about Earl and Dunlap, the suspects. Who are they, and how do they fit in?" I said.

"They're common labor. Karl hired them to do odd jobs, lifting, moving, that sort of thing. Karl was no youngster. He couldn't lift much, and as you can see I was no help. The men worked as needed, nothing steady. I had little to do with them."

"What about the fire?" I said. "Who started it and why?"

"I can't answer either of those questions. Some of the materials Karl worked with were flammable, but he knew how to do his work, and he was careful. I can't believe the fire was an accident. It must have been intentional."

We talked for a while longer. I asked questions. Hightower obliged with answers. His account matched the reports. Other than the sketchy information on Karl Weaver, I learned little I hadn't already read in the paper. He'd said everything he wanted to say. He glanced at a timepiece hanging behind me, a Vienna wall clock framed in oak. I'd noted it earlier.

He drummed his fingers on the arm of his chair and sipped lemonade. He kept his eyes focused on me. Hightower had been assessing me since the moment I arrived on his doorstep. I didn't think he cared for what he saw. What he saw was what he got.

I didn't care for him, either. I also didn't care to abandon those five orphans on the table. I wanted to adopt them and take them home.

"Tell me about the stolen piece you want me to locate," I said.

Like me or not, I was his only option. He'd already offered me the dough. He set his glass on the table next to the Franklins and leaned forward.

"It's a vase, antique Chinese, from the Qianlong dynasty. It dates back to the time this country's forefathers rebelled against the king of England."

He reached into a pocket again and withdrew a photograph.

"This doesn't do it justice, I'm afraid."

The vase looked to be a foot or so tall, tapered at the top, broad around the midsection, and narrower at the base. It bore the portrait of a man on its surface, elderly and obese with a long beard and mustache. The fat man was adorned in an ornate and flowing robe. His portrait was surrounded with delicate images of flowers and assorted Chinese pictograms.

"How did you happen upon this vase?" I said.

Hightower frowned, annoyed by my question.

"The vase was left to me by my father. How my father happened upon it, as you so casually put it, is both unknown to me and not germane to our discussion. What is important to me is its value. It's rare. It's valuable. It's mine, and I want it back."

"How valuable is it?"

He glanced at the bills on the table.

"Art is never easy to price. Its value depends on many things, the circumstances, the market, and most of all, the buyer. Under the right circumstances with the right buyer, the price can be very high. I've offered a reward of five thousand dollars for its recovery. That information will be published in this afternoon's newspaper. Five thousand dollars for the recovery of the vase. The money on the table is yours, Mr. Stone, if you agree to work for me. If you're successful, if you find the vase, then the reward is yours, too. Another five thousand dollars. That's how valuable it is."

The vase was worth more than the reward. I glanced at the table. Benjamin Franklin pursed his lips and stared at me from the C-notes. Hightower watched me and waited for my answer. I sipped my lemonade. Hightower didn't care for me. I couldn't blame him. I didn't care for him. I also didn't care for Christmas shopping or trips to the dentist, but I did them both. I'd always been a fan of Benjamin Franklin. I scooped up the bills and tucked them into my pocket.

"I'll be in touch," I said.

I left Terrance Hightower sitting alone in the great room of the Tudor house his father built.

5

gnes handed me a note when I entered the office.

"How was lunch?" I said.

She batted her eyelids and answered in a falsetto.

"Why, just wonderful. All we talked about was you. I gushed to Lucille that you were a terrific boss, and she delighted me with stories about how thoughtful you are."

"Such a comedienne," I said.

"Actually, Lucille is upset with you. She's hurt," Agnes said.

"I'm working on it," I said and glanced at the note.

"He called about an hour ago," she said.

"How did he sound?"

"The usual—upset."

Upset seemed to be the mood for the day. I dialed the telephone on my desk. A voice barked into the receiver.

"McCormick."

"You have such a way with words, Mac," I said, "a real charmer. Don't you ever say 'hello'?"

"Can the corn, Stone. Talk to me. What're you up to? Why are you pestering the good citizens of College Hill? I'm getting complaints. You're poking your nose into the Hightower affair. What's your angle?"

Lieutenant Thaddeus McCormick, homicide detective. All business.

"I'm just doing my job, looking after the interests of my client," I said.

"Who's your client?"

"A good citizen."

"Don't give me that. One of those good citizens called my office and complained about you."

That would be the back alley cyclops with the facial scar.

"I canvassed the neighborhood," I said.

"Yeah, we canvassed the neighborhood, too. Only when we did it, we got no complaints."

"You know me, Mac. Every stranger is a friend I haven't met."

"Yeah, and every enemy is one you have met," he said.

"I don't know. I thought the poodle and I got along famously."

"Poodle? Oh yeah, Fifi."

"Lily."

"Lily, whatever. Answer my question. What's your angle?" he said.

"My client wants me to find a man," I said, "one of the suspects in the Saturday night shenanigans. My client wants me to bring him in. My client wants to be there when the suspect turns himself in."

"Quit waltzing across the dance floor with 'my client' this and that," he said. "Give me the straight scoop. Your client is Ethan Alexander. Ethan Alexander is looking for his war buddy, Bobby Lopez, aka Earl. We already know that. The question is, why does Alexander want to bring in a gumshoe? The police will find those men. I've spoken to him. He knows we'll find them. Why mix you into the batter?"

"He has his reasons," I said. "It goes back to the trenches. Alexander and Lopez fought together during the war. There's a bond, a code between war buddies. It's about being there for a friend."

"Don't roil the waters, Stone. The last thing I need is muddy water. What did you find out today?"

"First you bark, then you beg for a bone."

"Answer my question."

"I didn't learn much. It's a quiet neighborhood. Nobody had much to say. The only one talking is Lily."

"The complainant said you picked up something in the alley," he said.

It was the pebble I'd picked up and put in my pocket. I explained it to Mac, and he snorted. We discussed the conversation I had with Hightower, including my impression that he cared more about locating the fat man than he did about apprehending the suspects.

"Fat man?" Mac said.

"The who's-it character painted on the missing vase," I said. "The guy could be royalty, a king or an emperor. For all I know, it's the artist's uncle. Whoever it is, the guy is old and fat."

"Watch your step," he said. "These men are violent. If you're not careful you'll never get a chance to grow old and fat. They've already shot one man."

"Allegedly," I said. "Hightower told me his assistant carried a firearm."

"We found a .22 with spent shells near the body."

"What put Weaver down?"

"The coroner pulled a .38 slug out of his chest," he said.

"There was a hole in the wall of the house," I said. "It looked like a bullet hole."

"We pulled a slug out of the wall, a .38. It looks like the suspects plugged the dead man. A stray bullet hit the house. The .22 had been fired. Hightower reported that a suspect appeared to be wounded."

"I've told you what I know," I said. "All I have on Karl Weaver is the moniker. What have you got? The dead man can't speak for himself."

There was a pause in the conversation.

"We're looking into Weaver," he said. "We're on top of it. We haven't located next of kin."

Something smelled fishy. Hightower told me he knew little about Weaver. The police had little on Weaver. Somebody knew something about the man.

"Listen, Stone, we'll find these guys," Mac said. "In the meantime, stay out of our way. And stay out of harm's way. One man is dead. Another man was shot. Maybe he's dead, too. You could end up on a slab yourself."

Mac uttered a harsh laugh.

"You shouldn't joke," I said.

"If I were joking, I'd agree," he said.

The phone went dead. I heard the outer door open followed by a familiar voice. Agnes laughed and greeted the visitor. They chatted, and the door closed. I glanced out the window to the sidewalk below. A green bike leaned against a lamppost. It belonged to Rusty, the newspaper boy.

I thumbed my book for a phone number and directed the telephone operator to place a call to Kansas City. Another familiar voice came on the line.

"If it isn't the prairie peeper blowing on the horn," Aaron Bernstein said. "Is Cowtown running low on bullets and bourbon? You came to the right guy."

"You're always prepared. That's the motto of a good Boy Scout," I said. "Be prepared."

Bernstein laughed.

"I was never a Boy Scout," he said. "Too many meetings, not to mention those uniforms."

"So, you hooked up with the mob," I said. "You've been known to pal around with the FBI, too. Which is it? Are you fighting crime these days or committing it?"

That brought another harsh laugh.

"Can't a guy do both?" he said.

Aaron Bernstein belonged to the Jewish mob in Kansas City. He ran numbers and controlled a sports betting operation. He did other things I didn't know about. I met Bernstein when my pal died in a plane crash. Bernstein worked with the FBI at the time, on loan from the mob. That relationship floored me. Then I learned that Bernstein wasn't the only mobster on the Fed payroll.

The FBI was stymied by smuggling operations on the east coast. The director of the FBI, J. Edgar Hoover, discovered that the way to uncover crime was to enlist the aid of the criminals themselves. With Hoover's blessing, G-men and gangsters began playing together in the same sandbox. When I met Bernstein, he worked with the FBI in Wichita unraveling espionage in the aircraft industry.

"I'm looking for information on a recently deceased victim of lead poisoning," I said. "He bought it Saturday night."

I gave Aaron Bernstein a summary of the crime, what I knew and what I didn't know. We discussed Terrance Hightower's assistant, Karl Weaver.

"All I've learned is that the man came from Kansas City," I said.

"Never heard of him," he said. "Let me do some checking."

"Thanks," I said and rang off.

Agnes came into my office carrying the *Beacon*, the afternoon edition of the newspaper.

"Rusty stopped in," she said and handed me the paper. "So, what were you up to while Lucille and I were at lunch?"

"I met a lady from France, another lady who's bored with her life and concerned about her weight, a woman who passed on tea and scones, and a grumpy cyclops. That all took place before I met Terrance Hightower."

"This better be good," she said and sat down across from me.

I brought Agnes up-to-date on my investigation. She raised an eyebrow once or twice but remained silent until I finished. I showed her the picture of the vase.

"This is what that man is so excited about?" she said. "His priorities are out of whack, if you ask me. I don't think I like Mr. Hightower."

"I didn't care for him, either," I said, "but I took his dough."

I handed her the money and told her to lock it in the safe. I reached for the newspaper as she left my office. Five desperadoes escaped from the Kansas State Reformatory at Hutchinson, including twenty-three-year old twins named Durbin. The men were seen in a southbound 1937 Ford coupe and were suspected of kidnapping a Mount Hope man. In other news, stocks were up, Roosevelt campaigned for reelection, and a new business, Fields Clothing Store, opened downtown. The paper carried a photograph of Howard Hughes who'd landed his twin-motored Lockheed in the Air Capital, an overnight stop on his flight from Los Angeles to New York City. The follow-up article on the Hightower episode mentioned the reward, five thousand simoleons, for information on the vase.

The Seth Thomas banjo clock on the wall told me the day was winding down. I heard Agnes gathering up her things in the outer office. I hadn't eaten since breakfast, and my stomach growled for chow. Agnes said she'd lock up. We said our goodbyes, and I left.

I steered my roadster west on Douglas. Pedestrians entered and exited the new Fields store. It was encouraging to see a new business downtown. We'd lick this Depression, yet. I crossed over the Arkansas River, rolled through the Delano district, and turned right onto Seneca. Several blocks later, I pulled up at the curb in front of a tavern. The sign read, "Tom's Inn."

The owner shouted my name when I crossed the threshold. A frothy glass of Storz beer appeared on the bar. I took a stool and reached for the beer in one motion.

"Thanks, Tom," I said. "That hits the spot."

"You haven't stopped by in a while," he said.

"Tell me about the Cardinals," I said.

"Meh, the Birds hosted the Cubbies at Sportsman's for a pair."

"How'd they do?" I said.

"They kissed their sister."

Tom grew up in Missouri. He followed his beloved St. Louis Cardinals as a youngster and remained a fan. His team had played a double-header against their biggest rival, the Chicago Cubs. Each team won a game. Not good, not bad. Like kissing your sister.

"First they lose four to three, then they take the next one by the same score, four to three. Go figure," he said.

"A split's not bad. The Cubbies are tough this year," I said.

"Don't remind me," he said.

A female voice said, "Hello, Pete," and I turned.

A round lady with gray hair stood at my elbow. She squinted and grinned.

"How about something to eat?" she said.

"Mabel, sweetheart, you read my mind. Dear old Dad was partial to simple fare. One of his favorite meals was a hamburger with a side of mashed potatoes. Could you do that for me?"

She squeezed my arm and tottered into the kitchen. I turned back to Tom.

"How's our gal?" I said.

He shrugged.

"Determined?" he said.

"That's a good thing," I said.

"She's not a quitter, but the stroke slowed her down."

Tom's wife had suffered a stroke the year before.

"Slower is okay. She's still with us," I said.

"That she is. I'm thankful. She loves that kitchen. It keeps her going. I wouldn't mind if she stayed home and rested. I'd rather close the kitchen than have it work her to death, but she won't hear of it. She works shorter days. Cooking keeps her occupied. When she gets tired, she stops. Nothing wrong with that. Maybe slow is good. To tell you the truth, she's not the only one slowing down. I've slowed down, too. Eh, enough of that talk. How's Lucille?"

"The waters are rough these days," I said.

"Don't quit on her, sailor," he said. "She's good for you. What's new in the detective business?"

I told Tom about the Hightower case. I showed him the picture of the soldier buddies in uniform, and I showed him the picture of the vase.

"I read about this," he said.

"There's a five-thousand-dollar reward for the doo-dad," I said. "Keep your eyes open."

"Sure I will, just in case that relic waltzes into my tavern," he said and laughed. "I could always use five G's."

Mabel returned with my food. I kissed her on the forehead. She stood at my elbow while I took a bite of the burger.

"Mmm. What did Dad always say? Beastly good. You're the aces, Mabel."

Mabel smiled and went back to the kitchen. I savored the food from my perch on the barstool.

"Your tavern has it all, Tom, the smells, the sounds, the flavors. Drink, chow, and camaraderie. I love a good saloon. Have I ever mentioned that?"

Tom put a fresh head on my glass of beer and returned it to the coaster.

"Only about a thousand times," he said. "Who's counting?"

Between bites, Tom and I talked baseball. The Yankees and Senators had played a pair. The Yanks took the first game. The second contest went thirteen innings and ended in a tie when the umps called the game due to darkness. The Yanks were knotted with the Cleveland Indians for the top spot in the American League. I followed the hamburger and mashed potatoes with another glass of beer. Tom moved to refill the empty glass. I waved him off.

"No thanks, pal. That's all for tonight. I've got to keep a clear head."

Tom raised an eyebrow but made no comment. We settled the tab and called it a night. I left and drove to my place on Lewellen.

Wednesday

July 6, 1938

6

gnes's black coffee brew warmed me and brought me to life. I hadn't eaten before I left home that morning. After I got ready for the day, I wound the clocks, the Black Forest cuckoo, the Seth Thomas grandfather, the Austrian Zappler Animated. Then, I sat down at the kitchen table and placed a telephone call.

"Good morning, Pete," Lucille answered. "The flowers are lovely."

It was early. Lucille didn't sound animated or enthused.

"Lucille, I'm trying to apologize," I said.

There was a pause.

"I know," she said.

"I'm sorry," I said. "I let my work get in the way."

"It isn't that," she said. "I'm not upset with your work. I'm upset because you forgot me. You didn't even think of me."

"I do think of you. I care for you, too," I said. "Let me take you to dinner tonight. We need to talk."

There was another pause.

"I'll think about it," she said. "Call me later."

I cradled the receiver. I didn't feel like breakfast. Instead, I drove to the office for a cup of joe and a cigarette, typical fare for a gumshoe.

I was midway through each when I heard voices in the outer office. Agnes ushered Ralph Waldo through my door. He carried a cup Agnes had filled for him. The young man looked dapper in a brown suit and matching fedora. He doffed the hat and took the chair across the desk.

"How was Kansas City?" I said.

"The best."

"Perry's barbecue?"

Ralph gave me a thumbs up.

"His sauce is aces," he said.

"I agree. It's not as sweet as others," I said, "just the way I like it."

"The Father of Kansas City barbecue. We started with a platter of ribs. Then we moved over to 18th & Vine for toe tapping and dancing."

"We, huh? Your dad gave me the scoop," I said. "He figured jazz and barbecue were a cover, an excuse for a little romance."

Ralph replied with a grin. We discussed his detective agency and recent business. He went over a case he'd closed a few days earlier.

"Have you read the papers? The incident in College Hill?" I said.

"I caught up with the news this morning. It sounds messy. Is that why I'm here? Are you involved in that?"

"If I am, would you be available? I need your help. It would mean a day or two, maybe longer. How about it?"

"I'm available. Count me in," he said.

"Good."

I refilled our cups, and we huddled over the desk. I went over the details of the case, starting with my conversation with Ethan Alexander and his relationship with one suspect, Bobby Lopez. I covered my visit to College Hill the previous day and my meeting with Terrance Hightower.

"You do realize the cops will find these guys," he said.

"I've explained that to Alexander. There's something else. A man appeared on Alexander's porch Saturday night not long after the shooting took place. The man fidgeted in the shadows. He spoke in rhymes and riddles. Alexander gave me a description that fits a man we both know."

"Rum-Rum," Ralph said. "It's been a while since we crossed paths. How does he figure in?"

"I don't know. That's where you come in. Try to locate Rum-Rum. Find the answer to your question. How does he fit into the picture? Why was he there that night? How did he come to be on Alexander's doorstep? Did he know the suspects? Was he involved in what happened or merely an observer? See what he knows. Look for Dunlap, too. Dunlap is a mystery. He and Lopez may or may not be together. One or both of them may be injured. Alexander hasn't seen Lopez recently, but he gave me his last known address. I'll start there. The professor knows nothing about Dunlap. Hightower considers both men nothing more than common laborers, his words. He doesn't know either one or care about either one."

Ralph studied Hightower's picture of the missing vase.

"The paper said there's a reward for this," he said.

"Yeah. I'm on Hightower's payroll to find that vase. As of now, you're on the payroll, too. He laid out five hundred smackers to locate his missing jewel. The reward goes with it if we find it."

"I wonder how Hightower would feel about a Negro detective working for him?" he said.

"He'd feel the same as he feels about me, a necessary evil beneath his consideration. You can always stop by and ask him yourself."

Ralph smiled and stood up.

"I'll reserve that pleasure for another day," he said.

He put on his hat and left the office.

Alexander's address for Lopez took me to an area of Wichita called the North End near Twenty-first and Broadway. Railroad workers from Mexico lived in the neighborhood. I parked in front of a building with a sign over its entrance that read, *Casa Grande,* an ambitious moniker for the sagging, three-story structure. A smaller sign near the door read hotel/rooming house.

I climbed the two steps up to a porch where a shrunken old man in dungarees and a straw hat rocked in a chair. He pretended not to notice me. I entered the lobby through a screen door. Two men in undershirts and khakis played a card game at a table in the corner. Cigarettes burned in an ashtray. Opened bottles of beer stood at the ready. One of the men gave me the eye-ball. That caused his partner to turn and glance my way. He gave me the once-over and turned back to his cards.

A frayed sofa with suspicious stains sat beneath a picture window. Its lone occupant was a cat likely responsible for the frays and the stains. A few chairs were scattered here and there. A ceiling fan screeched overhead. Neither the men nor the cat seemed to notice.

I moved to the counter and tapped on the bell. After a moment, a short man with a large belly appeared from the back. He, too, was dressed in an undershirt and khakis, the uniform of the day. I showed him my card. He ignored it.

"The cops already been here," he said.

"I'm not a cop. I'm private."

He shrugged at that revelation.

"Bobby Lopez," I said. "Is he in?"

"Bobby Lopez is gone. He left in a hurry."

"When was that?"

"Recently."

The man was a font of information.

"I'd like to take a look at his room."

"Room's occupied. New tenant," he said.

Empty rooms filled quickly at the *Casa Grande.*

"So, you know Lopez. Where I can find him?" I said.

He gave me an expression that suggested a stupid gringo was wasting his valuable time. He showed me his back and disappeared into a room behind the desk. The men at the table held cards in their hands and blank expressions on their faces. I pushed open the screen door and stepped onto the porch. The wrinkled raisin rocked in his chair. He continued to ignore me. I noticed a weathered magazine on a table near his elbow. I reached for it.

"May I?" I said.

The man came alive. He turned toward me and looked stricken. He extended an arm, but he was too late. I picked up the magazine. Its cover read, *Le Sourire de France*. It was dated two decades earlier, 1918. I couldn't read French, but the illustrations were artistic, intended for art enthusiasts. The magazine belonged to Lopez.

"Is this yours?" I said.

The man stared and didn't reply. I reached into my pocket.

"Trade?" I said.

He looked at the silver dollar I held and rubbed a hand over his chin. He didn't meet my eyes. He no longer cared about the magazine. He stared at the silver dollar and offered an upraised palm. I dropped the coin into it. I touched two fingers to the brim of my fedora.

"Thanks," I said and left the man on the porch of the grand hotel/rooming house.

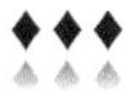

7

From the North End, I dropped south on Broadway. My fingers drummed the steering wheel. Lopez hadn't moved out of his room at the boarding house. He never returned after the episode on Saturday night. Lopez split. Fast.

Lopez studied art at Bethany College. His interest in the subject began before that, probably in France. Lopez held onto that art magazine for all those years. He probably kept more of them, souvenirs carried home from France. Souvenirs he wouldn't leave behind unless he had no choice. Where did he go? I wasn't gaining on Lopez. The cops were ahead of me. Every step I took landed in the footprint of a cop.

The suspects may or may not be together. Lopez had been loyal to Ethan after the war. Ethan said Lopez stayed by his side at Walter Reed Hospital. If Dunlap was wounded, Lopez would stick with him. I couldn't figure Dunlap. What if Lopez had taken a bullet? Would Dunlap stay or run? I had no answer to that question. I knew nothing about Dunlap's loyalties. Then again, loyalty wouldn't play into it at all if one of the men were dead.

I turned right on Central and motored several blocks. I neared the junction of the Arkansas River and the Little Arkansas, north and west of downtown. People who hailed from other parts of the country pronounced the name of the river as they would the name of the state, Arkansas. If a Jayhawker heard someone say that, he'd correct them. In the Sunflower state, the river's name was pronounced R-Kansas.

The Little Arkansas began as a tributary in the western plains and connected with the larger river near the heart of the city. Nestled at their confluence was the Riverside District, a neighborhood known for shady streets and ritzy homes, homes like the Campbell mansion. The Wichita Art Museum had opened in the neighborhood a few years earlier.

I located the Hightower Gallery and parked on the street beneath the limbs of a lofty elm. The gallery was a handsome structure similar to Hightower's Tudor across town but smaller.

I stepped through the door, and a young lady behind a desk greeted me. A killer smile spread over her freckled cheeks and drifted into eyes as green as springtime. Blonde curls spilled onto pale shoulders. Her image was as fresh as the Guernsey's milk.

"Hello," she said.

"Hello," I said.

"Welcome to Hightower Gallery."

I introduced myself and handed her my card. The young lady studied it. Her brow furrowed. That concerned me. I hoped it wouldn't leave a wrinkle.

"I spoke to the police," she said. "They've already been here."

Big surprise.

"I'm private," I said, "working with the police."

That wasn't exactly true, so I added, "Mr. Hightower hired me."

"Mr. Hightower left for home earlier," she said. "He didn't mention this to me."

"Why don't you phone him?" I said. "He can explain it."

Her brow furrowed again. She didn't want to question her boss over the telephone. I didn't want to cause a wrinkle. She came to a decision.

"I guess it won't hurt to talk," she said.

"I have a few questions," I said. "It won't take long. Maybe you can give me the nickel tour while we talk."

That worked. The gallery gave her home-field advantage. She popped up out of her chair.

"Sure," she said.

Her name was Susie Donovan, and Susie would be pleased to show me around, her favorite part of the job. We strolled, and she pointed. We began with the large room behind her desk. Hightower showcased the works of lesser known artists vying for the attentions of collectors and speculators. Susie gushed over some paintings but lowered her voice to a whisper when she saw one she didn't care for. I had to agree. Some paintings looked terrific. Others did not.

"Do you own paintings?" she said.

"I collect books," I said.

"Books?"

"A thousand words are worth one picture," I said.

We moved on to smaller rooms. Susie pointed out paintings and named artists, most of whom had respected reputations. There was a western scene by Charles M. Russell and a pair of portraits by Robert Henri. An Edmund L. Davison painting depicted a local scene in Wichita. A painting by Grant Wood depicted a small town. We walked past a room with a closed door.

"What's in this room?" I said.

"That's just an office," she said.

She opened the door. A desk occupied the middle of the floor. A chair behind the desk and a couple of customer chairs left little room for anything else. A telephone was the only object on the desk.

"This is a quiet place to meet with clients," she said. "Mr. Weaver uses—used—this room. Sometimes Mr. Hightower uses it."

She closed the door. We moved to a smaller room with a display of sculptures.

"What can you tell me about the vase that's missing, the fat man?" I said. "Why was that piece in the studio and not here on exhibit?"

"The fat man, that's a good name for it," she said. "I have no idea why that piece was in the studio. It left the gallery a few weeks ago. I'd forgotten all about it. I assumed someone bought it."

That puzzled me. The vase left the gallery weeks earlier. Why? We moved to another room that exhibited contemporary pieces. As we toured, we talked.

"Tell me about Earl and Dunlap," I said. "How well did you know them?"

"Not well. I mean we spoke to each other, hi, hello, that sort of thing. They seemed nice. They weren't here all the time. We didn't spend much time together."

"I understand they did the lifting and moving. They drove a truck. Did they use their truck to transport pieces from the gallery to the studio?"

"Oh, no," she said. "We have a panel truck for that. It's in the garage out back. It's outfitted with racks and ties to hold the art. The men loaded it, but Mr. Weaver drove that truck himself."

"What else you can tell me about them?"

She pondered a moment.

"The one they call Earl, I read that his real name is Bobby Lopez. He'd come around once in a while when he wasn't working, just to look. The other man, Dunlap, wasn't with him then. Bobby Lopez didn't say much. He was quiet. Even when he spoke it was almost a whisper. Maybe he was shy. He seemed thoughtful. He was always thinking, lost in thought. I guess he had a lot on his mind. That sounds bad, doesn't it? I don't mean it to be. It sounds like he was trying to figure something out. What is it you detectives call it? Casing the joint?"

"Some say that," I said. "Mostly in the movies."

"Well, I don't mean it that way. He looked deep in thought and peaceful. When he stared at a piece, I swear he'd go someplace else. In his head, I mean. Almost like he was in a trance. It would've taken a shake to snap him out of it, not that I would ever do that. You know how you hush up when someone's taking a nap? That's the way I was when he got like that. That sounds silly, doesn't it? I don't mean it to be silly."

"It doesn't sound silly at all," I said.

"I can't believe those two shot a man. They seemed nice, you know?"

"What do you think happened that night?" I said.

"All I know is what I read in the newspaper. I can't stop thinking about it. No one actually saw them shoot a gun, did they? And it was dark. The paper said Mr. Hightower heard the shots and found the body. Doesn't that mean no one knows for sure who the killer was?"

"The police are confident the suspects are guilty," I said.

"But they don't know for sure? Isn't that right?" she said.

"One person knows," I said.

Her eyes widened.

"Who?" she said.

"The killer," I said.

She frowned. There went that brow again.

"How about Mr. Weaver? How well did you know him?" I said.

"I didn't know him well, but I knew him well enough, if you know what I mean."

I didn't know what she meant. She read my expression.

"I don't like to speak ill of the dead," she said, "but he did do something once. He tried to get fresh with me. Buster, I set him straight. I warned him that Billy—Billy's my boyfriend—I said to him that Billy is over six feet tall and husky as an ox. Billy would box him on the nose if he didn't behave himself. He got the message. He left me alone after that. Even when we worked together he kept his distance."

She giggled.

"That was a little white lie I told him," she said. "Billy's not six feet at all, and he's skinny as a rail. Billy does have a temper, though."

She giggled again.

"What did Weaver do here at the gallery?"

"Well, he was in charge when Mr. Hightower wasn't here. Mr. Hightower comes in most days, but he let Mr. Weaver manage the gallery. Mr. Hightower never stays very long. He gets tired and leaves. It depends on who's visiting that day."

I didn't understand. She explained.

"You see, in this business there's buyers and there's browsers. Everything in the gallery is for sale, but serious buyers usually make appointments. They spend a lot of money, and they want advice and attention. Mr. Hightower meets with those people. Sometimes Mr. Weaver would meet with them. The gallery is open to anyone, though, and browsers are always welcome. I give them tours, just like now. If browsers want to buy, I call—I called—Mr. Weaver. Then there are the exhibits with a featured artist. Mr. Weaver made those arrangements. I assisted. Mr. Hightower attended, too, of course."

"And when there were no buyers in the gallery, what did Weaver do?" I said.

"Right," she said. "When there were no appointments, Mr. Weaver arranged displays and maintained the pieces. He handled all of the art, except lifting and moving. He supervised that. We both cleaned the gallery, but we divided the labor. He cleaned the pieces and the areas surrounding the pieces, the walls, pedestals. I do the floors and open spaces. Mr. Weaver also worked in Mr. Hightower's studio, restoration and cleaning. He painted there, too. It was his hobby. He loved to paint. He showed me some of his paintings. I think he spent more time on his hobby than he did with restoration. Most pieces don't require much work."

We approached her desk near the entrance.

"What's your role behind the desk?" I said.

"I'm a gal Friday. I'm the receptionist. I greet visitors and give tours if they request one. Otherwise, they're free to wander on their own. I answer the phone, type letters, whatever I'm told to do."

An envelope on the desk bore an address from Grant & Gray. I didn't know the firm.

"Who keeps the books?"

"Mr. Hightower does the bookkeeping. He handles the money and writes the checks, but he doesn't do that here at the gallery. He does that at his home, I suppose. I handle small bills, but I don't handle the big stuff that's bought and sold."

I scanned the gallery. The furnishings were plush, and the building itself set Hightower back a pretty penny.

"These are nice digs. The inventory must be worth a bundle. How does a guy make a buck in this business?" I said.

"Not everything belongs to the gallery. Some of the pieces are here on consignment," she said. "You're right, though. A lot of the work belongs to Mr. Hightower. It must be expensive. Mr. Hightower probably doesn't need the money. He loves art."

I thought that over. Even art lovers had to eat. I figured the income from Daddy's oil wells kept the wolf away.

"What about the pieces that aren't on consignment? How do they find their way here?" I said.

"Mr. Hightower works through an art dealer in Kansas City. He buys and sells with them."

Susie reached into a desk drawer and handed me a card that read, Carmichael's of Kansas City. She glanced at a clock on the wall. I'd taken enough of her time. I thanked the young lady. She flashed a smile and extended her hand. I took it in mine.

"You've been very helpful, Susie Donovan," I said. "I'd kiss your hand, but I wouldn't want to incur the wrath of Billy the ox."

Susie Donovan giggled. I left.

The Wichita Art Museum overlooked the Little River a few blocks to the south. I didn't know what I hoped to find there, but Lopez had maintained his interest in art over the years. I figured he must have visited the place. If he had, maybe someone would recognize his picture and have something to say about him.

I glanced at my watch. The afternoon had dwindled. The museum might be closed for the day. I pulled up and discovered that my hunch was correct. The building was locked up. I'd have to return another day.

8

It took another telephone call and a bit of groveling before Lucille relented and agreed to have dinner with me. I chose Green Gables, a roadhouse outside the city limits. Green Gables owned a reputation for live music, good food, a well-stocked bar, and a casual disregard for rules and regulations.

I'd considered a movie. The air-conditioned Miller Theater beckoned, a downtown oasis in the desert. The Miller kept its slogan, "Refreshingly Cool," emblazoned on its marquee. I passed on the theater in favor of the roadhouse. The evening called for conversation and intimacy. I still had explaining to do for my behavior on Monday night.

Green Gables, formerly a farmhouse, featured a gambling den that held little interest that evening. The well-stocked bar was enticing. A drink, a dinner, and with luck dancing, were just the ticket.

The guy manning the door gave me the once over. We recognized each other by face but not by name. He knew I was on the square and not looking for trouble. We shook hands, and I slipped him a couple of bucks. He held the door and swept us in.

The bartender made eye contact and hoisted a bottle.

"Good to see you, pal. Bourbon rocks?"

I gave him the thumbs up. He turned to Lucille.

"And for the lady?"

"Gin and tonic?"

"Gin and tonic it is," he said and went to work.

"I've never been here," Lucille said.

"Yeah, my first time, too," I said.

Lucille nudged my ribs with a gentle elbow.

"Nice try, mister bourbon rocks," she said.

She scanned the tables arrayed in the dining room. Music drifted from above. She wore the hint of a smile.

"This is a nice place. I like it," she said.

Just the words I wanted to hear.

"Let's sit at the bar before we get a table," I said. "There'll be dancing upstairs after dinner. I'd like to squeeze my gal."

The bartender served our drinks and moved to another customer. I lit two cigarettes and handed one to Lucille. She sipped her gin and tonic and tapped a toe to the music.

"Yum, tastes good. Thanks," she said. "Pete, Agnes explained that you were with Ethan Alexander when you forgot me. I want you to know that I'm not upset at you for working on a case. I understand that. Just promise me you won't forget me next time."

"You have my promise," I said. "I won't forget you."

"Agnes didn't tell me why you were there. I want you to know that, too. She doesn't tell me details about your work. I'm not prying, but I am curious about Ethan. I haven't seen Ethan in a while. I hope he's doing well."

"He's fine, but he's worried about a friend, an old Army buddy," I said. They fought together in France. His pal is in trouble. That's why he called me. His pal is on the lam, and he asked me to find him."

"His pal is on the lam? I hope it has nothing to do with that story in the newspaper, that terrible murder. If it does and you don't want to talk about it, tell me to take a hike."

"Tonight belongs to you, kiddo. I didn't bring you here to talk shop. Tonight let's talk about us."

She took my hand and squeezed it.

"Sweetheart, don't you understand? If it's about your work, it is about us," she said.

Notes from a trumpet blasted from the floor above. A clarinet joined in. A drum kept the beat. Traffic picked up. Couples entered and took tables in the dining room. I signaled the bartender and raised two fingers.

"Let's find a quiet table," I said.

We were ushered to a table for two in a corner. Fresh drinks from the bar followed us. I lit cigarettes and sipped bourbon. Lucille loosened up. She tapped her toes to the music and smiled at me over her gin and tonic. A waiter took our dinner orders. Piano keys tinkled from above.

A sultry alto broke into a rendition of Bessie Smith's, "Any Woman's Blues." The singer cried the lyrics, "I feel blue, I don't know what to do." The blue lyrics, the sweet notes, and that angelic voice carried me on a flying carpet.

At that moment crime halted on the streets. Murder and arson ceased to matter. Politics, poverty, the Depression all fell away. A chicken simmered in every pot. Every John Doe wore a look of serenity on his mug.

The song ended. I looked over to Lucille and smiled.

"I guess I went away for a moment," I said. "Blues, bourbon, and a beautiful woman. Those killer bees get to me. You are a beautiful woman, Lucille."

"You and your bees," she said. "You had your bees growing up as I recall. Remind me."

"Baseball, books, and a bicycle," I said, "everything a growing boy needed."

We sipped and smoked.

"Ethan is a good man," Lucille said. "I hope his friend is okay."

"Nothing about this case makes sense," I said. "If his pal is innocent, and Ethan Alexander claims he is, what were those men doing at the Hightower place on a Saturday night? Ethan is certain his friend swore off firearms after the war. Somebody shot the assistant. Who?

"I figured the suspects would be behind bars by now. The cops have been sweeping the city. I should be out of work. I said as much to Ethan. The cops have manpower. The cops are a step ahead of me.

"One of the men may have been shot. The cops put out the word to the medicos. You can bet they're on the lookout for a gunshot wound. There's been nothing so far. Nobody's turned up dead or alive. I wonder if they're still in the city. If not, where are they?

"I brought Ralph Waldo on board today. Our old friend Rum-Rum is in the picture. Keep that tidbit under your bonnet. Why Rum-Rum is involved, I don't know. Ralph is looking for him. Maybe he can tell us something."

"So, now what?" Lucille said.

Our waiter arrived with our food.

"Now, we tie into these rib eyes," I said.

The steaks were tender and cooked to perfection. We enjoyed the food and listened to the music. The roadhouse was not a high-toned establishment. It didn't boast the décor of Delmonico's. No matter. For my money, the beef and the booze couldn't be beat. Other patrons agreed. Couples entered, and the joint filled up. Some couples headed upstairs toward the music.

The waiter cleared our table. We declined dessert and opted for coffee and brandy. Cigarette smoke curled through candlelight. The sultry voice delivered a hypnotic version of "Bye, Bye, Blackbird." The notes swept down from above and lifted me to another place. Lucille's voice brought me back to earth.

"Are you still with me?" Lucille said.

"Tonight and always," I said.

"You told me what's happened on your case," she said. "You didn't tell me what's next. Those men haven't been located. So, what's next?"

I crushed out my cigarette and leaned forward.

"Put yourself in their shoes," I said. "Suppose you're on the lam. You or your accomplice has been shot. What do you do? You can't go to a doctor. You'd walk into the arms of the police if you did. You can't go to your place. The cops are waiting there, too. Lopez never returned to his room. He knew better. Dunlap is the wild card. No one knows anything about Dunlap. Let's speculate. Where would you go?"

Lucille thought that over.

"Could I go to a friend?" she said. "A friend might hide me for a night or two. A friend would offer food and shelter. I don't know about medical attention. How serious is the injury?"

"I don't know," I said. "No one is certain about the injury."

"A body hasn't been found. We're both alive," she said. "We're desperate. We need medical attention and a place to rest and recover. A safe place."

"Good," I said.

"Nix going to a friend. Nix going to a doctor. Nix going to my place. The police are on my trail," she said.

"Don't forget the reward," I said. "There's a reward for that vase. Joe Public would love to get his mitts on that money. A person on the street could recognize you. Anyone could drop a nickel and call the police."

"Nix showing my face. I need a safe place out of the public eye, medical care, food, shelter," she said.

She mulled it over.

"You're scared. You're alone. There's nobody you can trust," I said.

"No, you're wrong. There's one person I can trust," she said.

Lucille's eyes met mine. She placed her cup on the saucer and leaned forward, elbows on the table. She laced her fingers beneath her chin.

"When the chips are down, there's only one person to turn to," she said. Lucille uttered a single word, "Mommy."

Bingo. Mommy. That was my thought exactly.

Thursday

July 7, 1938

9

My feet were propped up on my desk. I nursed a cup of coffee and thumbed the French magazine, ignoring the verbiage and pausing over pictures and illustrations. I checked the clock and dropped my feet to the floor. I dialed the telephone. When Ethan Alexander answered, I gave him a report on what I'd learned so far. It wasn't much. I had more questions than answers.

"I thought they'd be behind bars by now," I said. "I was wrong. The birds are still in the bush. I think they've skipped town. They're too hot to be harbored in the city. Somebody would've cracked by now, given them up for the reward."

I shared my theory that the men had skedaddled.

"There's nothing like home cooking to put a man back on his feet," I said. "If I'm right, they've gone home. The question is, where is home?"

Ethan and I agreed that taking flight to Lindsborg was a stretch. Lopez hadn't spent much time there after he completed his studies at Bethany College. He might chance a visit alone but not together. Together, a white man and a brown man would stick out in a small town populated with Swedes. The cops knew Lopez had family in Lindsborg. They'd have local authorities on the alert. Lindsborg was too risky. I ruled it out. That left

Dunlap's family, assuming he had family nearby. If he did, where would they be?

"I recall that magazine you found," Ethan said. "It belonged to Bobby. I'm sure of it. Bobby read that in France. He stowed several issues in his duffle bag before we shipped out. He must've kept them all these years. You're right that Bobby left in a hurry. He wouldn't have left a magazine he carried home from the war. He must not have gone back to the boardinghouse Saturday night. What happened caught him by surprise. He didn't plan what happened.

"He loved reading those magazines. *Le Sourire* means smile, by the way. I believe Gaugin published the first issues. Languages came easily to Bobby. He spoke Spanish and English all his life. He picked up enough French to converse with the locals and charm the young ladies."

We chatted for a moment longer. I told Ethan I'd call when I had something to report and hung up the phone. I tossed the magazine aside and retrieved a state highway map from a desk drawer. I unfolded the map across the desk, lit a cigarette, and studied roads and towns within a reasonable distance from Wichita. A gentle rap on the door interrupted me. Agnes swept into the room wearing a Cheshire cat grin beneath wide eyes. She stopped in front of the desk and waited for me to say something.

"Why the smug mug?" I said.

"Come on, Romeo," she said. "You don't fool me. You waltzed in here this morning with pep in your step and a glint in your eye. You were whistling. 'Bye, Bye, Blackbird.' For crying out loud, Pete, you never whistle. Talk to me. Things went well last night? I take it you're back in Lucille's good graces. Has she forgiven you?"

Lucille and I enjoyed dinner and drinks at the Green Gables. After dinner and our chat about the case, we sat at the table and tapped our toes until the sounds of jazz and blues lured us to the dance floor above.

A combo played the tunes. The singer, a blonde stunner in a black evening gown, trilled the high notes like a canary. One musician played the piano, another blew the horn. A skinny kid with lowered eyelids kept the beat on the drums. Lucille and I danced cheek-to-cheek until the carriage turned into a pumpkin. I woke up that morning in Lucille's bed. She nudged me and suggested coffee. I leered and suggested something else. Later, I washed up and dressed at my place on Lewellen, then hustled to the office.

"We enjoyed a pleasant evening," I said.

Agnes lost the grin. She wanted more. She didn't get it.

"C'mon, give. That's all you have to say?"

"Can't a guy have some privacy?" I said.

The grin returned.

"You're right. A gentleman doesn't talk. Besides, I'll see Lucille later. Women tell each other everything."

I rolled my eyes. Agnes handed me a note.

"Ralph called," she said.

She swirled an about-face and headed for the door. She looked back over her shoulder, whistled a few bars of "Bye, Bye, Blackbird," and closed the door behind her. I dialed the number on the note. Ralph Waldo answered on the second ring.

"Give me good news," I said.

"I don't have any news, good or bad," he said. "Those two men are ghosts. I can't find a trail. They used to loiter around Union Station but not lately. The station is where men looking for work hang out. Sometimes the boss man stops by when he needs cheap help. It could be that Weaver fellow found our boys there.

"A couple of guys I talked to knew them by name, Earl and Dunlap. That's all they could tell me, though, just the names. They knew about the reward, too. If they could tell me where they were, they'd talk. They're hungry. Those joes would sell out a twin brother for a buck."

"Anything on Rum-Rum?" I said.

"Nah, nothing. You don't find Rum-Rum. Rum-Rum finds you. I put out the word. If he's willing to talk, he'll find me. He comes around after dark. There was no sign of him last night. He's probably scared. I know I would be."

"Let's give him another night," I said. "In the meantime, I'm working on another angle I'd like to run past you. Can you stop by this afternoon?"

"Will do."

Ralph rang off. I pored over the map. I didn't notice the time until Agnes knocked and came in carrying a grease-stained sack. A pleasant aroma wafted through the air.

"White Castle burgers," I said. "Agnes, you always know what's best."

I pushed the map aside. She laid out napkins and arrayed the feast over the desktop. The scent of savory sliders fried in onions stirred my appetite. I hadn't realized I was hungry.

"This is swell, Agnes," I said.

We munched burgers and drank coffee. Agnes was curious about Green Gables, the food, the drink, and the entertainment. I gave the place high marks and suggested she and Percy pay a visit.

"I heard you through the door talking to Ralph. You mentioned another angle," Agnes said.

She finished a slider and tossed napkins and wrappers into the trash. I leaned back and lit a cigarette. Agnes gestured toward the map.

"What's your plan?" Agnes said.

I repeated what I'd said to Ethan Alexander about the men leaving town.

"Those men would be in custody by now if they were in town. So far, not a trace. I think they've left the city."

"And you don't know where they've gone?"

"Not yet. Something's gnawing at me. Dunlap's a puzzle, the unknown quantity in the equation. Ralph and I will put our heads together this afternoon. I have an idea."

I patted my midsection.

"Kiddo, the burgers were delicious," I said. "You always know what I need. How is that?"

Agnes sighed and rose from her chair. She spoke in a stern voice.

"Pete, you're a simple man, a simple man with simple tastes. Be careful with Lucille. Treat her right or you'll lose her. That's a warning."

"Why the lecture?" I said.

"You don't need much, but you do need a woman's attention," she said. "You're right. I do know what you need."

"And?" I said.

"I know what you need," she said, "but I don't have what you need."

She moved toward the door.

"What do I need?" I said.

"A clue," she said.

The door closed behind her.

I opened my book. The business card Susie Donovan gave me at the art gallery fell onto the desk. I picked it up and dialed the operator who connected the line. A gentleman answered in a baritone, his voice as smooth and mellow as warm brandy.

"Hello and thank you for calling Carmichael's of Kansas City. My name is Mr. James. How may I help you?"

I gave the man my name and told him why I was calling. Mr. James acknowledged that he and Mr. Hightower had a business relationship, and he was aware of the episode at the art studio.

"I don't understand why a private detective is calling me," he said. "Isn't this a police matter?"

"Yes it is," I said. "Mr. Hightower has hired me to protect his interests. Specifically, he wants me to locate a missing vase. Are you familiar with the piece in question?"

"Only by description. I read the newspaper, but I have not seen the vase. I am familiar with art from that period. If you're asking if Carmichael's handled that item, the answer is no."

That checked with what Hightower had told me. He said that he'd inherited the vase from his father.

"You're familiar with the art and the period," I said. "Who might be in the market for such an item?" I said.

The warm baritone cooled a degree.

"Mr. Stone, your insinuation is insulting," he said. "We are proud of our relationships with our clients and hold them in the highest regard. The integrity of our clientele is beyond reproach. I know of no one who would buy stolen art."

"I apologize for the insult," I said. "Mr. Hightower's assistant was murdered during the theft. The man's name was Karl Weaver. What can you tell me about him?"

"I never met Karl Weaver. We deal solely and directly with Mr. Hightower."

"Hightower is quite elderly," I said. "I was under the impression he delegates many tasks. Karl Weaver must have accompanied Hightower on visits to Kansas City or acted as an emissary on Hightower's behalf."

"Mr. Stone, you're delving into Mr. Hightower's personal matters. We at Carmichael's do not discuss personal matters involving our customers. We are aware of the recent misfortune surrounding Mr. Hightower. Please extend our best wishes to him during this difficult time. We value our relationship with Mr. Hightower. That is all you need to know. Good day to you, sir."

The phone went dead before I thanked the man for his time. I didn't waste my breath on a dial tone. I hung up the phone.

The envelope I'd seen on Susie Donavan's desk came from Grant & Gray. The telephone operator kept me on hold while she investigated. A minute later, she reported that it was an insurance outfit in Kansas City and made the connection.

A male voice answered in a crisp tone.

"Grant & Gray, Stu Kelly speaking," he said.

I identified myself and told him why I was calling. Kelly informed me that Grant & Gray was in the business of insuring fine art and volunteered that Terrance Hightower was a client.

"Of course we are aware of the recent situation at the Hightower residence," he said. "That information is confidential. I cannot discuss that with you. I'm sure you understand."

"Yes, I do understand," I said, "Valuable art was destroyed in the fire. I'm sure Grant & Gray is on the job. Mr. Hightower has hired me to locate a stolen vase. He's offered a five-thousand-dollar reward for its recovery. Five G's is a lot of dough. The vase must be worth a lot more. Something that valuable must be insured. You must be interested in its whereabouts."

"What is your question?" he said.

"Are you investigating the loss?"

"Any insurer would investigate such a loss. I can tell you that Grant & Gray has received no claim from Mr. Hightower for the vase you describe."

"That surprises me," I said. "Art went up in a fire. What can you tell me about that?"

"Not a thing, Mr. Stone. That's strictly confidential, as I've already said. I do wish you the best with your investigation. Should you ever have the need to insure collectibles, I hope you'll consider Grant & Gray. Goodbye."

I thanked Mr. Kelly and cradled the receiver. Rusty's voice came through the door. He carried the afternoon edition of the newspaper. When I went through the door, he grinned and said, "Hiya, Mr. Stone." I tapped the lad on the shoulder and thanked him for the newspaper.

The door was standing open when Ralph Waldo arrived. I waved him into my office while Rusty and Agnes chatted.

"Thanks for coming," I said. "It's good to see another human. I've been yammering with faceless voices on the telephone."

"What'd the voices tell you?"

"Not a thing of note. Nobody wants to talk to a gumshoe. The easiest way to get rid of an unwanted caller is to hang up the telephone."

I gave Ralph a rundown of my conversations with the art dealer and the insurance agent.

"Suppose you had this stolen vase," I said. "What would you do with it?"

Ralph looked surprised.

"Are you kidding? I'd go for the reward. Five grand is a lot of cabbage."

"No, no. Suppose you were the thief," I said. "You have it. Now, what do you do with it?"

He gave that some thought.

"I'd try to unload it. Sell it fast. What's a guy like me going to do with a high-dollar relic like that vase? I'd want to get rid of it."

"Sure you would, but how would you do it? Who'd you sell it to? Who'd buy it?"

Ralph looked puzzled.

"A fence," he said, "someone with connections."

"An experienced thief would use a fence. Not you. You've never stolen anything. What went down happened fast. A murder, a theft, a fire. You grabbed the vase on the fly."

"A loaded dandy would buy it," he said.

I shook my head.

"No. You're a criminal. The doodad is stolen. A person who dealt with you would become a criminal, too. Put yourself in their shoes. Lopez and Dunlap are a couple of everyday joes who work at this and that for their bread and beans. How would they know what to do with the vase? Who would they know in the art world or in the criminal world? How many rich guys do you know?"

"I see your point," he said.

"Lopez is troubled, not stupid. He struggles with demons that haunt him from the war. He would have known that taking the vase would bring trouble. He would've known they couldn't deal it. He took it anyway. It doesn't add up. He didn't grab the fat man for the money. He kidnapped the fat man for another reason."

"What reason is that?" Ralph said.

"When we find him, we'll ask him," I said.

I gave Ralph my suspicion that the suspects left town. I stood to refill our cups, and he pulled his chair around to my side of the desk. We sipped coffee and pored over the roadmap together. I pointed out Lindsborg on the map.

"Lopez's family is here. It's seventy or eighty miles, but the cops know about it. They're watching the Lopez place. That leaves Dunlap. He remains a mystery. Who is he? Where is he from? Maybe Dunlap isn't even his real name."

Ralph raised his eyebrows.

"What're you driving at?"

"You talked to those men at Union Station, a hard lot, down and out. Some of them knew Lopez and Dunlap by name, nothing else. That's the way it is. Hardened guys thrown together keep to themselves. Their secrets are all they own. Personal stuff, where they've been and what they've done, stays hidden. They swap stories, all right, but they hide the truth."

"What's your point?" Ralph said.

"A man who owns nothing has only his identity and his history. He doesn't share his identity and his history. The men you talked to, what were their names?"

Ralph sipped coffee and thought.

"I didn't ask for names," he said, "but I heard a few. There was a big guy someone called Bear, and Lone Jack, a quiet man. He sat by himself in the shade. Glide claimed to be the best dancer in Doo-Dah."

"Nicknames," I said, "not their real names. Bobby Lopez goes by Earl."

"So, you think Dunlap's name is phony?" he said.

"Your dad said something to me that's been running through my head," I said. "He talked about freed slaves that came to Kansas after the Civil War. Kansas is sprinkled with settlements of Negroes. Those were your dad's words. Former slaves banded together and founded towns or settled into established neighborhoods and white communities."

"He talks to me about that," Ralph said. "Pop knows folks in Nicodemus. Is that what you think? Our guys lit out for Nicodemus?"

"Nicodemus is too far to travel if a man has been shot. They'd go someplace they could reach from Wichita. I've been looking over the map, wondering if Dunlap might have family nearby."

Ralph looked dubious.

"Even if you're right, how could we find Dunlap's family?" he said. "Pop said this state's sprinkled with Negro communities. Maybe they did go to his people, but where? Which town?"

"I have a hunch. Look here," I said.

I pointed to a spot on the map. Ralph followed my finger, then he looked up at me.

"It's about a hundred miles," I said. "Far enough from Wichita, but still doable if the man's injury isn't fatal."

We both stared at the spot on the map.

"It's a longshot," he said. "A hundred miles? That's a good number. I'll give it those odds. A hundred to one."

"It's a longshot," I said, "but it's the only shot we've got."

We considered our options. Was the trip worth the time? Would we find the men at the spot on the map or were we spinning our wheels? I was convinced the men had left the city. The dot on the map represented a better possibility than hanging around Wichita.

The longshot was located in Morris County, a tiny settlement nestled in the Flint Hills, home to a mix of Caucasians and Negroes. The longshot lay a hundred miles north of Wichita, a small town named Dunlap.

Friday

July 8 , 1938

10

10

We picked up K-11 east of El Dorado and headed north. Officially, K-11 no longer existed. The state renumbered it earlier in the year. The route's official number became K-99. The new number hadn't caught on yet. People were slow to change, and my map never would. Both Kansas travelers and my map still referred to the route as K-11. The highway ran north and south from border to border, extending into Nebraska to the north and Oklahoma to the south. It also passed through the city of Emporia en route to our destination, the town of Dunlap.

Friday morning was another hot one. On Monday, I met with Ethan Alexander in his kitchen. The following day I met with Terrance Hightower in his great room. There was still no sign of Lopez or the fat man vase. I owed a personal debt to my friend, Ethan. I also had five hundred of Hightower's dollars stashed in my safe. I owed the man a report.

I'd telephoned Hightower before we left the city. The call didn't go well. I informed him I was following a hunch that would take me out of town, probably for a day or two. I was on the trail of the suspects. To his credit, Hightower kept his yap shut while I explained. When he replied, he spoke in a low, even voice that he strained to control.

"I don't give a hoot about your hunch," he said.

He adopted the tone of a sucker who'd made a bad bet.

"I might as well have flushed my five hundred dollars down the toilet," he said. "I told you I don't care about finding those men. I care about the vase. Where is my vase?"

"I'll find the suspects. They'll have your vase," I said.

"I wish I shared your confidence," he said. "I do not. So far, my five hundred dollars has bought me nothing but your hunch. Now, you're spending my money on a wild goose chase. You disappoint me, Mr. Stone. I do not wish to be disappointed."

The phone clicked, and I got an earful of dial tone.

Ralph and I traveled in shirt sleeves and ties, our jackets folded on the backseat of the roadster. The temperature hovered in the nineties, a cool wave after the hundred-plus heat the previous day.

We briefly considered wearing khakis and work shirts and posing as laborers, but we lacked the sunburned necks and calloused palms to pull it off. People would be suspicious of out-of-town detectives. It couldn't be helped. We stayed with suits and ties.

A drive in the country worked like a tonic. It cleared my head. Quiet miles on backroads gave me time to mull things over. We rolled along the edge of the Flint Hills. Spent miles fell behind us.

The Depression pounded Kansans. Those who worked the land struggled against the elements. Dust storms blacker than midnight had rolled across the plains, choking cattle and humans alike. Topsoil rose into clouds and trickled back to earth as distant as New York City.

Some folks succumbed, driven from the land. Others thrived. They made money. We smelled money as we rode through the countryside. Hydrogen sulfide drifted from oil rigs sucking black blood from the ground and spiking the air with a stench like rotten eggs. Feedlot cattle and manure added pungent scents, fragrant to the cattleman, rank to the passerby.

As I drove, I wondered what we'd find in Dunlap. The town lay nestled in the hills between Emporia to the southeast and Council Grove to the northwest. I was encouraged that neither of those places were sundown towns.

Kansas owned a proud and bloody legacy as a free state. The state was born months before the beginning of the Civil War. Its citizens sided with northern states in opposition to slavery. Still, Kansas harbored sundown towns, white-only communities whose citizens intended to keep them that way. They did not welcome the Negro. Sundown towns got their name from signs posted at the city limits. Those signs bore vulgar messages, usually a racial slur followed by, "Don't Let the Sun Go Down on You in This Town."

I glanced over at Ralph. He was reading a newspaper he'd brought from home, *The Negro Star* published in Wichita. Ralph and I both knew Negroes encountered troubles when they traveled. He carried a copy of *The Negro Motorist Green-Book* in his bag, a guide to hotels, restaurants, and other places Negroes would be welcomed without facing ignorance and hatred.

We crossed over Slate Creek at the southern edge of Hamilton. I pulled into a service station where a sign over a pump read, Homer's. A man in faded bib overalls came out of the garage wiping his hands on an oily red rag. He eyed my car and my passenger. His face broke into a grin.

"I haven't seen one of these in a coon's age," he said. "She's a Jones, ain't she?"

"Jones Six roadster," I said. "That's right."

"She's a beaut. How old is this lady? They quit making the Jones quite a spell back, didn't they?"

"The last one rolled out in 1920," I said, "just before the factory burned down. This one was built the year before."

"1919. Heck, she's still a teenager," he said. "She purrs like a kitten. You must have a good mechanic."

"The best," I said. "My mechanic built these cars before the company closed. He keeps this one running."

Homer nodded his appreciation. The man had a few miles on him. His beard was salt and pepper. He began pumping the gasoline. Ralph walked toward an outhouse in the shade. Inside the station, I spotted cigarettes on a counter display and walked out with a pack of Chesterfields. I held them up, and Homer nodded. He finished pumping the gas and lifted the hood.

Ralph walked toward me as I stared at a vacant lot across the road where young boys played baseball, an abbreviated version with four or five lads on a team.

"Sandlot baseball, the best baseball in America," I said. "No umpires, no uniforms, not many rules. Just pals having fun. Duke it out on the field and leave it between the lines. Still pals after the game. How about you? Did you play baseball?"

"Sure," Ralph said. "I pitched."

"Any good?"

"I held my own. No Satchel Paige. How about you?"

"Centerfield, no Joe DiMaggio," I said.

Homer finished under the hood and wiped the windshield. We settled up inside. I handed over a couple of bucks and pocketed the change.

"Thanks, Homer," I said.

"Where're you headed?" he said.

I told him we were detectives and showed him the picture of Lopez.

"This guy and his accomplice might have come through here," I said. "It would have been Saturday night, maybe Sunday."

Homer shook his head.

"I lock up at night and stay closed on Sunday," he said. "Me and the missus go to church."

I thanked him again, and we hopped into the roadster. Thirty miles up the road we crossed the Cottonwood River at the outskirts of Emporia. The highway became Commercial Street and sliced through the heart of town.

Reeble's Grocery looked busy. At Sixth and Commercial shoppers entered Newman's Dry Goods. To the east, construction of a civic auditorium was underway. Downtown bustled with auto and pedestrian traffic. Folks visited J.C. Penney's and the Emporia State Bank next door.

It was midafternoon, and we hadn't eaten lunch. I pulled over at a diner. The Granada Theatre across the street advertised a vaudeville act on its marquee. A newsboy on the sidewalk hawked the *Emporia Gazette*. I gave the boy a nickel and waved off the change. We took a booth in the diner and gave the waitress our orders.

"What's the news?" Ralph said.

I unfolded the *Gazette*.

"We just missed the Emporia National Salesmen's Crusade," I said. "They brought in a speaker from Kansas City last night."

I turned to the sports page and pointed at a photograph.

"Here's Joe DiMaggio chatting with Johnny Vander Meer."

The pair had faced off two days earlier in the All Star game. Vander Meer pitched for Cincinnati, and Joe D. played centerfield for the Yankees. The National League prevailed four to one. Vander Meer earned the victory. I returned to the front page.

"Get this," I said. "A man here in town was sentenced to fifteen months in Leavenworth for possession of marijuana seeds."

"That's rough," Ralph said.

Ralph knew what he was talking about. Some years earlier, Ralph had been arrested for selling marijuana in Wichita. The police locked the young man in the hoosegow. His father, Waldo, asked if I could help.

Ralph was behind bars, despondent and scared. I asked questions. Ralph talked. He gave me a tip, and I went to work.

Cops wanted to hook a big fish. They weren't interested in a small fry.

I investigated and snagged a big fish. I dropped a nickel on a honcho who ran a drug ring. I gave it all to the cops and stayed out of the limelight. In exchange, the cops dropped charges against Ralph. He escaped hard time behind bars.

"Being a detective doesn't pay much," Ralph said, "but it's good to be free. I make enough jingle for off-the-rack threads."

"Pinstripes wear better than prison stripes," I said.

I turned the page. Crown Drugstore advertised electric fans for ninety-eight cents. Hordes of grasshoppers were reported over Neosho Rapids. A full-page advertisement brought a chuckle. "Comrade . . . Want to Buy a New Car?" was a spoof on Russia's dictatorship and its Communist Party, declaring they were no match for the U.S. of A.'s democracy and capitalism. Bursting with humor and wit, the advertisement bore the fingerprints of William Allen White, editor of the *Gazette*.

The waitress brought our food. We munched on hamburgers and sipped iced tea in silence. I wondered if Lopez and Dunlap had come this way. Would my hunch prove valid or would our trip be a waste of time? Sometimes my hunches panned out. Sometimes they didn't. Even a hall-of-famer struck out from time to time.

No one in Dunlap would be eager to share information with a couple of out-of-towners. Ralph must have read my mind. He lowered his empty glass to the table, wiped a napkin over his mouth, and leaned forward.

"How do you want to play it in Dunlap?" he said.

"We'll say as little as possible," I said, "and we'll listen a lot. If they're there, we'll find them."

Outside, a heavy-set man on a bench crossed his legs and gave us the once over. He doffed his straw hat and wiped his brow with a red bandana. I asked him if he knew the best way to

Dunlap. He wiped his neck and tucked the bandana into the front pocket of his bib overalls.

"You boys aren't from around here," he said.

"We're out of Wichita," I said, "private detectives."

"A white man and a Negro," he said and mulled that over. "You two wouldn't be on the trail of a white man and a Negro, would you?"

I glanced at Ralph and back to the man.

"What makes you say that?" I said. "Do you know something?"

"We read the news here in Emporia," he said. "Mr. White runs a pretty fair newspaper. You folks had a dustup in your town recently. Is that why you're here? Do you suppose those men are in Dunlap?"

"It's possible," I said. "We intend to find out."

"Well, let's see now. Dunlap is what, fifteen, sixteen miles as the crow flies?" he said. "Not that that matters, of course. A car can't fly, and a crow never built a road. Your best bet is Highway 50. Go west ten miles. You'll come to a county road. It's marked. That'll be Chase County. Turn north a dozen miles. You'll cross into Morris County. There's Dunlap."

He put on his hat and squinted at my roadster.

"Three counties, a couple dozen miles," he said. "You'd better go easy on those roads. That flint rock will chew a man's tires."

I thanked the man. We climbed into the roadster and headed west.

11

The directions were simple and accurate. I spotted the marker ten miles west of town and turned onto the gravel road.

"A lady librarian in Wichita gave me some background on Dunlap," I said. "We'll see for ourselves what the town is like today."

"What'd the lady have to say?" Ralph said.

"Dunlap had a rough start," I said, "like many communities did. Folks arrived with optimism, poor but hopeful. The dirt turned out to be poor, too, for farming anyway. This is grass country suited for raising beef. Grassland is unforgiving, difficult to farm. The settlers scratched and fought. They'd never known a soft life.

"The town teetered on its edge, crop failures, brutal weather. Wind and dust these past years broke more than a few. Some moved on."

"Pop talks about that," Ralph said, "about those Negroes from plantations."

"Pap Singleton was the pied piper who sounded the call," I said. "Without him the Negroes wouldn't have come. It was tough, but compared to slavery, it must've been paradise."

Dust and wind and heat had exacted a toll. The community staggered like a boxer in the late rounds. We idled down the streets. Weather buildings bore siding sanded gray by winds. Structures here and there lay toppled in the weeds.

Children, dark-skinned and light, played together in a schoolyard. The cornerstone on the two-story brick schoolhouse read 1918.

"Only twenty years old. That's encouraging," I said.

A small boy rolled a hoop. A few kids played kick the can. A cat stalked a robin, primed to pounce, then strolled away when its prey took flight.

We drove past homes. A dog languished in cool earth beneath a porch. A mother hanging laundry looked our way and hollered at her little ones to come here. A man under the hood of a car raised up. Ralph waved. The man scowled.

"Not the friendliest looking folks," Ralph said.

"Children look happy," I said.

"Children are always happy. They're too young to be suspicious," he said. "They haven't learned how to hate."

"Folks wonder who we might be," I said. "They're afraid of outsiders."

The bank was closed. Across the street, a few people gathered beneath a maple tree standing next to the church. A man pointed at the eaves. Another man nodded. A woman turned and watched us. The men turned and watched. Ralph waved again. No one waved back. The trio wore stoic expressions.

In the church yard, a couple of boys kneeled in the dirt. Marbles glistened in the sunlight. A small girl swatted a tire dangling from a rope tied to the limb of a cottonwood tree. A mutt crouched beside her with its tongue hanging out.

We came to a small store further up the street. A dark woman with white hair was seated on the porch, a corncob pipe clenched between her teeth. Licorice stick limbs poked out of her faded dress. She leaned forward and shuffled playing cards atop an overturned barrel. A coonhound lay in front of the screen door.

I pulled up and cut the engine. The woman continued shuffling her cards. The dog snoozed. Neither one acknowledged us.

"We make quite an impression," I said.

"You think she doesn't notice us? Or maybe she just doesn't care?" Ralph said.

"Pick 'em," I said.

The engine ticked. Flies buzzed. A cat meowed. A meadowlark sang in the distance.

"Damn," Ralph said.

"Yeah," I said.

"Two men on the run," he said. "What brings them here?"

"Home cooking," I said. "If this is Dunlap's home, he'd come here and bring Lopez with him."

"Do you think she'll talk to us?" Ralph said.

"We'll soon find out," I said.

We got out of the roadster and climbed the steps. The woman on the porch played solitaire. She studied the cards and didn't look up.

"Is there anything cool to drink?" I said.

She played a card and kept her eyes on the game.

"Two men decked out in fine suits drive through these dusty hills on a road bound to nowhere," she said. "They roll to a stop at my store for something cool to drink. Gives a body pause."

"While you're pondering, granny, why don't you answer the man's question?" Ralph said.

The woman gave Ralph a sharp look and played another card. A chair and a broom stood against the wall. In a single motion, Ralph snatched up the chair, plopped it down across from the woman, and straddled it backwards. He leaned forward. The woman's head rose. Her eyes met Ralph's.

"Two men drove through the hills and the heat," Ralph said. "They didn't do it to watch grandma play solitaire. That gentleman asked a polite question. He expects an answer."

The woman held the tip of her tongue between her teeth and looked up at me.

"There's a pump out back, no charge," she said. "Coca-Cola's in the icebox. Put ten cents on the counter."

The vigilant hound exhibited less interest in us than its owner did. It didn't budge when I stepped over it and went through the door. The store's sparse inventory consisted of a few grocery items.

I retrieved the colas from the icebox. A bottle opener hung from a hook on the wall. I popped off the caps and tossed coins onto the countertop. I went outside and placed a bottle on the barrel in front of Ralph. I placed another bottle in front of the woman and took a swig from mine.

"I left fifteen cents," I said.

Ralph uttered thanks. The woman said nothing. She took a pull on the bottle and laid a deuce on top of the ace of hearts.

"Solitaire's what I play," she said. "I used to play gin rummy. Not anymore. Not since I lost my ace."

Two aces lay face up on the barrel top, the ace of diamonds and the ace of spades. A deuce covered the ace of hearts. The ace of clubs was missing. The woman turned cards and spoke.

"You drove a piece. You might as well state your business. You the law?"

"We're private," I said, "out of Wichita."

The woman looked up and turned her head from one us to the other. She cackled.

"Private law? A white man and a Negro? Well, these old eyes have seen it all. What could be of interest to private law in this town?"

She answered her own question.

"Not a thing would be my guess," she said. "You best finish your soda pops and move along, private law."

She turned back to her cards. Ralph looked at me and shrugged. A young boy with several ears of fresh corn in his arms climbed the steps. His little sister tagged behind. The girl used all fours to navigate the stairs. The boy waited while the woman scanned his inventory.

"These are fine. Go ahead in," the woman said.

The boy went inside. The girl squatted and scratched the hound behind the ear. The lad returned with two peppermint sticks. He handed one to his sister, and they went back down the steps.

"How do you know there's nothing here for us?" Ralph said. "You don't know what we're after."

The woman's game reached a dead end. She scooped the cards up and leaned back in her chair, pipe in hand.

"Look at you and your fancy suits. You ain't worth the nickels you spend on soda pops. Folks in this town don't cotton to outsiders snooping around. You're not welcome here."

Ralph shook his head.

"You aren't curious," he said. "You don't know why we're here, and you don't care. You just want us gone."

He turned to me.

"Does that sound right to you?" he said.

He turned back to the woman.

"You act like you're not interested," he said. "Maybe that's because you know why we're here and you're afraid to talk to us."

The old gal flinched. If the game had been poker, she'd have lost the hand. I pulled Ethan Alexander's picture from my pocket and placed it on the barrel top. I pointed to the image of Bobby Lopez.

"This man. Have you seen him?" I said. "He's older now."

The woman glanced at the photograph. She stared at the barrel and refused to look up.

"I've got nothing to say to you," she said. "Git now. Leave the bottles."

She said enough. Ralph swallowed the last of his cola and lowered the empty bottle to the barrel top.

"Thanks for the refreshment," he said.

The lady snatched up her cards and shuffled in a fury. We got back into the roadster and pulled away.

"You handled that well," I said. "She knows something, and that means everybody in town knows something."

We continued up the street. Windows were raised to admit a breeze. Laundry hung on a line. We saw signs of people, but we didn't spot another soul. No children played. No adult sat on a porch. Dogs and cats roamed the streets. People had gone indoors.

"Must be suppertime," Ralph said.

"It's a bit early," I said.

A sign at the edge of town read "Cemetery." An arrow pointed east. We drove a half mile and stopped in the shade beneath a row of trees near the entrance. We got out and walked through the graves. Stones were carved with dates of deceased that went as far back as the 1870s.

"No fresh gravesites," Ralph said.

Another road led to the north where a copse of trees stood along the road.

"What's up there?" I said.

We drove the short distance and pulled over in the shade. A fence surrounded the acreage. A sign read, "Dunlap Colored Cemetery." I glanced at Ralph. He stared at the sign. We walked through the gate.

Stone markers lay helter-skelter amid patches of bluestem grass and goldenrod. Carved headstones decorated a few graves. White-washed stones sufficed for most. The name of a man who had died two years earlier was etched into a marble headstone atop one plot.

I pointed to a mound of earth beneath a tree. The freshly turned soil was unmarked.

"Dunlap? Maybe he didn't make it," Ralph said.

I walked around the grave and found nothing. We stood in silence for a moment.

"It could be Dunlap," I said. "Then again, it could be Lopez."

Ralph frowned.

"Lopez? How do you figure?" he said. "You saw the sign."

"Yeah. I saw it," I said. "Suppose Lopez bought the bullet. What if Lopez was shot, and Dunlap is alive?"

"Where are you going with this?" he said.

"If Dunlap is alive and Lopez is dead, what better place to bury the body than right here?" I said. "If the law comes snooping, they'll find this grave and move on. They'll keep looking for Lopez and forget about Dunlap."

"That would make sense," Ralph said.

"It could be Dunlap underground," I said. "It could be Lopez. It could be neither one. Maybe they're both alive and another body is planted six feet under."

A pickup truck pulled up next to my roadster. Two men, Negro, beefy and muscled, got out of the truck. One wore bib overalls with no shirt. The other wore khaki slacks and an undershirt. Neither carried flowers to put on a grave.

"This must be the welcoming committee," I said.

The men crossed their arms and glared at us. We walked over. The man in the overalls spoke.

"You two aren't welcome here," he said. "Get out."

"We're just paying our respects," I said.

He moved fast for a big man. His fist snapped out and caught me in the solar plexus. I doubled over and gasped.

"Maybe you didn't hear me," he said. "We want you gone."

"We're hunting down criminals," Ralph said, "wanted for murder. Maybe you know something about that."

"You're in the wrong place," the big man said. "Get out while you can."

The men got into their truck and drove away. I stood up and took deep breaths.

"How're you doing?" Ralph said.

"Okay," I said. "I'll ache tomorrow."

The truck kicked up a rooster tail of dust and rounded the corner.

"That was just a taste," I said. "We're on to something."

We went back into town and rolled down the streets. We kept out an eye for the pickup. The late afternoon sun begged a body to find a shady spot. Not a soul sat on a porch or beneath a tree. They'd all gone indoors. The streets were empty. Porches were empty. The place was buttoned up. At the south end of town, I made a U-turn.

"They can't stay indoors forever," I said, "but we're done for the night. Council Grove isn't far. We'll get a room and come back in the morning."

I drove past the church and the locked up bank. The porch at the store was vacant. The woman and her hound were not in sight.

"She's gone and so is the dog," Ralph said. "So is the broom."

"Maybe she went for a ride," I said.

Down the block, Ralph raised a hand and said, "Hold on."

I stopped in the street. Ralph looked toward a house on the right.

"What's that in the window?" he said.

A sun-faded sign in handwritten capitals was difficult to read. I rolled closer.

"Room to let," Ralph said.

The layout didn't look promising, neither the sign nor the house.

"Let's go to Council Grove," I said.

"I'll check here," he said.

I pulled over. Ralph got out and knocked on the door. No answer. He knocked again and then knocked a third time. The door cracked open. A dark face appeared, an elderly woman. Ralph and the woman exchanged words. The door swung open, and Ralph went inside. I sat behind the wheel and listened to the crickets. In a few minutes Ralph returned.

"I'll stay here," he said. "You go on."

He reached into the back of the roadster for his grip.

"Widow lady owns the place," he said. "She's hard up for cash. She'll put me up and throw in some chow."

I tapped my fingers on the steering wheel and scanned the area.

"Those guys may be back," I said.

"They aren't going to hassle me while I'm under that old lady's roof," he said. "You go ahead. See you in the morning."

Ralph was a grown man.

"See you in the morning," I said.

I left Ralph in Dunlap and drove northwest to Council Grove.

12

I reached Council Grove, and the roadster fought the steering wheel. I pulled into a Standard Oil station near the corner of Main and Vine. The attendant walked around the car and pointed out the problem.

"Low tire," he said.

"I've been driving backroads," I said. "I must've gotten into flint rock."

"You probably picked up a nail," he said. "If you'd met up with flint, you'd be running on the rim. This won't take long to fix."

He went to work. I walked to a phone booth on the corner. The operator placed my call, and Agnes answered on the first ring.

"I was just locking up," she said. "What's up with you two?"

I brought Agnes up to date on our talk with the wiry solitaire player in Dunlap and our visit to the cemetery. I didn't mention the men in the truck.

"So your hunch paid off?" she said. "You think that's where they went?"

"The signs are there," I said. "We'll knock on doors in the morning. Anything on your end?"

"Ethan Alexander called. He's anxious. He wondered if you'd found anything. Sitting and waiting for news makes him antsy, I suppose."

I told Agnes I'd give Ethan a call. We said our goodbyes. The operator rang Ethan's number, but there was no answer.

"He's in a wheelchair," I said. "It takes him a few minutes. Try it again."

She called again and gave it several rings. Ethan came on the line.

"Yes, hello," he said. He sounded out of breath.

"It's me," I said.

"Good," he said. "Go ahead."

He listened and didn't speak while I gave my report.

"Ralph and I will canvass the area in the morning," I said. "Someone will talk. We just have to find that someone. Dunlap is a small place. If the men are there we'll find them. I'll let you know as soon as I have something."

The station attendant had mounted the repaired tire. He looked my way and pointed to the gas pump. I gave him a thumbs up. It made sense to top off the tank. I might not see another station soon. Ethan and I finished our call, and I walked back to my car.

The attendant held up the culprit he'd pulled out of the tire, a bent nail. I thanked the man and settled up.

"I need a room for the night," I said. "Any suggestions?"

"There're several hotels in town," he said. "My sister lets rooms. Her place is clean, quiet, and cheap."

"That's the ticket," I said.

"I'll call her and let her know you're coming," he said.

He gave me his sister's address, and I left my card. I drove downtown and pulled up at the Hays House. A drugstore across the street looked closed, but I walked over to check. I wanted to question the druggist. The summer sun burned in the late afternoon. The door was locked up and no one stirred inside.

I walked back across the street. The Hays House was familiar to many. Seth Hays, a great-grandson of Daniel Boone, built the establishment in the 1800s and drew folks traveling the Santa Fe Trail. Decades later, it remained popular for food and shelter.

I took a stool at the bar. The bartender put down the glass he was wiping and flipped the towel onto his shoulder.

"What'll you have," he said.

I pointed to the tap. He pulled on the stick and placed a frothy glass of beer in front of me. It was quiet, and he was amiable, so we talked a little baseball. We discovered that we both rooted for the New York Yankees. Neither one of us could explain why.

"Don't tell anybody," he said. "I may have to get another job."

The bell on the door tinkled, and another customer took a stool. The bartender moved over to serve him. I picked up a menu. The café featured meat and potatoes, but I nixed the idea. I'd spent the day in the heat. The thought of hot food didn't sit well. I settled on a ham and cheese sandwich.

I ordered and browsed the *Council Grove Republican* while I waited. The high school had hired an English teacher, a recent graduate of the Kansas State Teachers College in Emporia. She'd begin teaching in the fall and was excited to be a Council Grove Brave. A new bookstore on Main Street invited citizens to stop in and buy a bestseller.

The sandwich arrived, and the bartender refilled my glass. I scanned the room while I ate. Framed photographs of Kansas Rotary Club district governors hung behind the bar. A Rotary Club banner hung on the wall next to an American Flag on a pedestal. The Rotary Club held their weekly meetings at the Hays House.

I finished my sandwich and handed the bartender my cash. He rang up the sale, and I noticed a photograph taped to the cash register. Several women shoveled snow in front of the café. The gals looked to be having a swell time.

"That was three months ago, the seventh of April," the bartender said. "Hard to believe, huh? In April? That's my wife right there. It snowed like crazy. We got a kick out of it. The skies dropped nearly ten inches of snow in April. Can you believe it?"

I recalled the snowstorm.

"I can believe it," I said. "That snow dropped on Wichita, too."

"Now here we are, one hundred degree days," he said.

"That's Kansas. Go to sleep in the Arctic and wake up in the tropics," I said.

I left and drove to the address the station attendant had given me. His sister lived in a two-story frame house on Belfry. She expected me and smiled when I arrived. She had a room prepared.

"You'll be upstairs, Mr. Stone. The door to your room is open. I put a fresh pitcher of water next to the bed. You'll find clean linens and towels. The bathroom is down the hall. You're my only guest, so you won't be disturbed."

I thanked her and started to go up but changed my mind. It was warm indoors. I dropped my bag at the bottom of the stairs and went outside to sit on the porch. I took a seat in a wicker chair and lit a cigarette. I looked over my notes on the case. My hostess joined me on the porch with iced tea.

"I just took cookies out of the oven," she said. "They're cooling in the kitchen. Shall I bring a plate?"

Her iced tea hit the spot, but I declined the cookies. She took a seat in a wicker chair.

"It's nice to have a visitor," she said. "Most nights my rooms stay empty."

Alma Noonan volunteered that she lived alone, a widow. She was a young widow, still in her thirties. She told me her dearly deceased had yet to reach his fortieth birthday when he died.

"When the grim reaper calls, he doesn't consult a birth certificate," she said in a matter-of-fact tone. "One day my husband pecked me on the cheek and said goodbye, just as he did every day. Then, he went to work and had a heart attack."

Her eyes focused on the memory.

"I was in the kitchen cutting up chicken to fry," she said. "A knock came at the door."

She dabbed her eyes with a hankie.

"We had no children," she said. "I'm alone in this house. I rent rooms. I give piano lessons and play the organ at the Congregational Church, too."

She paused and apologized.

"Listen to me go on," she said. "Forgive me. I must be boring you to tears. My brother said you were a private detective, Mr. Stone. I'm a shameless snoop. May I ask what brings a private detective to our town?"

"Murder, theft, arson," I said. "That all took place in Wichita. I'm on the trail of the suspects. They've led me to Morris County."

Her hand went to her chest.

"Here? We have murderers in Council Grove?"

"I believe they're close by," I said.

"That's awful. Your work sounds dangerous," she said. "Is it risky?"

"Risk is a part of life," I said. "We face risk every day."

Mrs. Noonan looked doubtful.

"Some roads are riskier than others," she said.

"What did your husband do for a living?" I said.

"He was an accountant, brilliant with numbers. He had an office downtown. He kept the books for—oh. Oh, I see what you're saying."

"When the grim reaper calls," I said.

"Still, tracking down criminals is violent work. You must carry a gun. Is it worth it?"

"Do you mean is what I do worth the money? I ask myself that question from time to time. Danger and low pay suit me, I guess. That's me all right, high risk and low reward."

I laughed. Alma Noonan looked bemused. She possessed poise and a quiet charm. Her pleasant face could have used a few laugh lines. She looked attractive in her cotton dress and styled curls, but it didn't tax the imagination to see the widow Noonan in a bustle and a bun.

We chatted until the sun dropped and the fireflies flickered. Alma said goodnight and moved inside.

I sat beneath the porch light and made notes in my book. The old lady at the store in Dunlap had been wary of strangers. There was nothing unusual there. Folks are usually wary of strangers. The tough guys at the cemetery were another matter, though. Those men had something to hide.

I drained my glass of tea and rose from my chair. I went inside and climbed the stairs. As billed, the room was clean and quiet. I undressed and raised a window. My head hit the pillow, and I was gone.

Saturday

July 9, 1938

13

A rooster crowed. I sat up in bed and groaned. My midsection was tender. My thoughts turned to Ralph Waldo in Dunlap. I threw back the covers. Council Grove would be waking up. I had business downtown before returning to Dunlap.

I cleaned up in the bathroom, dressed, and went downstairs. Morning sounds came from the kitchen. The aroma of fresh, brewed coffee drew me.

"I apologize for that rooster," Alma Noonan said. "My neighbor raises chickens. Would you like breakfast? How about bacon and eggs?"

A skillet rested on the stovetop. Eggs lay in a basket on the counter. On another day, I would have accepted her offer, but I needed to get to Ralph Waldo.

"No, thanks, on breakfast, but that coffee smells good," I said.

Alma poured coffee, and we sat at the table. I kept my eye on the clock over the stove. Alma asked how I'd slept, and I assured her everything was aces. I'd had a restful sleep. We finished our coffee, and I settled the bill.

"Take care of yourself, Mr. Stone," she said. "Catch those desperadoes. And stop again if you're ever in Council Grove."

I thanked her for her hospitality and left. Pedestrians strolled the walks downtown. Farmers and Drovers Bank hadn't opened its doors, but there was movement inside. Customers gathered on the corner at Main and Neosho. A door stood open at Durland and White Hardware. Vehicles lined the curb outside the Hays House café. I pulled over at the drugstore as the druggist flipped the sign in the window to Open.

"First customer of the day," he said when the bell tinkled above the door.

I found what I wanted, a deck of playing cards on a shelf of sundry items. I placed my purchase on the counter. A magazine on a rack caught my attention. The colorful cover screamed "ACTION COMICS" in bold, red letters. An illustration featured a brawny he-man decked out in blue tights and a flowing red cape. A red S adorned his chest. The muscular character hoisted a green sedan over his head. Citizens scattered in panic. I picked up the magazine and thumbed the pages.

"The guy's name is Superman," the druggist said. "That's the first issue, hot off the press. My kids love him. Got it just this week."

"I look at the funnies in the newspaper, but I know a swell young man who'd go for this," I said.

The price on the cover said a dime.

"I'll take this and the cards," I said.

The druggist punched keys on the register. I placed coins on the counter.

"You're not from around here," he said.

"I'm a private detective working on a case," I said. "Maybe you can help me."

The man furrowed his brow. I reached into my pocket.

"I'm looking for a man who may have stopped here. It would have been sometime within the week."

I showed him the photo and pointed out Lopez.

"That was taken twenty years ago," I said. "He's in his late thirties now."

He stared at the picture.

"What did this guy do?" he said.

"He's a murder suspect along with an accomplice," I said. "One of them may have been injured. If so, they may have needed medical supplies."

"Twenty years ago. That's a long time," he said and studied the photo. "A man changes. There was a fella, though. He came in needing bandages and alcohol and such. Just a few days ago. The man was in a hurry."

"The man I'm looking for would've been in a hurry."

"I can't say it was your man. I wouldn't have thought of him if it hadn't been for his shirt," the druggist said.

"What about it?" I said.

"His sleeves were rolled up. One sleeve was stained with blood."

"That could be my guy," I said.

"What's this man's name?" he said.

"The guy in the picture is Bobby Lopez. His accomplice goes by Dunlap," I said.

"Nah, it must have been someone else who came in," he said. "This fella had his name tattooed on his arm. His name was Earl."

Ralph was waiting on the porch when I pulled up. He tossed his grip in the back seat and climbed aboard.

"I found something last night," he said.

"I found something this morning," I said. "They're in Dunlap all right."

"Drive up the street," Ralph said. "Go slow."

I coasted forward. Ralph sat on the edge of his seat with his head turned to the right.

"I stepped out back last night to visit the outhouse," he said. "It was moon bright. I figured I'd stroll around town, see what I could see. Slow down here. There, in the back."

Ralph pointed to a patch of weeds behind a house.

"See that lean-to?"

A shed stood in the weeds.

"It's empty," I said.

"It's empty now. Last night there was a pickup truck parked there. I took a peek inside and saw smudges, stains on the seat. In the moonlight, it looked like blood. I snuck back at dawn to get a better look. The shed was empty. That truck was gone."

"Did you see the vase?" I said.

"Nah, the truck was empty," he said.

The townspeople were awake. A door slammed. A dog came off a porch, trotted toward a bush, and lifted its leg. A baby cried. A man stood outside his doorway and lit a cigarette. He watched us drive by.

At the store, the crone sat on the porch and leaned over her barrel. Her broom leaned against the wall. The hound lolled in front of the door.

"Déjà vu," Ralph said.

As before, the woman didn't acknowledge our presence when we climbed the steps. She'd dealt herself a hand of solitaire. She looked over the cards and ignored us.

"I bring a peace offering," I said.

I placed the deck of playing cards on the barrel. She glanced at the deck and grunted. She didn't look up.

"They're new. The seal hasn't been broken. All the aces are there," I said.

That got her attention. She looked at me. Then she leaned back and laughed. I glanced at the cards she played. All four aces lay visible atop the barrel. She puffed on her corncob pipe and gave me a tobacco-stained grin.

"You're an odd man, private detective," she said.

"The men are here in Dunlap," I said. "We know they're here or they were here. We intend to find them. You want us to leave. I get that. We don't like being here, but we're not leaving until we get answers. The sooner you talk the sooner we'll be gone."

She considered my words. She took her pipe in hand.

"You might see the oracle," she said. "Won't matter. She won't see you."

Then the old woman cackled and dismissed me with a wave of her hand. She returned to her game of solitaire.

"What's that old hen talking about?" Ralph said in the car. "Who's the oracle?"

"I have no idea, but we're going to get answers. Everyone knows we're here. They know why we're here. Let's knock on doors."

We stopped at the house with the shed. We knocked and waited and knocked again. The door cracked open. A nose and eyes appeared. I held up my card and started to speak but never got the chance.

"I know who you are. Those boys aren't under this roof. Git. Go on, now."

The door started to close. I stopped it with a stiff arm.

"Their truck was parked in your shed last night," I said.

"That don't make 'em mine," she said. "A skunk lives under the house. That don't make it mine neither. Now get your hand off my door."

I removed my hand from the door, and it slammed shut.

We tried the next house and the next one and so on down the street, all with similar results. Our presence was no secret. Everyone knew we were private detectives looking for suspects on the lam. No one wanted to talk about it.

"We've found the right place," I said. "Now, we have to find the person who will talk to us."

"The oracle?" Ralph said.

"The oracle," I said. "We have to find the oracle."

We neared a house where a couple of youngsters played in the dirt. Two boys pushed toy trucks and made throaty noises. They looked up as we approached. One of the boys stood up and dropped his truck. He balled his hands into fists.

"You the man who shot my uncle?" he said.

"No, I did not shoot your uncle," I said. "Is he here?"

The boy swung a leg and kicked me in the shins. He socked my knee with his fist. I bent over and picked him up and held him at arm's length. He squirmed and struggled.

"Easy, young fella," I said, "settle down. Who told you I shot your uncle?"

He twisted and tried to kick me again.

"Granny said so! Granny said a white man shot my uncle!"

"I did not shoot your uncle. Where's your Granny?" I said. "Is she inside?"

He wriggled, and I let him go. The boy turned and raced around the corner of the house. His playmate ran after him, hot on his heels. Ralph chuckled.

"Wipe that grin off your face," I said.

The grin grew into laughter.

"Some detective," Ralph said, "saving the world from angry six-year-olds."

I knocked on the screen door. A woman appeared who was no granny. The young woman would've been attractive had she lost the scowl. She adopted a fists-on-her-hips pose and appeared to have thoughts of kicking my shins.

"Hold it," she said. "Say what you came to say and be on your way."

I reached into my pocket for my card. Another woman's voice came from inside the house.

"Now wait a minute, Wilma Jean. Wait a minute. You hear me? You show those men inside. I intend to have words with those men."

"Hush, Momma," Wilma Jean said.

"Don't you hush your momma, little girl. You do what I say now."

Wilma Jean glared through the screen, fists on her hips. Wilma Jean did not welcome strangers coming into her home. Wilma Jean did not welcome an argument with her irate mother, either.

She tapped her foot and scowled and weighed the options. When the scales balanced, she shook her head and gave the screen door a shove. The door slapped against the side of the house. Her irate mother was more threatening than unwelcome strangers.

She ushered us in with a sweeping gesture. We stepped over the threshold, and she pointed to a couch. Ralph and I sat down.

A gray-haired woman shuffled into the room. We rose to our feet. The woman took tentative steps with her arms extended forward. She groped for a chair. When she reached it, she ran her hands down the back and over the seat. Then she lowered herself.

The woman was blind. She turned toward us and spoke.

"Sit down," she said.

We sat down.

"Now then," the woman said, "you gentlemen state your business. I know what you've been saying to my neighbors. Say it to me as if you were saying it for the first time. I want to hear your piece from your lips."

I spoke. The woman listened. I told her that I'd been hired to find a man named Bobby Lopez who sometimes went by Earl. He was wanted for murder. The man who hired me wanted Lopez to surrender himself to the police to avoid further violence. Lopez had an accomplice who went by the name of Dunlap. He, too, was wanted for murder.

"Those men are the focus of a statewide manhunt," I said. "They can't hide forever. They'll be caught. Their best hope for staying alive is if we get to them first."

The woman remained stoic.

"We want no harm to come them," I said. "The police don't share our concern for their safety. If the police get to them before we do, they'll use whatever force is necessary to take them in."

The woman considered my words.

"They're accused of murder," I said again. "Throw in arson and theft. Valuable art perished in the fire. According to a witness one man carried an antique vase when they fled the scene. We're looking for the men and the vase."

"I know nothing about a vase," the woman said.

"When the police learn that those men came to Dunlap, they'll swoop down on this town like a swarm of locusts," I said. "They'll search every nook and corner until they find them. They'll be on your doorstep. They'll be in your home, in your closets, in your attic. They'll be armed. They'll shoot anyone who gets in their way.

"My partner and I don't judge the men. Guilty or not, the courts will decide. Our job is to locate them, get them to surrender peacefully, no gunplay. Let the men tell their story without more violence."

She turned her head and faced Ralph.

"Do you have anything to say, or are you just this man's lackey?" she said.

"I'm nobody's lackey, ma'am," Ralph said. "I'll kindly ask you not to suggest it. I'm a licensed private investigator. What this man said is the truth. We want no harm to come to the men we're chasing."

The old woman sat in thought. She didn't speak.

"Lopez's accomplice goes by Dunlap," I said again. "It's that name that brought us to your town. Is he family?"

A large man came into the room. He wore the same bib overalls he'd worn the day before at the cemetery. He still wore a scowl. He leaned against a wall, arms crossed, and chewed a toothpick. He didn't speak.

Wilma Jean moved over to her mother and draped an arm over her shoulders.

"Momma, we don't know these men," she said.

Her mother patted Wilma Jean's arm.

"No we don't, but what they say about the police is true," she said. "We can't have the police."

The woman turned toward us.

"His given name is Benjamin, Benjamin Carter. He's named for the man who led our people to these hills, Benjamin Singleton. Our community has many boys christened Benjamin. It can be confusing. My Benjamin took to calling himself Dunlap when he was a boy. The name stuck."

She gestured toward a spinet piano against the wall.

"Dunlap played that piano," she said. "That boy is blessed with the gift of music. He never had a lesson. He hears a piece of music and plays it. He makes his own music, too. He carries music in his head, in his heart. It springs from his soul. Dunlap Carter is my son. Sybil Carter is my name."

"Sybil," I said. "So, you're the oracle."

"You've been speaking to my sister," she said. "Some folks call me the oracle. I'm blind, but my sister believes I see things other folks don't. That may be true."

"Your sister is the woman at the store? The woman who plays solitaire on the porch?" I said.

"She's my sister," she said.

"Dunlap is your son," I said. "You say that in the present tense. I take it Dunlap is alive."

"My son is alive. You've met his sister, Wilma Jean. That's his brother Edward brooding in the background. Edward, we'll have no trouble in this house, you hear your momma?" she said.

Edward heard but didn't reply. He removed the toothpick from his mouth and glared. I sneered. Edward gave me the finger.

"Dunlap was wounded," I said. "We spotted a fresh grave at the cemetery. We thought it might be his."

"A bullet grazed my boy. It didn't kill him, praise the Lord. It took some of his blood but not his life. That grave you mention holds the remains of my sister's husband. He passed last week. Those two were never apart. They spent their days at their store, played gin rummy for hours on end. Now Celia is alone. Asa is dead and buried. Now she plays solitaire."

"Her husband's name was Asa?" I said.

"That's right. She called him Ace."

The woman had said she lost her Ace. I assumed it was a playing card. She'd lost her husband, her Ace.

"Both men are here or they have been," I said. "Their truck was parked in a shed down the street. That shed is empty now. Where did they go?"

"We don't know," Wilma Jean said. "They left in the middle of the night. They pulled out without a word while we slept. I'm angry, but I'm beginning to see why they didn't talk. They expected someone to show up and ask questions. They didn't want us to have answers."

"They left for Wichita," her mother said.

"Momma, you don't know that," Wilma Jean said. "They never said. Why Wichita? The police are looking for them there. That'd be the last place they'd go."

"They went to Wichita," Sybil repeated.

"Wilma Jean is right," I said. "The Wichita police are on the lookout there. Those men would be flies in a spider's web."

No one spoke. Edward leaned against the wall, arms crossed, a fresh toothpick in his mouth. Wilma Jean ran a hand over her momma's shoulders.

"My Dunlap sat at that piano last evening," Sybil Carter said. "My Dunlap tickles the keys, makes sorrowful music. Such sorrow in that boy. Blue, blue notes. Sorrowful notes inch their way into a body's soul. I hear those notes now. I sat here last night and wept."

She dabbed her eyes with a handkerchief.

"I cried. That Earl wept, too," she said.

"I sat here and heard my brother play," Wilma Jean said. It was beautiful and sorrowful, but that white man didn't cry."

Sybil smiled.

"Earl didn't weep tears," she said. "Earl wept inside."

Sybil patted her breast.

"Earl carries a pain," she said. "Has for much of his life. My boy's music brings relief. It heals a tender soul. It's the medicine a momma brings."

"What does this have to do with returning to Wichita?" I said.

"Earl is in love," Sybil said. "He pines for a woman who calls him. The men drove into the night so Earl could be with his woman."

"I never heard mention of a woman," Wilma Jean said.

"There never was mention of a woman," her mother said, "not in so many words. A woman lives in his head, his heart. I heard her voice with every word he spoke."

Sybil Carter lifted her head toward a vision only she could see.

"I hear a silver bird," she said, "a siren call. A song wafts through the shadows and embraces a shattered soul, caresses a creased brow. A silver bird sings blue notes beneath a blue moon, icy and cool. A silver bird whispers in the dark of night."

Sybil Carter lowered her head. Then she turned toward us.

"You men leave now," she said. "Follow that siren's song. Find the silver bird. The silver bird will lead you to Earl. Earl will lead you to my Dunlap. Find those men before the police do. Mind you, private detectives. Let no harm come to my son."

14

Ralph Waldo and I headed south through the Flint Hills and didn't stop for gasoline or lunch. We rolled into Wichita that afternoon.

Ralph Waldo hadn't heard from Rum-Rum before we left, and he was concerned. We talked it over. Rum-Rum lived in the shadows and made an appearance when it suited him. In the past, he'd appeared when Ralph beckoned, but so far he'd remained hidden. No one had seen him since he knocked on Ethan Alexander's door. Ralph wanted to find him.

"I figure he's scared," Ralph said. "I'll put out the word that we mean him no harm. I'll let you know."

I pulled up at Douglas and Emporia. Ralph grabbed his grip from the backseat, gave me a wave, and motored off in his car. I looked at the Lawrence Block Building and raised my eyes to the window of my office on the top floor. I tapped a finger on the steering wheel. My office would be empty on Saturday. Mail and messages would wait.

I edged back into the traffic and drove to Ethan Alexander's place near the university campus. I arrived unannounced, but Ethan was happy to see me. He was eager to hear my report.

"Come in, come in," he said.

He gestured toward the kitchen table and retrieved beer from the icebox. I removed my hat and took a seat while he popped the tops on the bottles. We each took a pull, and I began my report. Ethan was all ears. He furrowed his brow when I told him about the woman the oracle described.

"A woman? That's news to me," Ethan said, "but we haven't spoken in some time. I'm not surprised. Bobby's a man, after all. He was popular with the ladies in France. Who's the oracle?"

I gave him the lowdown on Sybil Carter, Dunlap's mother.

"She called the woman a silver bird," I said. "The oracle said the bird cast a spell over your pal and drew him back to Wichita."

Ethan Alexander puzzled over the news.

"I've been out of touch with Bobby," he said. "I'm encouraged by this news, though. In twenty years, this is the first I've heard of a serious relationship. Bobby's dated women, but not one who cast a spell."

"I wonder how this woman figures into what took place a week ago," I said. "Love makes a man do crazy things."

"You don't believe me," he said, "but Bobby is innocent. You don't know if this woman exists. If she does exist, how do you find her?"

"That's the question," I said. "The oracle may be wise or she may be off her rocker. I'm working on a tip from a blind woman. I could be going on a wild goose chase."

"A wild goose chase. That's what you said about going to Dunlap," he said. "Look what happened."

"If there is a woman, she could hide the men," I said, "for a while. Let's assume they're holed up together. If anyone spots a change in the woman's behavior, they'll get suspicious."

"How so?" Ethan said.

"People watch each other, and they don't like change. When someone acts out of character, someone else scratches his head. A grocer sees a customer buy a dozen eggs and two loaves of bread when she usually buys half that. The milkman delivers an extra bottle of milk. A lamp burns after midnight, and neighbors wonder why. Changes in behavior trigger suspicions."

"Are people really like that?" Ethan said.

"All it takes is one," I said. "Not everyone is a snoop. This crime is still fresh. It's in the newspapers. The city knows the men are in the bush. That makes people nervous. Don't forget that reward. Money changes the game. Money makes people pay attention."

"So, what's next?"

"If she exists, I have to find her. Rum-Rum should be in the picture. We haven't found him. Rum-Rum is hiding, and Ralph is beating the bushes. Then, there's the dead man, Karl Weaver. Weaver gnaws at me. Weaver's an unknown quantity. I asked Lieutenant McCormick about Weaver, and he hedged. He said the police were on top of it. I don't buy it. They hadn't found his next-of-kin. That doesn't spell on top of it to me. Mac knows something he's keeping close to the vest. Shots were fired. Weaver bought it. Who was Weaver, and why did that bullet have his name on it?"

The Lawrence Block Building was locked and quiet. My key unlocked the front door, and I stepped into the eerie silence. Pete Stone Private Investigations, shared the building with a law firm, a couple of accountants, an insurance office, and various tenants that came and went. They all had something in common. They knew how to take a day off.

I climbed the steps to the third floor. Agnes had straightened my desk and stacked the mail and messages next to the telephone. I read the message on top and picked up the receiver. The operator placed a call. The phone rang four times, and a female voice came over the line.

"Hello?" she said.

She sounded tentative, like she wasn't sure.

"Pete Stone calling for Aaron Bernstein," I said.

I waited a beat.

"What's this about?" she said.

"Aaron Bernstein left a message for me to call him. That's what I'm doing."

"What's your business with Aaron?"

"Don't worry, lady. I'm not a bill collector, an irate husband, or an insurance salesman. Bernstein and I are pals. How about it? Is he in or not?"

"You don't have to get snippy," she said. "Aaron Bernstein is not in at the moment. I can take a message."

"Just tell him Pete Stone returned his call. I'm in my office."

"Does he have your number?"

I rolled my eyes.

"He called me, remember?"

"Oh, yes. Okay. I'll give him the message."

"Thanks," I said and hung up the phone.

The next message was from Ethan Alexander. I'd just left his place, so I tossed that note into the trash. Terrance Hightower wanted me to call. I owed him a report, but I wanted to leave the line open for Aaron Bernstein. I set Hightower's message aside. Police Lieutenant McCormick left a message. That would wait, too.

I lit a cigarette and turned to the mail. A charity I'd helped in the past was desperate for loot. Would I help? They were always desperate. They always asked but never bothered to say thanks. They kept asking for more.

The next envelope contained a letter from an insurance agent who touted a policy that promised financial security. In the last envelope, an investment firm promised wealth and prosperity. Riches, security, and peace of mind awaited me. All I had to do was wedge a crowbar into my wallet and let the vultures feast on my dough.

I thought it over. I liked the idea of more money. Rich sounded good to me. I scanned each letter, stacked them into a pile, and tossed the pile into the trash. I felt richer immediately.

The telephone rang.

"Cow town cops, Sheriff Stone speaking."

"Heh, heh. Looks like I've got the right number."

"Talk to me, Bernstein. What's the word?"

"My gal said a rude man called. She forgot the guy's name, but I figured it was you. You annoyed her."

"I do that. Let me apologize to her. What's her name?" I said.

Bernstein laughed.

"You always ask the tough questions," he said. "She's gone."

We bantered, then I asked my question.

"Karl Weaver," I said. "Did you learn anything?"

"Weaver had a past," Bernstein said. "I've got the lowdown on the guy, but I have to be someplace. I'll talk to you tomorrow."

"Tomorrow is Sunday," I said. "How about a face-to-face?"

"Tell me when and where," he said.

"Afternoon, Twenty-second and Brooklyn," I said.

Bernstein chuckled.

"Heh, heh. Sure. See you there," he said.

We rang off. I dialed Terrance Hightower at home and got no answer. I tried the art gallery in Riverside and struck out again. I dialed the police station. McCormick was out till Monday. Three strikes, game over.

I stood to leave, and the telephone rang.

"Pete Stone," I said into the receiver.

A male voice spoke.

"You're in over your head, gumshoe. Back out now or you'll end up like Weaver."

The phone went dead.

Sunday

July 10 , 1938

<h1 style="text-align:center">15</h1>

Game time was an hour away when I pulled up at Twenty-second and Brooklyn in Kansas City. The crowd outside the stadium was small. Kansas City baseball fans were a rabid bunch. They'd be along soon. An exciting match was on tap. Folks drifted toward the ticket window in twos and threes and trickled through the turnstiles.

I parked in the shade, top down on my roadster. I lit a cigarette and leaned back. I thought about my mystery caller from the day before. The anonymous voice wanted me gone and warned I'd end up on a slab if I didn't back off the case. Hightower hired me to find the vase. I figured Bobby Lopez was the person with something to lose if I kept digging. Had Lopez made the call?

I eyeballed the crowd. The stadium had long been known as Muehlebach Field, home of the Kansas City Blues. That changed the year before. Colonel Jacob Ruppert, owner of the New York Yankees, bought the stadium and the minor league team. Flushed with hubris, he slapped his own name atop the facility.

Ruppert Stadium was also home to one of the greatest baseball teams in the Negro American League, the Kansas City Monarchs. On that summer Sunday, the Monarchs would be hosting a game against the rival Memphis Red Sox, another fine team vying for the top spot.

I flicked the dead cigarette onto the gravel. A voice over my shoulder spoke.

"They've got seats inside. All you have to do is buy a ticket," the voice said.

I looked up at a wolfish grin. The jutted chin bore a scar he hadn't gotten from a shaving accident.

"I've been sitting here watching people do that very thing," I said. "I almost had it figured out. It's a good thing you came along."

Aaron Bernstein wore a blue seersucker suit and a scarlet tie in a Windsor knot. His red pocket square was folded just so. The hatband on his straw boater matched the tie and the pocket square. Another joe in seersucker would've looked ordinary. Bernstein looked sharp enough to cut diamonds.

We shook hands in the parking lot.

"Lead on," he said.

We made our way to the ticket window. I bought a pair of ducats, and we went inside.

"I haven't eaten," I said. "You?"

"I rolled out of bed an hour ago," he said.

"I'll buy breakfast," I said.

The guy at the concession stand leaned forward.

"What'll it be?" he said.

"A couple of dogs with mustard," I said, "along with beer and baseball. That's how Grandad ate them."

The guy went to work. He placed hot franks in buns, slathered mustard, and wrapped them up in paper. He pulled the stick and filled cups with frothy brew. Colonel Ruppert kept Muehlebach beer on tap. I handed Bernstein a dog and a beer.

"You're giving a hot dog to a Jew?" he said.

"Breakfast of champions," I said.

We found our seats behind the first base dugout. The stadium roof provided welcome shade. We watched the teams run through their pregame routines. I scanned the crowd and sipped my beer.

"Some of these Negro players could be all-stars in the big leagues," I said. "Did you ever hear of the Monrovians?"

"The Mon-who?" he said.

"The Wichita Monrovians."

"Never heard of them," Bernstein said.

"Something triggered a memory," I said. "The Monrovians played a game twelve, thirteen years ago. People still talk about it."

Bernstein took a bite of hot dog and nodded approval.

"Not bad," he said. "What happened?"

"The Monrovians were colored ballplayers," I said. "The Ku Klux Klan had a team, too. The Klan was active then. This was before Kansas courts put the kibosh on the Klan."

Bernstein snorted.

"Yeah, right," he said.

"The Klan was legit then," I said. "Somebody came up with the idea of staging a game between the two teams, Negroes versus whites. The Monrovians usually played for gate receipts, winner take all. When they won they shared the dough with the community. Fans loved them. The players were good, and they won a lot.

"This day the teams played for charity. The ballpark is gone now. It used to be on Ackerman Island in the middle of the river. The stands were packed with folks, dark and light."

"Break out the shells and the shivs," Bernstein said.

"No guns and no knives," I said. "The umpires announced that any culprit who started trouble would be hauled to the hoosegow. Fans were boisterous, but no one got hurt."

"What happened?"

"The game was a nail-biter," I said. "Both teams played well. Pitchers controlled the outcome early. Midway through the game, the score was one apiece. Then bats came alive. Each team started scoring. The lead changed hands, back and forth. The final score was ten runs to eight, Monrovians over the Klan. Newspapers called it the greatest game ever played in Wichita."

The Monarchs finished their warmups.

"It makes you wonder," I said. "How good would baseball be if Negroes and whites played on the same field every day?"

We finished our hotdogs and beers. The Monarchs took their positions. The umpire yelled, "Play ball!" The crowd roared.

Fans arrived from church services, dressed to the nines in Sunday finery. Women wore hats featuring feathers and fruit. Men wore dress shirts and ties.

Fans cheered. Some players acted aloof, but fan favorites acknowledged the attention with a tip of the hat. First baseman Buck O'Neil waved to fans. He spoke to the crowd when he left the field for the dugout.

The first few innings were scoreless. Hilton Smith of the Monarchs and Lefty Wilson of the Red Sox were locked in a duel, each man the ace of his team's pitching staff. On a different day, I would have kept a scorecard and followed every play. On that day, I had other things on my mind.

Bernstein puffed a cigar. I lit a Chesterfield.

"Karl Weaver," I said.

Bernstein grinned.

"Karl Weaver," he said. "A name he used. He used others."

"I didn't figure him for a Boy Scout. Was he connected?" I said.

Bernstein shook his head.

"Not connected," he said. "Weaver was penny-ante. He spent time in jail, passed bad paper, petty theft, that sort of thing."

"He never learned," I said. "Weaver was no kid when he was retired to the pine box."

"As he grew older, his rap sheet grew along with him," Bernstein said.

Lumber smacked horsehide. The crowd came to its feet and roared. Buck O'Neil one-hopped a line drive against the left field fence. He slid into second base with a double.

"How long was that rap sheet?"

"Weaver grew older, not wiser," he said. "Cops busted a counterfeit ring, a half-dozen crooks. One of those crooks died during the bust, a fatal gunshot but not from a cop. They suspected Weaver killed the guy, but they couldn't make it stick. They recovered weapons and prints but nothing definitive. Weaver did a nickel in Leavenworth on the counterfeit charge."

The crowd roared again when Mex Johnson laced a single down the left field line. O'Neil sprinted around third base and crossed the plate. The Monarchs led one to nothing.

"The cops have this," he said. "McCormick knows this."

Of course Mac knew it.

"I suspected the cops had goods on Weaver," I said. "They kept a lid on it. The press never gets everything. According to Hightower, Weaver painted. He pooh-poohed the man's talent. I can't draw a line between Hightower and Weaver. What connected Weaver to art?"

Bernstein's grin ran cold. Bernstein survived in a violent world. People lived. People died. Death came with the territory. Bernstein lived by his own code. He once taunted a cop for not shooting a criminal. He also crippled a man for shooting a dog.

"Weaver did his time," he said. "The warden believed prisoners could be rehabilitated. He encouraged his houseguests to read and learn. Weaver painted."

"Weaver painted behind bars. He did his time," I said. "He was released. How did he get from prison to Wichita?"

Bernstein rolled his cigar ash to a point on the sole of his shoe.

"He landed in Kansas City after prison," he said. "I never met him. He rubbed elbows with some of my associates."

"From Leavenworth to Kansas City," I said. "Did he stay clean here in K.C.?"

"Who knows? He didn't get caught dirty," he said. "He worked in art. That doesn't mean he went straight. Crooks like Weaver don't go straight. I wouldn't make that bet with your money."

"Not with his record," I said. "How many ex-cons do you figure go straight?"

Bernstein laughed.

"They could hold a reunion in a broom closet," he said.

"He worked in Kansas City. He wound up in Wichita," I said. "I still can't draw the line. Is that all you've got?"

"That's what I've got," Bernstein said.

"It's more than I had," I said. "What drew him to Wichita? What exactly did he do in Kansas City?"

"He didn't paint for dough," Bernstein said. "He worked for a dealer. I don't know what he did for the dealer."

The mid-afternoon sun bore down. Temperatures hovered in the mid-nineties. I heard Bernstein's words and felt a chill.

"Do you have the name of the dealer?"

Bernstein retrieved a note from his pocket.

"A place called Carmichael's," he said. "Carmichael's of Kansas City."

Karl Weaver had worked for Carmichael's of Kansas City. That was the dealer Susie Donovan mentioned at Hightower's gallery. Hightower did business with Carmichael's.

I had telephoned Carmichael's. I spoke to Mr. James. Mr. James refused to discuss Hightower's business. I asked about Karl Weaver. Mr. James told me he'd never met the man. That was a lie. Karl Weaver had worked for Mr. James.

The game ended with no other runs. The score held one to nothing, the Kansas City Monarchs over the Memphis Red Sox.

Bernstein said he had someplace to be. We shook hands. I thanked him for digging the dirt on Weaver.

"I owe you one, pal," I said.

He touched the brim of his boater. I watched him move into the crowd. Monarch fans celebrated. Memphis fans were disappointed. That was baseball. I remained in my seat and stared at the ballfield and wondered why Mr. James had lied to me.

Sunday

July 10, 1938

to

Monday

July 11, 1938

16

I hadn't planned on spending the night in Kansas City. My plan was to meet with Aaron Bernstein, learn what I could about Karl Weaver, and drive back to the Air Capital after the final pitch of the game. Lucille and I had planned a quiet dinner at her place. After Bernstein revealed his nugget about Weaver's time at Carmichael's, my plan changed. I'd stay over in Kansas City and question Mr. James face-to-face on Monday morning.

My first stop was a phone booth on Brooklyn near the stadium. Lucille was disappointed I wouldn't make it for dinner, but I scored a run by calling her before she'd prepared our meal.

"I'll call you as soon as I get back into town," I said.

"Don't call tomorrow. Tomorrow I'm seeing a friend in Newton," Lucille said.

"I hope this friend wears dresses," I said.

"He does. Luckily he has the legs for it," she said. "Call me Tuesday."

"Heh, heh. Tuesday, sweetheart. Clear your calendar," I said.

I needed to find a room for the night, but first things first. I was in the barbecue capital of the country. Other towns in the south and Midwest claimed to have the best barbecue in the land, but when they went up against Kansas City barbecue, they all fought for second place.

Ruppert Stadium was near the Nineteenth and Highland neighborhood. I drove there and pulled up at a trolley barn. The sign read Perry's Barbecue. Mr. Henry Perry was in his sixties, but he still operated the smoker in the back.

A trio of jazz musicians busked beneath an elm tree. One man blew a horn and another played a trombone. The third kept time by slapping his fingers and palms against an empty barrel.

I placed two-bits on the counter, and a fellow in a stained apron handed over hickory-smoked ribs wrapped in newspaper.

"I keep beer in the ice box," he said.

"Sold," I said and dropped another coin on the counter.

I sat on a stump and tapped my toe while I feasted. Perry was famous for his peppery sauce, not as sweet as most. It suited my palate. The trio played well. Their music was lively. I polished off the ribs, lit a Chesterfield, and sipped beer.

More people visited the trolley barn. A line formed at the counter. I stood up and dropped a few coins in the upturned fedora on the ground. The drummer nodded thanks. I climbed back into my roadster and headed downtown.

I stopped at a drugstore for a toothbrush and a razor and left with my purchases in a brown paper bag. Carmichael's was located near Tenth and Locust. A hotel two blocks over looked affordable. I pulled over and parked. I buttoned up the top on the roadster.

The lobby greeted me with holes in the carpet, dead bulbs in the chandelier, and an odor of dirty laundry. I needed a cheap flop, not a romantic getaway, so I walked over to the desk. The clerk wore a black bow tie and a white shirt that had gone yellow.

I placed my paper bag on the counter and signed the register. The clerk worked a toothpick with his tongue and tried out his banter.

"What's with the bag?" he said.

"That's my luggage," I said.

"Luggage, huh?" he said.

He spun the register and read my signature.

"Stone. You travel light, Mr. Stone. Staying long?" he said.

The man was a real Jack Benny.

"All night," I said.

"That'll be two bucks for all night," he said and eyeballed my paper bag. "In advance."

I forked over the bills. A bellhop appeared at my elbow. His face fell when he caught sight of my luggage. I told the man I'd manage on my own.

The hotel was a dive, but I'd slept in worse. The sheets were clean and free of bugs. The room smelled better than the lobby. I opened the window and listened to the night and fell into a dreamless sleep.

Morning traffic woke me. I washed up and shaved, got dressed, and left the hotel. I still carried my own luggage.

I had time, so I found a diner and ordered coffee and scrambled eggs. When the minute hand approached nine, I settled up and drove the two blocks to Carmichael's.

The business was open, but no one was in sight. Paintings lined the walls or were displayed on easels. I picked up a business card near the entrance. Unlike the card from Susie Donovan, this one bore the proprietor's name, Henry James. I doubted it was the guy who wrote the books.

"Good morning, sir. May I help you?" a man said.

I recognized the baritone from the telephone. The voice didn't jibe with its owner. The short, frail man wore a gray, double-breasted suit and a gray tie. Both his hair and his eyes matched his threads. I held up his business card.

"Henry James? Proprietor?" I said.

"That's right," he said. "And you are?"

"The American."

"Pardon me?"

He didn't get the reference. I was right. He didn't write the books.

"My name is Pete Stone," I said. "We spoke on the telephone last week. So, who's Carmichael?"

"You're that gauche private detective from Wichita. You're investigating the Hightower affair," he said.

"You remember," I said. "So, who is he?"

"Mr. Carmichael established this business many years ago," he said. "He's retired now. When he retired, I purchased his name along with the business. His is an old and trusted name, well-known in the art community. Why are you here? I thought I explained over the telephone that I had nothing more to say to you."

The door opened, and a matronly woman walked in. She glanced our way.

"Just browsing," she said.

"I was in the neighborhood," I said. "I thought you might give me a tour. We can discuss art. Maybe we could talk about your former employee, Karl Weaver."

Henry James looked stricken. He looked over at the woman.

"Perhaps we should go into my office," he said.

His office had a window that looked out onto the showroom. He sat behind his desk facing the window. I took the chair across from him. He removed a cigarette from a gold case on his desk. I lit a Chesterfield. He put his unlit cigarette into his mouth and opened a drawer on his desk.

"I've left my lighter in the back," he said. "May I have a light?"

I leaned over and lit his cigarette.

"You told me over the phone that you never met Karl Weaver," I said. "That was a lie. Why did you lie to me Mr. James?"

"It's true. Karl Weaver did work for me at one time," he said. "Mr. Hightower got to know Karl Weaver when he made his trips to Kansas City. They hit it off, I suppose. Weaver left my employ to work for Mr. Hightower with my blessing. That's all there was to it."

"So, why did you lie?" I said.

"Frankly, I didn't see how it was any of your business," he said. "And I didn't see how bringing Karl Weaver's death into my business would help matters in any way. Weaver died violently, shot during a robbery. That occurred at the Hightower residence two hundred miles from here. It had nothing to do with me or my business."

"Weaver was an artist and an ex-con," I said. "He painted in prison. He painted in the Hightower studio. Did he keep up his hobby when he worked here for you?"

"I was aware of Weaver's prison history and his artistic talent," he said. "He convinced me that he had reformed, and I hired him. I have no idea how Karl Weaver spent his free time."

He looked out the window.

"I have a customer on the floor, Mr. Stone," he said. "While I have sympathy toward Mr. Hightower for his troubles, I have nothing further to add. I'm afraid that's all the time I can give you. Please excuse me."

He gestured toward the office door and followed me out into the showroom. He pointed to the exit.

"Don't come back," he said.

Then he pasted a smile on his face, walked toward his customer, and worked his baritone. I opened the door and left.

17

That afternoon I was back in Wichita. I reached for the telephone on my desk and heard a familiar voice on the other side of my door. I replaced the receiver and retrieved an item from a drawer. In the outer office, the paperboy bumped gums with Agnes. A bag stuffed with newspapers was slung over his shoulder.

"Hiya, Rusty," I said.

"Hiya, Mr. Stone."

"What's in the news?"

He pulled a copy of his bag and handed it over.

"I haven't even checked the baseball scores," he said.

Something stuck out of his back pocket.

"What are you reading?" I said.

Rusty pulled out a paperback book, wrinkled and worn and bound with staples. He placed it on the corner of Agnes's desk and smoothed it with his elbow.

"The Son of the Wolf," he said and handed it over. "Jack London is swell."

The cover read Little Blue Book No. 152. It was published in Girard, Kansas, along with hundreds of others. People all across the country read Little Blue Books, cheap to buy and great to read. The books were the average Joe's gateway to literature.

"Jack London spins a good yarn," I said. "I like his books myself."

"I've read them all," he said.

"You're a smart lad. You enjoy reading."

"I sure do."

"Here's something new," I said, "hot off the presses."

I handed Rusty the comic book I'd purchased in Council Grove. His eyes grew large.

"Wow! Superman!"

Agnes gauged Rusty's reaction and smiled.

"Who's Superman?" she said.

"Superman is a hero!" he said. "All the guys are talking about him. I haven't read it yet. I've been saving my pennies for a copy. I don't have to wait any longer. Gee thanks, Mr. Stone. This is really swell!"

The lad was fourteen years old. Rusty worked hard and saved his pennies. Every dime he earned went to his folks. He helped out with the bread and the eggs and whatever else they needed. The kid delivered newspapers in the city seven days a week, rain or shine. Rusty never complained. He just did it.

"That's the first issue," I said. "The guy who sold it to me said it might be worth something someday."

"Don't worry about that," Rusty said. "I'll take good care of this! Thanks again!"

He tucked the comic book into his newspaper bag. He went out the door with a grin on his face.

"Rusty's a swell kid," I said.

"Yeah, well, you're pretty swell, too, Mr. Stone," Agnes said. "Mr. Hightower called again, and there's a message to call Lieutenant McCormick."

"Swell," I said.

The hands on the Seth Thomas banjo clock snuck toward three o'clock. I returned to my desk. My conversation that morning with Mr. James gnawed at me. First he said he never met

Karl Weaver, then he said his association with the man was none of my business. He lied to me. People lied to me all the time. I didn't have to like it.

I dialed Hightower at his home. The telephone must have been at his elbow. It rang only once, and he came on the line. He didn't bother with the amenities.

"Stone, what kind of detective are you, anyway? Why haven't you returned my calls? You're supposed to be working for me. You took my money, then you disappeared. You've left me in the dark. Is this your idea of professional behavior?"

"I told you that I was working on behalf of another client," I said. My client hired me to find Lopez. You hired me to locate the vase. One leads to the other. I'm working both ends. I've been conducting my investigation."

"You went to Kansas City. Why? You've been pestering Henry James. You call that investigating?"

It didn't take long for James to contact Hightower and complain about my visit.

"I hired you to find my vase," he said. "You took my money. You go gallivanting hither and yon spending my money to pay your expenses, no doubt. What have you accomplished? Not a thing, that's what."

"How I conduct my investigation is none of your business, Mr. Hightower. However, you do deserve a report. For the record, I've called you more than once. I called your home and your gallery. You didn't answer either time."

"I was out," he said.

"So was I," I said.

"All right," he said. "Go ahead. Give me your report. Have you found my vase?"

"No, I haven't found it, but I'm close. I will find your vase."
"When?"
"Soon."
"If you're close, why can't you get it? What's holding you back?"

"There are elements of this crime that puzzle me. I'm trying to solve the puzzle. I have more questions than answers, and the answers I do have are questionable."

"What's that doubletalk supposed to mean?"

"It means I need more time. A few days should do it," I said.

"A few days. Today is Monday," Hightower said. "Okay, Thursday. That's your deadline, Stone. If I don't have my vase by Thursday, I want my money and your hide."

I wasn't sure how my hide figured into it. I didn't get the chance to ask. The dial tone buzzed in my ear. A sensitive guy would've felt wounded. My hide handled it.

Agnes knocked and came in.

"Ralph is here," she said.

I didn't like the expression on Agnes's face. Ralph followed her in. I didn't like his expression either. Agnes went out and closed the door. Ralph took a seat and didn't speak, so I did.

"Rum-Rum?" I said.

He looked at my desk and nodded.

"Yeah, Rum-Rum," he said and looked up. "Rum-Rum is dead."

Neither of us spoke. We stared at nothing and listened to the same. I lit a Chesterfield.

"Rum-Rum never appeared. I got antsy, so I checked the morgues," Ralph said. "Some boys found him. They found his body, that is. The boys were playing baseball in a vacant lot, and their ball rolled under an old house. I drove there to look it over. It's more of a shanty than a house. One of the boys was on his hands and knees looking for his baseball and smelled something."

Ralph paused.

"He saw a pair of legs under the porch," Ralph said.

I asked Ralph if he'd like a drink of water or coffee. He shook his head.

"The body was a couple of days gone," he said. "Rum-Rum died like he lived, all alone. He wasn't injured, no foul play. The coroner figured the heat got him. Years of living on the street is my guess.

"I checked around the house. There was no sign of struggle. He crawled under the porch to sleep and never woke up."

"Did anyone claim the body?" I said.

"No. I doubt if anybody knows his real name. The coroner made a call to a Baptist church on Hillside. Those good folks saw that he was buried. They put him underground, spoke a few words over him. At least he got that. I went by the gravesite. It's unmarked, but Rum-Rum found a place to rest."

We chatted some more. Ralph felt awful. I felt no better. We talked it out.

"It was a lousy way to die," he said.

"Death is always lousy when the grim reaper calls . . . "

Ralph looked puzzled.

"Something I heard recently," I said.

"Listen, Pete, if you don't need me, I've got another case," he said.

"You go ahead," I said. "You were a big help in Dunlap and again with Rum-Rum. See Agnes when you leave. She'll give you an envelope."

We shook hands, and Ralph left. I sat quietly for a moment. Then, I reached for the telephone. Agnes interrupted me.

"Mac's here," she said.

Detective Lieutenant Thaddeus McCormick came through the door and ducked his head in the manner of tall men. He screwed his face into a frown.

"Another sour puss, just what I need," I said.

"What's that supposed to mean?" he said.

Mac's tone matched his face.

"Can I get you boys anything?" Agnes said.

We both declined.

"I'll leave you in your sandbox," she said. "Play nice, now."

She closed the door behind her.

"I was just calling you," I said.

"Sure you were," he said.

The phone was in my hand. I decided not to argue.

"Not now, Mac. I'm not in the mood."

"Get in the mood. Ralph Waldo just left," he said. "What's with you two?"

"Ralph was looking for Rum-Rum," I said. "He found him—dead."

Mac knew Rum-Rum. He'd been with me on that rainy night.

"I got a report on a John Doe. Some kids found the body," he said. "That was Rum-Rum? Was he involved in the Hightower affair?"

"That's what we hoped to find out," I said.

Mac and I were together when a killer had us in his sights, when Rum-Rum cried out a warning from the shadows. Rum-Rum sounded the alarm that saved our lives. Without that warning, Mac and I would each be wearing a pine box.

"He wasn't murdered," Mac said.

"No, he wasn't murdered," I said. "He was just a victim of a cruel world, a raw deal."

I gave Mac a rundown of Ralph's report.

"Rum-Rum had a rotten life," I said. "He deserved better. Maybe he never got a break or maybe he squandered it. He died in his sleep."

Mac looked at his watch. I checked the time.

"I need a snort," Mac said. "What's stashed in your desk?"

I pulled out a bottle of bourbon and reached for a pair of drinking glasses resting on the windowsill. I poured bourbon, and we clinked our glasses together.

"To Rum-Rum."

"To Rum-Rum."

We tipped our glasses. Mac reached into a pocket and pulled out a brown rope that masqueraded as a cigar. He lit the thing, and rancid smoke wafted. I lit a Chesterfield in self-defense and opened a window.

"Somewhere in this town is a good five-cent cigar," I said. "Do us all a favor and find it."

He studied his cigar and raised his eyebrows.

"What's wrong with my cigar?" he said.

I poured more bourbon. Mac remembered why he came to my office.

"You haven't been around the past few days," he said. "You've been out of town. What've you got? Give."

"That's why I was calling you," I said. "I just got back from Kansas City. A guy I know ran a check on Karl Weaver. Get this. It turns out Weaver was an ex-con, did five years in the slammer. What do you make of that?"

I was telling McCormick what he and every cop on the case already knew. Weaver's background was not news to Mac. He stared at me and worked his jaw on the rope.

"Okay, okay," he said. "So, Weaver was an ex-con. Now, you know."

"You could have saved me a lot of legwork," I said. "Why the secrecy? We're working the same side of the street, you know."

Agnes tapped on the door and opened it.

"I'm leaving," she said. "Do you need anything before I go?"

She spotted the bottle of bourbon on my desk.

"I guess not," she said. "You look like you have everything you need. I hope that bottle is not the only thing standing in the morning."

She pulled the door shut.

"You've been out of town. You did more than run down leads on Weaver," he said. "Where else have you been?"

"I've been tracking the suspects," I said. "They ran me in circles. I've been one step behind since the beginning. I'm still one step behind."

"What do you mean?"

"They skipped town. I went after them," I said.

Mac stared at me and raised his glass. His eyes held mine. He puffed on his cigar, leaned forward, and blew smoke.

"You followed the perps out of town? Where did you go?" he said.

I wasn't going to sic the dogs on Dunlap, Kansas.

"Where doesn't matter," I said. "They were gone. I chased my tail and ended up right back here. They're in Wichita. The question is why did they come back? Something brought them back to the scene of the crime. I'm working that angle."

Mac stared at me and chewed the stub in the corner of his mouth. He didn't believe my story. I told the truth, but he figured I was holding back. He was right. I wasn't ready to discuss the silver bird, a woman who may or may not exist. The bird would have to wait. So would Mac.

"They left, and they came back. You must have a thought on that. Why do you figure they came back?" he said.

I sipped my bourbon.

"They know the danger they're in," I said. "Maybe they want to be caught."

"They want to be caught. Sure, that must be it," Mac said. "First, they shoot a guy. Then they burn down an art studio and steal an expensive jug. That was all a lark. They did that so they could get nabbed and sent to the big house. Why didn't I think of that?"

"Maybe there's more to their story. Maybe they want to tell it," I said. "Maybe they're looking for a way to explain their behavior without getting nabbed or shot."

My argument sounded lame, like I was trying to convince myself. Mac frowned. When he'd heard enough, he tossed back the last of his bourbon and rose from his chair.

"You've been lapping up that history teacher's drivel," he said. "Don't go soft in the head. Watch your back. Those men are killers."

Mac blew a puff of foul smoke and left the office.

Tuesday

July 12 , 1938

18

18

The weatherman in the sky woke up on the right side of the bed Tuesday morning. A breeze drifted in from the north, a summer rarity. Temperatures dipped into the low eighties. Pedestrians welcomed the relief from relentless heat. They moved along the sidewalks with their shoulders thrown back and pep in their step. The city stretched and yawned and came awake.

I greeted Agnes at the office and poured a cup of joe. The *Wichita Eagle* lay on my desk. In the comics, Buck Rogers chased bad guys in outer space, and Daisy Mae chased Li'l Abner in Dogpatch. Locally, baseball was on tap at Lawrence Stadium. Two Negro teams, the Wichita Garst Brothers and Emporia's Humphrey Bakers were slated to face off at six o'clock. Baseball drew me, but an advertisement at the bottom of the page caught my eye.

Phil Harris and his dance orchestra were scheduled to perform that night. I'd had to cancel my date with Lucille Sunday night, and she'd spent the previous day in Newton. I'd promised to see her on Tuesday.

Old Curly's wit and mellow voice made him a popular entertainer. I often listened to him and his orchestra on the radio. His live show would be a hit. Wichita was fortunate to have him for the evening.

The Hightower case had kept me busy. I hadn't seen Lucille since our evening of dining and dancing at Green Gables the week before. Detective work made it difficult to keep to a routine. It was time we spent an evening together.

Phil Harris and his orchestra would be great entertainment. The tickets were steep, a buck and a half a copy. Lucille was worth it. The location of the gig intrigued me. Harris would play in a night spot on Oliver called the Blue Moon Club.

The oracle's words came back to me. "A silver bird sings blue notes beneath a blue moon," Sybil Carter had said.

Silver bird. Blue notes. Blue moon. I mentally kicked myself in the backside for dwelling on the words of the oracle. The gal was probably loony. Maybe I was, too. Still, I couldn't shake that vision of her looking at me, looking through me. She didn't see with her eyes, but she saw things all right. She knew what went on around her. She caught details that escaped others in the same room.

I'd discussed the woman with Ethan Alexander. I hadn't mentioned her to Lieutenant McCormick. I didn't intend to, either. If Mac knew I was chasing a silver bird, the vision of a blind woman, he'd have me confined to the loony bin. Who could blame him?

I left my office early and motored west on Douglas with the top down on the roadster. Fields Clothing and Hinkels Dry Goods boasted signs in bold letters that proclaimed "SALE." Eager shoppers filed in like ants on a windowsill. A clerk at Jones Shoes arranged a display on the sidewalk. A clerk at Whitney Jewelry wiped the store's window. The marquee at the Miller Theater featured Ginger Rogers and Douglas Fairbanks, Jr. in *Having a Wonderful Time.*

I crossed over the river and turned north toward the Riverside District where Hightower's art gallery was located. I intended to question Susie Donovan before Hightower arrived.

I pulled up at the art gallery and scanned the neighborhood. The burgundy Cadillac was not in sight. Private vehicles stood in driveways. The only car on the street was a gray LaSalle parked down the block. Hightower had not arrived.

"Mr. Stone?" Susie Donovan said when I walked through the door.

She sat at her desk with a puzzled expression.

"Bingo," I said. "You sound like you're not sure."

Susie giggled.

"I just didn't expect to see you, that's all," she said.

I glanced past her desk and looked into the gallery.

"Are you alone, Susie? No Mr. Hightower? No Billy the ox?"

She giggled again.

"No one else is here, Mr. Stone. It's early. Mr. Hightower will be here later. He usually arrives about an hour from now."

"Good," I said. "Susie, if you have time, I'd like to ask a few more questions."

She smiled and gave me a thumbs up.

"I'd love to talk to someone," she said. "It's been awful. Mr. Hightower has been in a bad mood, understandable of course, but still. I'd like to chat with someone else for a change."

"Tell me more about Bobby Lopez," I said. "You told me that Lopez visited the gallery to look at the art."

"That's right."

"Did Lopez come alone? Was there a woman?" I said.

She thought that over.

"A woman? No. His friend, Dunlap, was with him sometimes, but not a woman," she said.

"Did Lopez talk about a woman? Maybe he spoke to you directly or maybe you overhead a conversation?"

"No, nothing I remember."

Her eyes dropped, and she went silent. She stared at her desk. I waited.

"There was one time," she said. "It probably wasn't anything you'd be interested in. Something happened one day."

"Go ahead, Susie. Tell me about it," I said.

"Well, we were busy. Everyone was here," she said. "Bobby and Dunlap were helping Mr. Weaver set up the gallery. There was going to be a showing. I helped Mr. Weaver with arrangements. Mr. Hightower was in the office."

"That small office you showed me, where he meets his buyers?" I said.

"That's right," she said. "I thought he was alone, but I heard a woman's voice. That surprised me. I hadn't seen a woman come in, but like I said, I wasn't working at my desk. She must have come in when I was in the back."

"What did you hear?" I said.

"Their voices were low at first," she said. "I wasn't trying to listen, but I was working right outside the door. Then Mr. Hightower yelled. I heard that, all right. He said, 'No! No! That's not right!' I was embarrassed. I didn't want to be standing there hearing that. I stopped what I was doing and went to my desk.

"Mr. Weaver didn't leave, though. He stayed right there outside the office and pretended to wipe down a sculpture. He had an ear cocked, boy, and he was grinning like a raccoon in the corn crib. I didn't think that was very nice."

"Who was the woman? A dissatisfied customer?" I said.

"No, I don't think so," Susie said. "This was personal. I can't tell you why. She wasn't a customer."

"What did the woman look like? Can you describe her?"

"I didn't see her come in," she said again. "She ran by my desk when she left. She was crying and held a handkerchief over her face. She had blonde hair, almost white. She was too young to be gray, though."

"You returned to your desk. Weaver eavesdropped," I said. "What did Bobby Lopez do? How did he react?"

"After the woman left, Bobby came to the front of the gallery," she said. "Dunlap was with him. Bobby said something like, 'He shouldn't speak to her that way.' Bobby was upset the rest of the day."

"Did Mr. Hightower speak to anyone about this?" I said.

"Oh, no, not that I know of," she said. "He left without speaking to me at all, and he always tells me when he's leaving. He went out the back door. I didn't see him."

I glanced at my watch.

"Thank you, Susie. You've been very helpful," I said.

She threw her shoulders back.

"Really? I didn't know if that was important," she said. "I was afraid it might seem silly."

"It wasn't silly and neither are you," I said. "You have an eye and an ear for detail. In fact, Susie Donovan, if I were king I'd christen you Honorary Private Eye."

Susie Donovan beamed.

19

The Wichita Art Museum had been closed when I stopped the previous week. That morning I parked and took a moment to admire the structure. The museum was only a few years old. An architect back east designed the building in the modern French art décoratif style. The art museum made a splash when it opened. I attended the opening and returned from time to time.

The Public Works Administration footed the bill for the building. Louise Caldwell Murdock, an architect and designer in her own right, had bequeathed her estate to purchase art. The collection would be in memory of her late husband, Roland P. Murdock, a brother to Marshall Murdock, founder of the *Wichita Eagle*.

I never met any of those folks. I would like to have thanked them for their gifts to the community. We once walked the same walks in the same city, but our paths never crossed. I read the newspaper and eyeballed the art, but those folks lived in their neighborhood, and I lived in mine. We lived in the same pool but swam at opposite ends.

I got out of the roadster and climbed the steps. Inside, a woman at the front desk looked at my card and excused herself. She returned with another woman, the director of the museum. The director read my card as she approached.

"Yes, may I help you?" she said.

"I'm working on a case," I said. "I hope you can help me."

She glanced at my card again.

"Private investigator, your card says. What's this about?"

I pulled the photograph of Bobby Lopez from my pocket.

"I'm investigating the crime that took place at the home of Terrance Hightower, murder and art theft. It's been in the papers. One of the suspects has an interest in art. It's likely that he's visited the museum, maybe often. I thought you might recognize him."

I pointed out Lopez in the photograph.

"This picture was taken during the war," I said. "That's him twenty years ago. Since then, he's studied art and done some painting. He must have visited your museum."

"I don't recognize him," she said. "I'm usually in my office. I rarely see our visitors. Is this man dangerous?"

"He's a suspect in a murder."

The director handed the photograph to the woman at the desk.

"Jill, does this man look familiar to you?" she said.

Jill looked at the photo and shook her head. The director returned the photo to me.

"We have guides on the floors. They keep an eye on things, help with the patrons," she said. "You're welcome to walk through the museum and ask your questions. I'll ask you to speak softly and not create a disturbance."

I thanked the director.

"If nothing else, I can enjoy the art," I said. "You've collected an impressive inventory."

Her smile looked condescending.

"The art we have is impressive," she said, "but it doesn't belong to us I'm afraid. It takes years to build a museum-worthy art collection. Much of the art you see is on loan from other museums and private collectors. We'll have a collection to show in a year or so."

I thanked her again. Her offer to allow me to tour the museum and question the staff was generous. Her request to avoid a disturbance was reasonable. Nevertheless, my quest for information on Lopez proved to be fruitless.

The museum guides were a mix of high school teenagers working summer jobs and older people in retirement. All appeared knowledgeable about the exhibits. They were eager to discuss paintings and sculptures. No one recalled seeing Bobby Lopez. I showed the picture and asked my questions. His photo didn't trigger a memory. Blank looks and head shaking were all I got for my trouble. To the guides, one patron looked like any other.

I felt that the moment I left no one would recall Pete Stone, private eye, either. I chose to risk it and left.

I walked down the steps and approached my roadster. My hand was on the door when a voice addressed me from behind.

"Hold on, pal," he said.

I turned to face a rangy specimen in faded dungarees and a soiled shirt, sleeves rolled to the elbows. He flexed his muscles and grinned. A shorter, heavier companion in bib overalls shifted from foot to foot.

"I didn't know we were pals," I said. "Have we met?"

"You're a real wise guy," he said.

His short backup remained silent. The taller man was the mouthpiece.

"Look, I don't know who you are, and you don't know me," I said.

"We're here to deliver a message," he said.

"Let me guess," I said. "Some guy you never met gave you a couple of bucks to do his dirty work."

The men looked at one another.

"I don't suppose this fella gave you his name?" I said.

"Shut up," the man said. "We've got a job to do."

"What's the message?" I said.

"Cough up the vase and nobody gets hurt," he said.

I shook my head.

"Even if I had this vase," I said, "I'd never hand it over to a couple of bums like you."

"Then you get hurt," he said.

"Make it quick," I said. "You're blocking my sunlight."

They'd rehearsed their act, but their talent was strictly amateur hour. They were pretenders, long on tough and short on temper. They didn't know how to begin. They packed the muscle, but lacked the choreography.

The shorter one looked over at his taller buddy. Then, the men looked at me. Then, they looked at one another. Then, back at me.

"What's the matter?" I said.

The short one finally added his two cents.

"We thought you'd hand over the vase," he said. "We never figured you'd take a beating."

"I don't figure I'll take a beating, either," I said.

The tall guy was quick. He snapped a punch that missed my chin and landed on my shoulder. I countered with a punch that caught him on the ear. The shorter one dove for my legs. The toe of my shoe landed under his chin. He went backwards and groaned when he fell onto his bottom.

The tall guy shook off my punch and came back with left hook. I blocked it with my right forearm and clipped his jaw with a left jab. He staggered. I telegraphed a roundhouse that a decent fighter would have dodged with ease. My fist connected with his temple. His knees wobbled, and his eyes rolled back. He collapsed onto the ground.

I turned back to the shorter guy. He tried to stand but gave it up. He held both palms out in surrender.

"That's enough," he said.

I lowered myself to the running board of my roadster to catch my breath. The short guy rubbed his chin. His partner was out cold. A car's engine turned over down the street. I looked up as the rear end of a gray LaSalle disappeared around the corner.

20

"Oh, Pete, I'm so excited," Lucille said. "Phil Harris!"

Lucille's enthusiasm was contagious. I pulled into the parking area and killed the motor. There was some daylight left in the summer evening. On the other side of Oliver, a DC-3 approached the runway and came in for a landing at the Municipal Airport.

"I've listened to Phil Harris on the Jack Benny Program," she said, "but to actually see him, to dance to his music, right there next to him. Your shoes better have thick soles. We're going to cut a rug."

Lucille's excitement pleased me. I needed something to smile about. The altercation at the art museum that afternoon left me more confused than rattled. Someone wanted me off the case. Was it the driver of the gray LaSalle? Lopez drove a pickup truck. I couldn't picture him in the LaSalle.

I opened the passenger door on the roadster and offered my arm. Lucille rose and squeezed my arm above the elbow. When I closed the car door, she held me back.

"Wait a minute," she said.

I faced her. She looked into my eyes. In the twilight shadows, we gazed at each other and smiled. I leaned in for a kiss and lingered for an embrace.

"Thank you, Pete," she said.

"My pleasure, sweetheart," I said.

We entered the Blue Moon Club and waited to be seated. I scanned the room.

"You did it again," I said.

"What's that?"

"You're the prettiest gal in the joint," I said.

I teased, but it was the truth. Her freshly styled pin curls framed her face. A blue sapphire teardrop pendant hung from her neck on a white-gold chain. The sapphire accented blue flecks in her slate grey eyes and matched the gown that fell below the knee and left her slender ankles exposed. My date was a knockout.

The club filled with couples and groups, a sellout crowd. A buck slipped into a palm got us a table near the dance floor. Our waiter made another bill disappear. He returned with a gin and tonic for Lucille and bourbon on the rocks for me.

Orchestra members filed in to polite applause and tuned their instruments. The air buzzed with conversation and laughter. The emcee stepped to the microphone and welcomed the crowd. The orchestra played low notes, and the emcee said, "Ladies and gentlemen, the man you've been waiting for, Old Curly himself, Mr. Phil Harris!"

The music crescendoed, and the applause grew louder. Phil Harris wore a big grin and entered with a wave. He reached for the microphone, and his mellow voice broke into a lively number called "Jammin'."

"First we had blues, then we had ragtime . . ."

People tapped their toes.

"Right now everybody is jammin'!"

When the song ended, the orchestra moved into, "I'd Love to Take Orders from You." After the song ended, Phil Harris addressed the crowd. He said he was delighted to be in Wichita, Kansas, and we laughed and applauded. He cracked a couple of corny jokes and invited everyone onto the dance floor.

The orchestra played "Too Marvelous for Words." Couples rose and began dancing. Lucille and I joined them on the floor.

The selections that evening were a mix of slow and fast numbers. We danced to several tunes before we returned to our table.

Our waiter brought fresh drinks, and I lit a pair of cigarettes. Harris announced the arrival of a female vocalist to accompany him. I turned my attention to the stage. Ruth Robin entered to applause. The lady performed a solo number followed by a duet with Harris. Her voice was wonderful, but she wasn't who I hoped to see.

"What's the matter?" Lucille said. "You look disappointed."

I filled in Lucille. I told her the story of the oracle in Dunlap, my search for a silver bird, a woman singing blue notes beneath a blue moon. Ruth Robin was a fine singer, but the petite woman was a brunette. Even with a birdlike name, the dark-haired woman didn't qualify as a silver bird.

"She isn't what I hoped for. No matter. The evening is perfect. You're here. Enough tilting at windmills. No more idiotic quests. I've won my Dulcinea," I said.

The music continued. The orchestra played "Jelly Bean," "Lazy River," and other songs. We danced on the crowded floor.

Harris spoke again.

"Ladies and gentlemen, Ruth and the boys need a break, and Old Curly needs to catch his wind."

The orchestra rose to exit. A man came onstage followed by a young boy. The pair carried drums and arranged the set near the piano. The orchestra pianist remained at the keyboard.

"Now, don't you folks go anywhere," Harris said, "We'll be back in a moment. In the meantime, I have a surprise for you. One of the pleasures of traveling across this great country is discovering new talent that rarely enjoys the spotlight. Well, get ready for a treat. The moment I heard this lady sing, I knew I had to add her to the bill tonight. Ladies and gentleman, please give your warm Midwest welcome to Wichita's very own, Ava Argent!"

A stunning, platinum blonde, came onstage. The crowd applauded.

Lucille squeezed my arm.

"Pete, isn't that the same woman?"

"Yes, it is," I said.

We'd heard the singer before.

"She wore black that night," Lucille said. "Now, look at her."

I looked. Everyone in the joint looked. The blonde wore a silver satin evening dress that clung to every curve.

The woman had performed at Green Gables the week before. As Lucille said, the woman wore black that night. Her dress had changed but not her hypnotic voice. She sang the tune that haunted me before. Once again, I was possessed. Husky, blue notes embraced me and drew me into a trance. The room dropped away.

"Pack up all my cares and woes, here I go, singing low . . ."

The silver bird cast her spell.

"No one here can love or understand me . . ."

She whispered.

"Make my bed and light the light, I'll arrive late tonight, blackbird, bye, bye."

My eyes never left the woman. The song ended. Lucille's voice brought me back.

"Pete, did you catch her name?" she said. "Her name is Ava."

"Yes, Ava Argent," I said.

"I have a cousin named Ava. Ava means bird," she said.

"And Argent means silver," I said.

"Silver bird," Lucille said.

"Silver bird," I said.

The pianist played. The drummer drummed. Ava Argent sang the blues. Blue notes dripped from her lips, spilled drops squeezed from her heart, her soul. Couples danced. We didn't move. We sat and listened.

The orchestra returned. Ava Argent thanked the pianist. She introduced the drummer, Ivan S. Baker. The young lad returned to carry the drums. Phil Harris moved to the microphone and led the applause that sent Ava Argent offstage. The orchestra started playing.

I turned to Lucille.

"Sweetheart, I have to—"

"I know," she said. "Go ahead. I'll be fine."

I moved toward the door that led backstage. A bouncer stepped into my path.

"Easy, pal. Where do you think you're going?" he said.

I handed the man my card. He gave it a cursory glance.

"I have to go backstage," I said.

"No can do, pal. Entertainers only," he said.

"This is important," I said.

"Sorry."

He didn't mean it. I didn't want to create a disturbance. Also, the bouncer was a mountain. If he came down hard, a landslide could be fatal.

I pulled a Lincoln from my wallet. The bouncer looked away and scanned the room. I slipped the bill into his jacket pocket. The bouncer stepped aside. I went through the door into a dimly lit room decorated with electric cables and dust. There was no sign of Ava Argent.

The drummer and the young lad packed the drum set. They glanced at me and returned to their task. The exit door was closed. I crossed the room and opened it and stared into the empty black beyond.

I turned back to the pair packing the drums.

"I'm looking for Ava Argent," I said.

"She's gone, man," the drummer said. "She did her gig and split. Twenty-three skidoo."

I muttered an oath under my breath.

"I'm a private detective," I said and handed him my card. "I have to speak to Ava Argent."

"Is she in trouble?"

"No, she's not in trouble. I'm looking for a suspect. She may know where he is."

"Sorry, man."

"Look, Ivan is it?"

"That's right. Ivan S. Baker. This is my nephew, Chet," he said.

"Hello, Chet," I said.

"Chet's a musician," Baker said, "up from Oklahoma."

The lad grinned.

"He blows a mean horn," Baker said, "already a prince on the trumpet."

The boy basked in his uncle's praise.

"Ivan, you played last week at Green Gables," I said. "I was there. You were onstage with the woman who left, Ava Argent. You were great, both of you."

"Thanks, but I still can't help you," he said. "I don't know Ava."

"But you performed together, last week and again tonight."

"Last week was a fluke. I answered an ad," he said. "We ended up together onstage. One of Harris's people heard us and got us an audition for tonight's gig. That's it. Maybe I'll see her again. Maybe not. Who knows?"

"Listen. Keep my card. If you do see her, give me a call. She's not in trouble, Ivan. You won't be ratting her out."

I turned to leave. Ivan stopped me.

"Hang on. Ava said something the other night that might help. We rehearsed, you know, before we went on. We introduced ourselves.

"We played a few numbers and took a break. She told me she had a confession. Argent was her mother's name. She used it onstage. I said that's cool. Lots of entertainers use stage names. Argent wasn't her name growing up. She said her name growing up was Ava Hightower."

Wednesday

July 13, 1938

21

The burgundy Cadillac with the whitewall tires and all the chrome sat in the driveway. Its convertible top was down. I pulled over in the shade of a sycamore near Bluff and English and turned off the engine. Then, I lit a Chesterfield and checked my watch.

Lucille and I had danced late into the night. We didn't leave the Blue Moon Club until Harris and his orchestra played their final set. It rankled me that I'd spotted the silver bird and lost her before we spoke. She'd flown into the shadows. The lady was not a figment of a blind oracle's imagination. The lady existed. Her name was Hightower.

After we left the club, I drove Lucille home. I kissed her goodnight at the door. We embraced. The next morning, Lucille kissed me awake in her bed. I stayed for breakfast—and dessert.

Later I cleaned up at my place on Lewellen and phoned Agnes at the office. I told her I'd be in later. First, there was someone I had to see.

Hightower told me he had no family. The drummer at the Blue Moon Club told me Ava Argent's real name was Ava Hightower. Susie Donovan said that a woman with blonde hair had words with Terrance Hightower behind closed doors. The conversation sounded heated and personal. I had questions, and I wouldn't get answers from Terrance Hightower.

The door on the Tudor house swung open. Hightower sidled out leaning on his cane and pulled the door closed. He climbed into the Cadillac, started the engine, and left for his gallery in Riverside.

That suited me. I didn't want Hightower to know I was in his neighborhood. When the Cadillac disappeared around the corner, I stepped out of the roadster. I left it parked in the shade and walked down the sidewalk.

I reached the house next door to the Tudor and knocked. The nurse in her white uniform opened the door and stepped back, eyebrows raised. She put her hands on her hips and gave me a once-over. She shook her head and laughed.

"I never expected to see you again," she said, "not today, not ever."

"I'm a bad penny. I keep showing up. I'd like to speak to Miss Devlin," I said.

"You may be a bad penny, but you're no quitter," she said. "I'll give you that. Why would you want to speak to Miss Devlin? Nothing's changed. Miss Devlin sits in the parlor, still deaf as a post."

"I understand, but I'd like to speak to her," I said.

"The last time you tried that it didn't go well, or have you forgotten?" she said.

"I have an idea," I said. "A conversation might do Miss Devlin some good. She sits all day in that big chair. She must get lonely. She might fancy some company."

The nurse considered my remark.

"She might at that," she said. "It's a waste of time, but I'm game if you are. Just don't upset her, now. Come on in."

I followed the nurse through the foyer and into the parlor. Hightower told me that his Tudor was one of the first homes built in the neighborhood. Miss Devlin's home appeared to be built at about the same time. If so, she'd lived next door to Hightower for decades. She could shed light on the Hightower family history.

Miss Devlin sat alone in the dim light just as she had before, a small woman in a large chair. The room was warm and stuffy. A blanket lay across the woman's lap and draped over her legs.

She raised her head when I entered. She nodded recognition but wore a questioning expression. She turned to her nurse and shrugged.

"Don't upset her," the nurse said. "Explain why you're here. If she wants you to leave, you'll have to leave."

I pulled my notebook from my pocket and scratched a note in pencil.

"May I?" I said.

I reached for a lamp on the table next to Miss Devlin's chair and pulled the chain. Light glowed over the table and chair. I handed her my notebook. She read my note.

"I'd like to visit with you, Miss Devlin, about the Hightower family."

She looked up at me. She turned to the nurse, her voice frail but clear.

"Wilma, dear, would you bring us some refreshment, please? I'll have tea."

Wilma, asked what I would like.

"Tea would be fine," I said, "iced if it's no trouble."

Wilma left the room. I pulled a straight-backed chair next to Miss Devlin and sat down. The woman was deaf, her body frail, but her mind was keen. On most days, she had little cause to use her voice, usual requests to Wilma, I figured. Her pipes were rusty but not broken. As she spoke, her voice gained in strength.

Wilma returned with beverages. She hovered and listened and approved of our arrangement.

"I've never seen her this animated," Wilma said.

She left the room with a smile.

Miss Devlin and I huddled together. I wrote down questions. Miss Devlin replied with her voice. Yes, she'd known the

Hightower family for years, since the early days when the neighborhood began.

"They came up from the south shortly after the war between the states. They settled in Kansas, young Terrance and his father, John. Terrance was just a small boy then. He was born the day Lee surrendered to Grant."

I smiled.

"Oh, of course, he's told you that," she said. "He tells everybody that. They came north together, father and son, just the two of them. John never spoke about Terrance's mother. I think she must have died shortly after Terrance was born."

Miss Devlin preferred her tea hot. Her hand trembled when she reached for the sugar. I picked up the bowl.

"One lump or two?" I said.

She didn't hear my words, but she understood the question.

"One, please," she said.

I added a lump of sugar with silver tongs. She smiled and stirred it into her cup. I sipped iced tea and waited for her to continue.

"John Hightower was a stern man, tough and bitter," she said. "He was a determined man. He'd lost most everything he had in that war. He'd been raised on a cotton plantation, raised to work the land and oversee the plantation when the time came. He worked, but he lived in luxury. After the war, everything he'd grown up with was gone. John Hightower lost more than his plantation. He lost a way of life. He never choked down the bile that loss brought. He remained a bitter man the rest of his days.

"First came the Yankees, the fighting, the pillaging, the destruction. After the war, the carpetbaggers swooped in. John's folks were gone by then. John owned land, but everything else was destroyed. His livestock was gone. His farming equipment was gone. No slaves were left to work the land. Carpetbaggers hovered like vultures until he sold out on the cheap. He and Terrance came north to Kansas."

"How did he make a living?" I wrote.

"I didn't know them at that time. I understand John put his money into cattle. He'd never ranched a lick, but like I said, the man was determined. He carved a living for himself and his boy. Terrance grew up, went to school, did his chores.

"According to his father's accounts, Terrance never took an interest in ranching. He worked because his father insisted, but Terrance didn't like it. He hated to get his hands dirty. He studied art while he was in school and cared for little else. That's according to his father. They lived on a ranch east of town. Then they struck oil and moved into Wichita. That's when we met."

"Hightower told me his father made money in oil," I wrote.

"That's right. After the oil came in, John Hightower quit on the cattle business. He sold the livestock and put his money into the ground. He hoped Terrance might prove to be an oilman, but Terrance hated the oil business even more than he hated ranching. Oil provided a handsome living, but the work was dirtier. Roughnecks and roustabouts are a rugged bunch. A hard life didn't suit Terrance Hightower. Terrance was always a bit soft, if you ask me."

"Does he manage his oil business today?"

Miss Devlin furrowed her brow.

"Oh, no. He never did. I thought you knew. The family hasn't been in oil for years. John Hightower sold the business not long before he died," she said. "I guess you didn't know."

I shook my head.

"John Hightower realized that his son would never have what it takes to run the business, so he sold out. John's been gone nearly thirty years. He died before his granddaughter was born. John Hightower died and never got to meet that sweet little girl."

Miss Devlin caught my expression.

"Are you okay, Mr. Stone?" she said. "Was it something I said?"

I swallowed the last of my tea. Wilma returned to the parlor to see how we were getting along.

"Let's freshen our drinks," Miss Devlin said, "and we'll have some of those oatmeal cookies you baked yesterday, Wilma. They're so delicious. Oh, and bring an ashtray for Mr. Stone."

Wilma left, and Miss Devlin turned her attention back to me.

"I grew up in a household of men," she said. "My father used tobacco, as did my brothers. Smoke doesn't bother me one bit. To tell you the truth, I miss that smell. They're all gone now, the men in my family. I know you're a smoker. I can see the cigarettes in your pocket. You go right ahead and light up."

Wilma returned with refreshments. I passed on the cookies but lit a Chesterfield and reached for the ashtray.

"I guess you didn't know that Terrance had a daughter," Miss Devlin said.

"Terrance told me that he had no family," I wrote.

"Well, that's true, I suppose. It wasn't always true. Terrance had a beautiful family, a lovely wife and a darling child. Back before the accident, that is."

I raised an eyebrow.

"Terrance didn't marry until he was almost forty," she said. "By then, his father was slowing down and ready to sell the business. John had been successful, but success didn't dampen the hatred he carried. He remained a difficult man.

"John raised a son and built a life, but his days were numbered. He sensed the end. He wanted Terrance to leave him an heir before he died, a child to carry on. Terrance had been seeing a woman, and when he popped the question, she said yes.

"They married and moved into their own place not far from here. Terrance and his wife checked on his father every day. Marie, that was her name, was the sweetest thing. She took care of John. The couple seemed happy together.

"A year went by, then two, and no heir arrived. The couple didn't conceive. Marie visited often back then. She told me horrible stories about the teasing and tongue-lashing John inflicted on Terrance, questioning his manhood, you see. Why can't you father a child? It must have been awful.

"John continued to fade, and then he died. The couple moved in next door and took over the house. Not long after that, Marie discovered she was with child. They finally conceived, and John Hightower never knew that his grandchild was to be born.

"The baby arrived, a beautiful girl. That was such a wonderful time. Terrance strutted like a peacock, a proud papa, and a good papa, too. He seemed determined to be the father his own father never was, loving and kind."

I wrote, "What was the girl's name?"

"Her name was Ava. They called her Ava," she said.

I reached for my glass and swallowed tea.

"Little Ava was so beautiful, delicate features and thick blonde curls," Miss Devlin said. "I was delighted to have the family next door. Watching a child grow is a joy. When Ava took her first steps, her papa walked beside her, the little one hanging on to his finger.

"He opened his art gallery in Riverside, and he took Ava along with him most days. Marie came to visit me, and when she did she'd bring Ava with her. The little one brought music. When Ava learned to speak, she sang her words. Her greeting was a lilt. She had a lovely voice. 'Hello, Miss Devlin,' she'd sing, and I'd sing back to her, 'Hello, Miss Ava.'"

"You mentioned an accident," I wrote.

Miss Devlin's face grew dark.

"Yes, the accident. That was the summer before Ava was due to start school. She had a bicycle and was learning to ride. Terrance walked beside her to keep her steady. She wasn't allowed to ride the bicycle on her own, not without her parent alongside.

"Well, she was only a small child. One day she took the bicycle out by herself, to ride on her own. She fell over, like children do, but this fall was serious. She hit her head and lost a lot of blood.

Her parents were afraid they'd lost the child altogether. An ambulance arrived, and away she went. That was the last time I saw that little girl."

Miss Devlin dabbed her eyes with a handkerchief.

"The doctors saved Ava," she said. "That's all I know. I don't know what happened after that. Ava survived, but I never saw that child again, not her or her mother. Marie and Ava did not return home. One day a truck arrived. Their belongings were loaded up, and away the truck went.

"I spoke to Terrance Hightower. I demanded he tell me what happened to his wife and daughter. He answered with a stone-faced glare. I wouldn't be put off. I loved those two. I demanded an answer. What happened to Marie and little Ava? I pleaded and begged.

"His stony expression turned to a look of bitterness I hadn't seen since his father was alive. It was as if Terrance Hightower had morphed into his father. I can still hear that low, even timbre, that controlled rage in his voice. 'I have no wife. I have no daughter.' We never spoke of it again. Those were the last words Terrance Hightower ever spoke to me. All these years, and he hasn't offered so much as a hello to me. Terrance Hightower flipped a switch, and the light went out."

22

errance Hightower had a daughter named Ava. Whether estranged from her father or disowned was unclear. It was also irrelevant to me. What did concern me was her role, if any, in the crime at her father's house. Had she been a part of that? Had she been there that night, waiting in the alley, hiding in the shadows? Had she fired a weapon? What was her association with Lopez and Dunlap? Was she harboring the suspects?

Those questions ran through my mind as I stepped off Miss Devlin's porch. I started down the walk and paused when I heard activity at the Hightower residence. The backdoor opened and shut.

A hedge separated the properties. I stepped over and peered through the bushes. A figure stepped off Hightower's back porch and crossed the yard. I watched a man exit through the gate and walk into the alley. His face was turned away from me, but I knew it bore a scar and a patch covered one eye. The back-alley cyclops climbed the steps to his house and disappeared inside.

Hightower was still away from his home. His house was empty. Why had the neighbor been inside during Hightower's absence? I had no answer. I tucked the question away for later consideration.

I checked my watch. The morning was shot. Hightower would return soon, and I wanted to be out of the neighborhood before then. I walked to my roadster and drove away.

The blocks rolled by. I tapped a finger on the steering wheel as I drove. I figured Hightower and the man across the alley were old friends, neighbors for years. That didn't explain what he was doing in the empty house.

I arrived downtown and drove west on Douglas. I passed my office at Emporia, turned left on Market, and pulled up at a beanery on the corner of Beacon Lane. Valentine's diner was noted for good food, simple fare at a low price. My kind of eatery.

A man walked toward me and caught my eye. He looked at me and looked down. Dark, reedy limbs extended from his worn clothing. The sight of the man jolted me. A vision popped into mind that made me shudder.

"Rum-Rum," I said.

The man stopped and raised his head. The resemblance was striking, but he wasn't Rum-Rum.

"Sir?" he said.

I raised my palm in apology.

"Nothing, pal. My mistake. I thought you were someone else," I said. "You remind me of a guy."

"Yes, sir. No harm done," he said.

He moved away a step or two. Even from the back, he looked like Rum-Rum.

I called out, "Say, I'm going inside for a bite. Care to join me?"

He stopped and turned around. He rubbed his chin.

"I don't think so," he said. "If you're feeling generous, I could use a bracer."

"Have some food," I said. "Afterwards, I'll spot you that bracer."

The man looked me over. His eyes moved to the diner. He ran his tongue over his lower lip. He wanted food. He needed a drink. What he didn't need was trouble.

"Are you sure it's all right?" he said.

"It's all right," I said.

We went inside. The diner built by Arthur Valentine was simple and efficient, a row of stools at a counter and a kitchen alongside. Valentine fabricated his diner and sold the packaged product to entrepreneurs throughout the state.

We took stools. The gal behind the counter wore a yellow blouse with a hankie in the pocket that failed to cover a ketchup stain. Her hair was styled into a bird's nest held together with bobby pins and a pencil. She pulled out the pencil and picked up an order pad.

"What'll it be?" she said.

A sign read, "Fireman's Special—Fast and Hot." I pointed to it and said, "What's on the menu?"

"Today, it's a burger and fried potatoes, fifteen-cents. That includes coffee or tea."

"Sold twice," I said and turned to my dining companion. "Iced tea?"

He nodded, and the gal placed the order on the kitchen counter. She poured tea, and our plates appeared at her elbow. As advertised, the chow was fast and hot.

The man with a lined and weathered face kept his head down and chewed slowly. He seemed subdued and out of place. He might have been thirty or sixty. I couldn't hazard a guess as to which.

"I'm Pete," I said.

"Willie," he said.

Willie swallowed a bite.

"Rum-Rum is dead," he said in a soft voice.

I lowered my fork to my plate.

"You knew Rum-Rum?" I said.

Staring at his plate, he nodded.

"How did you know Rum-Rum?" I said.

He raised his head and offered a faint smile.

"We lived in the same neighborhood," he said.

I conceded a grin and raised my glass.

"Rum-Rum once saved my life," I said. "To Rum-Rum, Willie."

Willie raised his glass. We drank to Rum-Rum's memory.

The burgers were fresh, and the potatoes were crispy. We downed our meals, and I settled the tab.

Outside on the sidewalk, I extended my hand. Willie shook it and stared at the silver dollar in his palm. His long, narrow fingers closed into a fist over the coin.

"Never had a silver dollar," he said. "That's mighty generous."

"It's a pleasure to meet an associate of Rum-Rum's," I said.

"Associate," he said and grinned.

Willie opened his fingers and stared again. His head rose.

"No, sir, never had a silver dollar," he said. "I believe I'll hang onto this for a day."

"Hang onto it," I said. "That's a fine idea."

"Just for a day," he said.

"Just for a day," I said.

"So long, Pete," he said.

"So long, Willie," I said.

23

My office was a few blocks from the diner. I pulled up in front of the Lawrence Block Building at Douglas and Emporia. A secretary who worked at a legal firm on the first floor arrived from around the corner. She thanked me with a smile when I held the door for her. I followed her in and climbed the stairs to the third floor.

Agnes pecked the typewriter at her desk. She raised her eyebrows when I entered. I glanced at the Seth Thomas banjo clock.

"I was beginning to think this was a one-woman shop," she said. "Have you started working half-days?"

"I spent the morning in conversation with a deaf woman," I said.

"A deaf woman?" she said. "That makes two of us who didn't hear from you."

"I told you I'd be late," I said.

"This is a strange case," Agnes said. "First, you meet a blind woman, then you talk to a deaf woman."

"The blind and the deaf know more than I do," I said. "What can I say? I'm just the detective. I need to make some calls. You go on to lunch. I'll hold down the fort."

"I ate at my desk," she said. "Have you eaten?"

"I stumbled across the colleague of an old friend," I said. "We had a bite together."

"Speaking of old friends, you might want to call Mr. Hightower," Agnes said. "He called twice and sounded testy. In fact, he was loud the second time he called. I don't care for that man."

"Neither did the deaf woman," I said.

I went into my office and dialed Hightower. The telephone rang once, and he answered. He must have had the phone at his elbow.

"This is Hightower," he said.

"Pete Stone here."

"Finally. You are certainly not an easy man to reach," he said.

"Criminals rarely come to my office, Mr. Hightower," I said. "I have to go look for them."

"Do you know what day it is?" he said.

"It's Wednesday, the thirteenth," I said. "Is that why you called, to check the date? You could buy a calendar and save us both some time."

"Quit the wise remarks," he said. "I know today is Wednesday. I also know that tomorrow is Thursday."

"That sounds right," I said.

"Thursday, Stone, the day you promised to deliver my stolen vase. I hope you haven't forgotten your promise," he said.

"I haven't forgotten," I said.

"So, I can expect you tomorrow? You'll be here with the vase?"

"I'm a man of my word," I said.

"I'll be waiting. I suppose you expect that reward," he said. "You'll get it along with some questions. I want to know where you found my vase. I'll expect an answer."

"I haven't found the vase yet."

"You haven't found it? And you promise delivery tomorrow? What kind of game are you playing? Don't toy with me, Stone."

"I'm not toying with you," I said. "I'm telling you the truth. I'll have it tomorrow. I'll deliver it. When I do I'll want answers."

"What answers?" he said.

"I want to know about Ava, your daughter," I said. "You told me you had no family. That doesn't square with my investigation."

The line buzzed with a blistering barrage of vulgarities. I held the phone away from my ear until the vulgarities ceased.

"Your investigation? I hired you to find my stolen vase," Hightower said. "That's it! Find the vase. Why are you prying into my private life, sticking your nose in places it has no right to be?"

"I explained my situation when you hired me," I said. "I was already working on behalf of another client. You hired me to find your vase. Fair enough. I'm also looking for a suspect. The name Ava Hightower came up during my search for this suspect. It's possible she's harboring one or both of these men. She may figure into the crime itself. Your private life belongs to you. I don't care one whit about your private life. However, if your daughter is involved, I intend to get some answers."

The man lowered his volume, but the tremble in his voice was audible.

"Tomorrow. Bring me the vase tomorrow. We'll talk then."

"Tomorrow," I said and hung up the telephone.

I lit a cigarette and considered Hightower's situation. For a man of wealth and means, he seemed awfully desperate to recover a single piece of art. How could so much hinge on a lousy vase?

I thought about the back-alley neighbor. I hadn't mentioned that I'd spotted the man in the eyepatch leaving Hightower's house. I'd tell him face-to-face. I wanted to gauge his reaction in person. Maybe his neighbor had the privilege of coming and going when he pleased.

I dialed the operator.

"Do you have a number for Ava Hightower?" I said. "It might be a new listing."

"One moment, please," she said.

I remained on hold. Could locating Ava Hightower be as simple as asking the operator? The answer was no.

"I have a Terrance Hightower, residence and business," she said. "Nothing for Ava."

"Check Ava Argent," I said.

She came back a moment later.

"I'm sorry. I have no listing at all under Argent," she said.

I thanked her and hung up. I spent an hour calling talent agencies. I hoped to find someone who represented Ava. I struck out again. No one knew her name. A gal at one agency suggested I try the Wichita Musicians' Association.

I placed the call to Local 297 of the American Federation of Musicians. The lady who answered was pleasant and polite. She filled me in on the organization's history. They had been chartered thirty-five years earlier. Their membership included musicians in Sedgwick County and extended into a number of surrounding counties.

She assured me that the union welcomed new talent into their fold, but alas—that was her expression—alas, they did not have an Ava Hightower or Argent as a member.

Rusty arrived with the afternoon edition of the news. I took it into my office and turned to the classifieds. Ivan S. Baker, the drummer at the Blue Moon Club, told me he had answered an ad for his gig with Ava. I thumbed through the ads looking for calls for musicians and came up empty. I checked the entertainment section for promising looking venues that Ava might play. Nothing caught my eye. I tossed the newspaper onto my desk.

I placed one more telephone call. Ethan Alexander came on the line.

"Ethan, we have to talk," I said.

He listened while I spoke. I gave him instructions and told him I'd be at his place first thing in the morning. He told me he'd be waiting. I stared at the telephone for a long moment after I hung up. Then, I called it a day and went home to my place on Lewellen.

♦♦♦

Wilfred Owen was a tragic figure, a man who led a "pitifully brief" life according to Louis Untermeyer, editor of *Modern America Poetry, Modern British Poetry*. I opened my copy to page 444. Wilfred Owen, brilliant British poet, fought in the trenches in France during the Great War. For all I knew, he shared the battlefield with Ethan Alexander and Bobby Lopez. Owen translated his impressions of those nightmares into poetry.

I sipped bourbon and read and envisioned young men in those trenches. Ethan came home in a wheel chair. Bobby suffered a bruised mind. Wilfred Owen never made it home. He died at the tender age of twenty-five, one week before the signing of the Armistice. His remains were buried in northern France.

Owen's poetry carried the reader to those long-ago battlefields.

> "Men marched asleep. Many had lost their boots,
> But limped on, blood-shod. All went lame, all blind;
> Drunk with fatigue; deaf even to the hoots
> Of gas-shells dropping softly behind."

I thought about the two friends, Ethan and Bobby, and all the other young men who had fought side-by-side. Ethan and Bobby made a pact, a vow to always be there for each other no matter the odds.

The clocks chimed. I took a final swallow of bourbon and rose from my chair. I reached for the chain on the floor lamp between my chair and the window. A gun fired. A bullet shattered the window.

I dropped to the floor. Another bullet whizzed through the window followed by another. Shards of glass covered me. Outside, a car's engine roared. Tires squealed. I hugged the floor and listened to the roars and the squeals fade into the night.

◆ ◆ ◆

Thursday

July 14, 1938

24

The overcast sky complemented my sullen mood Thursday morning. I'd had a lousy night of sleep. My hands shook more from anger than fear when I cut up a cardboard box and covered the broken window.

I left my place on Lewellen with the top up on the roadster. A couple of blocks over, I dropped south on Waco to Douglas and rolled through downtown.

The route I chose wasn't the most direct. Thirteenth to Hillside would've saved time. Saving time wasn't important that morning. The day was young, and I needed time to think. Also, a man in a wheelchair needed extra minutes for his morning routine.

Somebody wanted me off the case. Somebody hired a couple of punks to rough me up. Somebody put bullets through my window. Somebody wanted me out of the picture.

Hightower was upset that I'd learned about his daughter, but he wouldn't try to plug me before I delivered the vase. Dunlap's brother, Edward, didn't want me involved with his family, but I figured he'd respect his mother's wishes and let me do my job. Would Lopez or Dunlap try to kill me? Not if Ethan Alexander's impressions were accurate. Somebody knocked off Karl Weaver. If Lopez or Dunlap had pulled the trigger, they'd be willing to kill again.

I decided to keep the attempt on my life to myself. I wouldn't mention it to Ethan Alexander. It had been ten days since our July fourth conversation at his kitchen table. Ten days since Ethan told me his war stories and talked about his friendship with his pal. Ten days since he asked me to find Bobby, to draw him out of hiding so Ethan could help him to go to the police.

I figured locating Bobby Lopez and his accomplice would take no time at all. Either I'd find them, or the police would find them. I was wrong. The mice remained hidden in their nest. I'd looked for them and come up empty. The cops had done no better. Maybe I could draw them out, bait the trap with cheese.

Downtown Wichita glittered beneath the clouds. Absent the glare of sunlight, neon signs and commercial lighting dazzled the eye. Banks sparkled, their interiors lit up. Fourth National Bank and Kansas State Bank down the street glowed that morning.

Men and women in suits and dresses clustered around a memorial in front of Farha Shoes. The city had chosen the location to honor The Salvation Army. A bronze tablet in the walk commemorated fifty years of service to the community.

Lights brightened the lobbies of the Lawrence Block Building and Hotel Eaton on the next corner. I passed through downtown and continued eastward to Hillside. At the intersection, I turned north until I reached the Municipal University. A few people strolled the walks. I circled the buildings and pulled up at Alexander's residence on the edge of the campus.

Three steps rose to the porch next to a ramp that Ethan's landlord had installed to accommodate a wheelchair. I climbed the steps. The door opened before I knocked.

"Come in, Pete," Ethan said.

We went into the kitchen. I took a seat at the table. Ethan poured coffee at the counter and placed steaming cups on the table. The usual clutter, newspapers, mail, and other papers had been cleared. Other than our cups and an ashtray, only one item remained on the table, an object wrapped in a towel.

"How long have you known?" Ethan said.

I sipped coffee and lit a cigarette.

"I suspected early on," I said. "It was the only thing that made sense."

Ethan reached for a pipe and tobacco on the countertop. He tamped tobacco into the bowl with his thumb and held a match over the pipe. He puffed and blew smoke.

"The men left town," I said. "I trailed them to Dunlap. They were there, and they'd gone. Dunlap's family acknowledged that. The family saw the men. No one saw the vase. Ralph Waldo inspected their truck. He found bloodstains. He didn't find the vase."

Ethan watched me sip coffee.

"Then, I thought about Rum-Rum's visit," I said, "and the words you quoted. 'The man says he don't shoot. The man says don't want no loot.' Rum-Rum had the vase. He left the vase with you that night."

"I didn't know what it was," Ethan said. "I didn't know what to do with it. When I read the news, I called you. I wanted you to find Bobby so Bobby could return the thing to its owner."

Ethan laid his pipe in the ashtray. He reached for the object. Holding it steady with one hand, he unwound the towel with the other and laid the towel aside.

The vase stood bare. We stared it. Neither of us spoke. Ethan retrieved his pipe from the ashtray and held another match to it. I smoked my cigarette. Smoke wafted toward the ceiling fan.

The vase had an ivory tone decorated in blue with the fat man figure and flourishes. We studied the sculpture for a long moment. I leaned forward and flicked an ash into the tray.

"I'd make a lousy art dealer," I said.

"Why so?" Ethan said.

I crushed out my cigarette and stared at the fat man.

"All the hoopla. All the fuss. A man is dead, paintings destroyed," I said. "Through it all, the only thing Hightower has shown an interest in is the return of this vase. You called me to find Bobby Lopez. You hope to establish his innocence. The cops want to nab the pair. They hope to establish their guilt. Hightower, meanwhile, cares about only one thing—the return of this vase. Does that make sense to you?"

"The man has skewed priorities," Ethan said.

"Skewed priorities don't begin to describe the man," I said.

I gestured toward the vase.

"I don't even like the thing," I said. "If you ask me, it's ugly."

Ethan considered that remark.

"I appreciate art as much as the next guy," he said. "This vase does nothing for me, either."

"And yet, this is what the men took," I said. "They didn't grab a painting. They took this."

"Bobby didn't take this vase because he wanted to own it," Ethan said. "He had other reasons for taking the vase."

"What reasons?" I said.

"I have no idea. I wish I did. I wish I could talk to Bobby."

"If my plan works, you'll be able to do just that," I said. "You'll talk to Bobby."

"What's your plan?" he said.

"Bobby Lopez and Dunlap left town together and stayed together. Bobby made sure Dunlap received medical care. They came back to Wichita together. They share a loyalty."

"Bobby is loyal," Ethan said.

"They left and came back," I said. "The question is why? Dunlap's mother told me Bobby has romantic feelings for Ava Hightower. If Ava shares those feelings, she'd harbor the men. I can't tie their romance to this jug, though. There's something else that drew the men back to the city. They have unfinished business."

"What unfinished business?" Ethan said.

"I don't know, but my instinct tells me I don't have much time to find the answer," I said.

"Are you sure they're still here?" he said. "Maybe they left and took Ava with them."

"They haven't left," I said. "Ava Hightower performed at the Blue Moon Club Tuesday night. That was risky, singing in public. If the cops connect her to the suspects, they'll come down fast. She's doing it because she needs the dough."

"Now what?" he said.

"I return the vase to Hightower," I said. "When Hightower gets the vase, Lopez and Dunlap lose their leverage. They'll be forced to act. The walls are closing in on them. I hope to get to them before the cops do."

Ethan looked doubtful.

"The plan is leaky," I said. "If it were a boat, I wouldn't take it out of the harbor. It can't be helped. I can't stall Hightower any longer. I have to return the vase."

"I guess we have no choice," Ethan said. "This unfinished business, do you think Bobby planned it from the beginning?"

"I don't think anything that happened was planned from the beginning," I said. "The events that night took all the players by surprise. If Bobby Lopez had planned to steal that vase, he wouldn't have done it there and then. Karl Weaver was armed and dangerous. Weaver died, but not before he wounded Dunlap. That wasn't planned."

"Bobby didn't fire a gun," Ethan said. "He didn't shoot Weaver."

I didn't argue the point. Ethan had claimed the same to the police. The cops didn't believe him. I had doubts. Ethan's assurance in Lopez's innocence didn't waver.

"Somebody shot Weaver," I said.

Ethan looked at the vase.

"Pete, you know I didn't want this thing. Everything that happened that night and since has caught me by surprise."

"I know that, Ethan. However, you do have the vase. The right thing to do is return it to its owner. I don't care for Terrance Hightower, but the vase belongs to him. He should get it back."

"Yes," he said. "I agree, but my loyalty is to Bobby Lopez. I made a promise to my friend long ago. I have to be there for him. He made the same vow to me."

"That vow kept you both alive in the trenches," I said. "Bobby Lopez's proper name is what? Robert? Roberto?"

"Roberto," he said.

"Roberto Lopez," I said. "Ethan Alexander. Roberto Lopez. E-A-R-L, the tattoo Lopez wears. Why do I suspect that you wear the same tattoo, Ethan?"

Ethan Alexander stared at me. He unbuttoned the cuff on his shirt and rolled up the sleeve. His inner forearm displayed the letters, EARL, in dark ink. The name hovered above the profile of a head with two faces.

"We were crazy kids," Ethan said, "fresh off the farm. We were thrust into a war half a world from home. We acted like brave soldiers, but we were scared. We landed in France and concocted our pact. We were determined to survive.

"We found a tattoo artist in France. EARL was Bobby's idea, using our initials. The profile of two faces is Janus, god of beginnings and endings. One face looks ahead. The other looks back. Janus was my idea."

"Janus is vigilant," I said. "That's appropriate."

Ethan rolled down his sleeve and buttoned the cuff.

"Hightower will be pleased when he gets his vase," Ethan said.

"He'll be pleased," I said.

"He's going to ask you where you found it," he said.

"He'll want to know," I said.

"What will you tell him?" he said.

A dog barked in the distance. A door slammed. Someone started an automobile engine and drove away.

"Hightower offered five thousand dollars for the return of the vase," I said. "He said it was mine when I delivered. I'll refuse the money on the condition I don't reveal where I found it. Hightower will want to know, but he won't be willing to pay five G's for the information. Greed will outweigh his curiosity. He'll have his vase. He'll let it go."

"Thanks, Pete," Ethan said.

"Friends take care of friends," I said.

25

The sun failed to show that morning. It hid its face behind the clouds, and I kept the top up on my roadster. The vase in the towel lay at my hip. I taxied the treasure through town.

Together we backtracked my earlier route down Hillside. Near the intersection at Central, a siren blared. Traffic slowed, and drivers pulled over. I braked with one hand on the steering wheel and the other over the vase. The ugly fat man fell under my protection. I didn't want the fellow to suffer an accident.

An ambulance sped by and turned, then disappeared behind Wesley Hospital. I crossed over Central toward Douglas further south. College Hill was to the east. I rolled through the neighborhood toward Bluff and English.

The overcast sky cast a gloomy spell I couldn't shake. A foreboding feeling weighed on me. I turned a corner and heard a pooch yap in the distance. I lowered my window. The yap sounded familiar. It sounded French.

A car door slammed, then another, and another after that. I braked to a stop in the middle of the street. To my left, a woman in a housecoat and slippers stood in her lawn, arms crossed. A gray cat circled her feet and rubbed against her bare ankles. Wilma, the nurse in her white uniform, stood on Miss Devlin's porch and observed the goings-on next door. Neighbors congregated on the walks and talked over one another.

Hightower's English Tudor buzzed with activity. A black van idled in the driveway, its rear door open. "SEDGWICK COUNTY CORONER" was printed in gold lettering on a side panel.

The burgundy Cadillac with chrome trim and whitewall tires was parked on the drive in front of the van. Behind the van, a police cruiser idled with lights flashing. Another police cruiser was parked on the street along with a dark sedan, unmarked. The sedan had a siren mounted on the hood.

A pair of uniformed cops huddled on the lawn and pondered the situation. Or they discussed baseball or where to have lunch.

On the other side of the Tudor, a woman and her poodle watched from the porch. Lily yipped and yapped. Mommy stood beside her and took it all in. The lady savored the feast like a body starved. She'd have something to talk about that night, all right. Wait until she told her husband. Wait until she told her mother-in-law. Lily barked. The woman ignored the poodle. No one complained.

At Hightower's place, two beefy young men rolled a stretcher out the door. A human-shaped figure lay beneath a sheet, covered head to toe. The men grunted and lifted. They hoisted the stretcher into the back of the coroner's van. One man went forward into the driver's seat. The other man climbed in the back and closed the doors.

The van was wedged between the Cadillac to the front and the police cruiser to the rear. The driver rolled off the circular driveway and crossed the manicured lawn. The vehicle exited onto the street leaving ruts in its wake. No one complained about that, either.

I edged the roadster to the curb and killed the engine. My feeling of foreboding grew stronger. Had Lopez and Dunlap paid a visit to Hightower? Had they completed their unfinished business?

I surveyed the onlookers. All eyes were trained on the activity at Hightower's home. No one paid attention to a gumshoe who slid a package beneath the seat of his car.

I left the roadster at the curb and walked down the block. I crossed over the lawn. The two uniformed cops glanced at me. I touched the brim of my fedora, and they returned to their discussion. A third uniform stepped into the doorway and blocked my entry.

"Hold it, pal," he said. "No one comes inside."

"I have an appointment," I said.

He placed his fists on his hips.

"And just who are you?" he said.

"The Jewel Tea man," I said.

He didn't care for that.

"You look like a private dick, and you act like a wise guy," he said. "Beat it."

A deep voice roared from inside.

"Let him through," Lieutenant McCormick said.

The cop glared. I grinned. The cop stepped aside.

"Watch your step," Mac said. "What brings a sleuth to the scene of the crime on this bright and cheerful morning?"

"Bright and cheerful? You better stick with being cop. You're a lousy weatherman," I said.

The great room was a shambles. A photographer sidled from here to there and snapped pictures from various angles. He snapped, and a flashbulb popped. He edged to a new spot and repeated the process. Snap. Pop. Snap. Pop.

Blood stains covered the chair next to the table.

"This was Hightower's chair," I said.

"He won't be using it again," Mac said.

A pearl-handled pistol lay on the floor. I looked toward the Buffalo Bill Colt .45s displayed above the mantel. One pistol was missing.

Two glasses of cloudy liquid sat on the table. The coasters beneath the glasses were dry. A sheet of notepaper also lay on the table. I read upside down, AVA, in capital letters. I couldn't make out the notations in script beneath the name.

"You didn't answer my question," Mac said. "Why are you here?"

"I had an appointment with Hightower," I said.

"You had an appointment why?" he said.

"We had business," I said.

"I thought your client was the history professor?" he said.

"You thought correctly," I said. "What happened here?"

Mac sketched an outline for me. The police responded to a call that came from Hightower's art gallery. The woman who called had been unable to reach Hightower by telephone, and she was worried. Would the police check on the elderly gentleman at his home?

"In light of the recent murder at this address, the cops came in a hurry," Mac said. "No one responded to the doorbell, and the door was unlocked. They came in and discovered Hightower's body right here."

Mac indicated the blood-soaked chair.

"Other than the body which the medics took away, everything is the way we found it," he said.

"Any chance it was suicide?" I said.

Mac shook his head.

"Two shots to the chest," he said. "It looks like Alexander's war buddy returned to the scene of the crime."

I surveyed the room. I didn't buy Lopez as Hightower's killer.

"When you check the gun for prints, check the casings, too," I said.

"We will, but why do you mention it?" Mac said.

"Those pistols were show pieces, never fired," I said. "The murderer was familiar with the layout and carried .45 slugs to do the job."

Mac noted that.

"There's no doubt about premeditation," he said.

"Susie Donovan called from the gallery?" I said.

Mac glanced at his notes.

"Miss Susan Donovan. You've obviously met her," he said.

"Hightower's routine was to go to his gallery in the morning," I said. "I had an appointment with him today. He must have told Susie his plans. What prompted her to call the police?"

"She was worried. She called here to discuss gallery business," he said. "She got no answer, so she waited and tried again. Hightower was always available by telephone, according to Miss Donovan. When he didn't answer, she grew worried. When she didn't reach him a third time, she called the police. According to Miss Donovan, Hightower wasn't in the best of health."

I glanced at the chair.

"Miss Donovan was right," I said.

The uniform who'd braced me at the front door came in for a look-see. He didn't care for the idea of a private eye monopolizing his superior's time. He got Mac's attention and tried out his deductive reasoning.

"According to the Donovan gal, Hightower arrived at his art gallery yesterday and stayed until noon. That was the last time she spoke to him," the cop said.

The cop glanced at his watch.

"We arrived at ten this morning. That makes our window twenty-two hours," he said. "Hightower died within the last twenty-two hours."

The cop clasped his hands behind his back and pasted a smug grin on his puss. He rocked back and forth from his heels to the balls of his feet.

"You've opened the right window," I said, "but you cracked it too wide."

He lost the smug look and jutted his chin.

"What do you mean?" he said

"Hightower died last night. The coroner's report will confirm it."

"How can you be sure?" he said.

I gestured to the table.

"Hightower drank lemonade," I said. "He served it to his guests, ice cold and tart. Those glasses have no ice in them. The ice has melted. There's no condensation on the glasses. The coasters are dry. They've been sitting there for hours.

"I spoke to Mr. Hightower by telephone yesterday afternoon. He expected me here this morning. Sometime after that telephone call he died by gunfire, probably that evening."

The cop didn't look happy, but he listened and didn't speak.

"Check with the nurse next door," I said. "Her name is Wilma. Wilma cares for Miss Devlin during the day and puts her to bed at night. Then she leaves. Miss Devlin is deaf and wouldn't hear gunshots, but Wilma would. Find out when Wilma left and if she heard anything. That will narrow your window.

"After that, talk to the woman who lives on the other side, the gal with the poodle. The poodle's name is Lily. The lady of the house may have heard something. She loves to talk. Say something to her in French. She likes that."

The cop curled a lip like he'd stepped in Lily's doo-doo, and I was to blame.

"Enlist some help," I said. "Your pals on the lawn aren't doing much but shifting from foot to foot."

The cop glared at me like I was a public nuisance. He did the smart thing. He turned on his heel and left without a word.

"Ever the diplomat," Mac said.

"Just offering my help," I said, "trying to be friendly."

"Says the guy without a friend."

"I have friends," I said.

"How many?" he said.

"Counting you?" I said.

Mac snorted.

"I rest my case," he said.

The photographer finished with his pictures. He told Mac he'd deliver the photographs that afternoon. He packed up his gear and went out the door.

"You had business with Hightower," Mac said. "What business?"

Mac was a dog with a bone.

"This, that, and the other," I said. "Hightower asked me to meet him here."

"This, that, and the other. You play your cards close to the vest," he said. "You eye-balled that note on the table. Who is Ava? What do you know about her?"

"I could ask you the same question," I said. "You know more than I do."

"I'm asking the question," he said. "Who is she?"

"That's something I intended to discuss with Hightower this morning," I said. "You know who she is. Why don't you tell me?"

Mac studied me.

"You intended to discuss her with Hightower," he said. "That means you know something. How did you come to know about Ava?"

"Her name came up during my investigation. A little bird sang in my ear," I said.

"Don't crack wise with me, Stone."

"I've never met the woman, Mac," I said. "All I have is her name and lots of questions. I hoped Hightower might enlighten me."

Mac looked at his notes.

"City Hall has a record of birth," Mac said. "Ava Ann Hightower, born to Terrance and Marie Hightower."

He read again.

"She was born in 1910," he said. "That makes her twenty-eight years old."

"You have a head for numbers," I said.

"That's it. That's what I have on Ava Hightower," he said. "The city has no school record. No record of a license to drive. No marriage license. She's not registered to vote. Ava Ann, born to Mister and Missus, then nothing else. The girl disappears along with her mother, apparently. Are you saying you know nothing about this?"

"I'm as baffled as you are," I said. "I'm trying to find Bobby Lopez. Hightower's personal life holds no interest for me, unless it has a bearing on finding Lopez. I hoped to learn if she is involved."

"You're late," Mac said.

"We're both late," I said.

"You're too late to save Lopez," he said.

"Lopez didn't do this," I said. "Someone close to Hightower did this. That wasn't Lopez."

Mac rubbed his chin.

"You figure Ava Hightower?" he said.

"I don't know," I said. "She's as good a candidate as any. Hightower wouldn't serve lemonade to Lopez."

"We'll find her," Mac said.

I studied the table. Something was missing.

"Hightower smoked cigars," I said. "He used a gold lighter. I don't see it."

"I didn't see a gold lighter," Mac said. "Maybe it's in another room."

The study was off the great room. We checked tabletops and the escritoire and came up empty.

"It could be anyplace," Mac said.

"I don't think so," I said. "Hightower smoked one cigar a day. It was a ritual, his way of cheating death. He smoked his cigar in that chair. The lighter should be here on the table. What was he wearing? Did you check his pockets?"

"He wore slacks and a smoking jacket," Mac said. "I checked his pockets myself. They were empty."

Hightower's pockets were empty. The gold lighter was missing. The killer left a pair of bullets in Hightower's chest. Would a killer commit murder and pick up a souvenir on the way out the door?

26

"Mr. Hightower is dead?" said Agnes.

I assured Agnes that the man was deceased. She toyed with her sandwich and lowered it to her desk. She'd ordered lunch from the diner across the street, ham and cheese on rye. The news I delivered dampened her taste for food. Neither of us shared a fondness for Hightower, but murder never piques an appetite. Another sandwich meant for me remained untouched.

I placed the towel-wrapped package on Agnes's desk. She sat quietly and listened while I talked. When I finished, she shook her head.

"Pete, you have to be careful," she said. "That's two murders. This killer is ruthless."

"Assuming there's only one killer," I said. "Lopez and Dunlap are on the hook for the Weaver killing. They had nothing to do with Hightower's murder. Someone else killed Hightower."

"You're sure it wasn't Lopez or Dunlap?" she said.

"It wasn't them," I said. "The cops are still looking for the pair, but they've added Ava Hightower to their wanted list. Their fishing expedition may snag all three. Ava's wanted for questioning. I don't blame the cops. I'd like to ask the lady a few questions myself."

Agnes turned her attention toward the object on her desk.

"Is that what I think it is?" she said.

I removed the towel and steadied the vase.

"I promised Hightower I'd delivery this today. I arrived too late."

"Is this why he was killed?" she said, "for this vase?"

"I don't know. It's a possibility," I said.

Agnes took the piece in both hands. She rotated the vase and studied the artwork. Then she released it, leaned back, and sighed.

"I don't get it," she said. "Is this thing worth five thousand dollars? Who'd kill for this?"

"We live in a crazy world," I said.

We gave up on lunch. I puzzled over where to keep the vase. It belonged to Hightower and would belong to his estate. I'd return it, but for now I needed to stash it. I wrapped it in the towel. The relic was too large for the office safe. The bottom drawer on my desk locked with a key, but I nixed the idea. A thief would jimmy the lock in a heartbeat.

"Do you have any suggestions on where to stash this thing?" I said.

Agnes thought for a moment. She got up from her desk and opened the closet door.

"A thief would check the closet first thing," I said.

"Give it to me," she said.

Agnes took a brown paper bag out of the closet and emptied its contents, her personal items, on the desk. She placed the wrapped vase inside the bag and surrounded it with her items, a makeup kit, a hairbrush and a comb, a toothbrush and toothpaste wrapped in a washcloth, a bottle of mouthwash, and a first aid kit in a zippered case. She propped a box of sanitary napkins on top.

"Tough guys get spooked when they see a box of Kotex," she said.

The paper bag camouflaged the vase. I admired Agnes's work. The bag didn't look like a hideaway for a priceless piece of art.

"I know the jug is in there, and I doubt I could find it," I said.

I went into my office and picked up the telephone. I asked the operator to place a call to Grant & Gray, insurers of fine art, in Kansas City. The insurance company's client, Terrance Hightower, was dead. I doubted if agent Stu Kelly would discuss much with me when he heard the news, but I wanted to gauge his reaction.

The operator dialed the number, and a woman came on the line. She explained she was with an answering service and Mr. Kelly was out of the office. She offered to take a message, but I declined and said I'd call back. I hung up.

I made another call, this time to the Hightower art gallery to check on Susie Donovan. Two murders in as many weeks was more than most people could handle, let alone a sweet kid like Susie Donovan.

Another woman with another answering service took my call. The lady informed me that the gallery was closed for the day. She didn't explain why, and I doubted if she knew. She also didn't ask if I wanted to leave a message which suited me fine. I hung up the phone.

I sat back and listened to the quiet and thought about bullets and who might shoot them. I thought about twiddling my thumbs and wondered if anyone really did that. I lit a Chesterfield instead.

I reached into my pocket for a slug I'd taken out of my wall the night before. It looked like a .38. The cops could tell me for sure if I bothered to ask them. The slug certainly wasn't a .45. The bullet I had in my palm might match the one that killed Weaver. The cops could tell me that, too. I decided to keep it to myself. If it came from a gun fired by Lopez, I'd find out soon enough.

The Seth Thomas banjo clock indicated three o'clock. Rusty opened the door bearing his trademark grin and the afternoon edition of the newspaper. Hightower's murder made the headlines. The police had issued a bulletin calling for information on Ava Hightower. She was named as a possible suspect. If anyone had information on the woman, or if anyone knew her whereabouts, they were to contact the police immediately.

I tossed the paper aside and put on my fedora.

"I'm going out," I said to Agnes. "I have a doctor's appointment."

Agnes was no dummy.

"I know all about your doctor's appointments," she said. "Say hello to Tom and give Mabel my love."

I tipped my fedora and left.

27

I drove west on Douglas, crossed the river, and rolled through the Delano District. The afternoon traffic was light. I continued west for several blocks then turned north. A few moments later, I pulled up at Tom's Inn.

Tom spotted me and waved hello as I crossed the threshold. He drew a glass of Storz beer from the tap and placed it on a coaster. I took the stool at the end of the bar. A couple of laborers in dungarees occupied a table in the corner. Kitchen noises came from the back. Tom leaned over the bar.

"Ask me about the weather," he said. "Ask me about my sick sister in Tulsa. Ask me do I think Bruno Hauptmann kidnapped the Lindbergh baby. Ask me anything you want, but for crying out loud, don't ask me how the Birds did today."

"How'd the Birds do today?" I said.

"We lost. The bums lost to the Bees, can you believe it? And at Sportsman's Park, too. The Bees slaughtered us ten to five."

Tom went on with his tale of woe. His beloved St. Louis Cardinals had dropped a tough one to the Boston Bees. The Birds managed fourteen hits, on most days enough for a win, but they plated only five runs. Jimmy Brown had gone three for four, a good day at the bat, and others in the lineup added punch, but when the score was tallied, the Birds fell short. Four pitchers for St. Louis combined to give up sixteen hits and ten runs. It was a tough loss.

I sipped beer and listened to Tom's lament. Several minutes later, he paused and noticed my empty glass. Tom freshened it and centered it on the coaster with a shrug.

"I told you not to ask me about the Birds," he said.

A customer came through the door and took a stool at the other end of the bar. Tom moved down to take care of the guy, a mechanic I recognized. He'd helped me out one night when I had a flat tire. Tom moved to the stick to draw the man a beer.

"That one's on me," I said.

Tom delivered the beer and whispered to the man. The man looked my way and hoisted his glass. I hoisted mine in return.

Business picked up. Men arrived from work in twos and threes wearing khakis and dungarees, the occasional suit. They huddled across a table or in a booth, drank a cold one and shared a few laughs before heading home to the wife and kids.

Tom worked behind the bar. He washed and filled glasses. Mabel shuffled out of the kitchen. She toddled over and squeezed my arm.

"Agnes sends her love," I said.

"Send mine back to her," she said.

We shared small talk. Someone ordered a sandwich, and Mabel went back to the kitchen. A trio of young women came in and looked around. Tom waved at them from behind the bar. They grinned and waved. One of the gals gestured to a booth along the wall, and they took it.

Mabel came from the back with the sandwich and delivered it to a customer. She spotted the women and shuffled their way. The ladies clapped when Mabel approached. They stood and hugged her. One gal slid a chair over so Mabel could sit down. The four of them laughed and chattered.

I lit a Chesterfield and sipped my beer and mulled over the case. I considered different angles and motives. Ava Hightower and her father had argued in loud voices at the gallery. According to Miss Devlin, the woman and her mother had left the home years earlier. Miss Devlin never saw them again. Why had they gone? When and why had Ava returned?

I sipped and mulled and came up empty. I had no answers. I glanced at the young women in the booth and felt my age. I reminisced about my boyhood, and that led to thoughts of baseball.

Tom surveyed the room. Satisfied that everyone was satisfied, he brought over a fresh beer for each of us.

"It's been a busy afternoon. You've been lost in thought," he said. "What's on your mind? Wait a minute. Let me guess. I can read you like a dime novel. Let me tell you what you're thinking."

"All right, go ahead," I said.

"You're thinking about sex," he said.

"That's not a bad suggestion," I said, "but no."

"Food?"

"Maybe later," I said.

"Give me one more guess," he said.

He rubbed his chin.

"You're not thinking about sex, and you're not thinking about food," he said. "You have a beer, so not that."

He snapped his fingers.

"You're thinking about that case you're working on," he said.

"I was earlier. Not now," I said.

"Okay, I give up. What's on your mind?" he said.

"Centerfield," I said.

"Centerfield. That was going to be my next guess," he said.

"I knew you'd get it," I said.

"Sex, food, booze, baseball," he said. "Basic needs for a guy like you. Add your work, whatever case you're on, and that sums you up."

"That's not everything," I said.

"Those are the things that occupy your mind," he said. "What else is there?"

"There's more, much more. I contain multitudes," I said.

"You contain multitudes. Some poet said that, didn't he?"

"He did," I said. "That poet was also a fan of baseball."

"Okay, I'll bite. What makes centerfield so interesting?"

"I played centerfield back in the day," I said.

"I played in the infield," Tom said. "Second base, sometimes first. I liked the infield, close to the action."

"Fair enough. Every position in baseball requires unique skills," I said. "Centerfield calls for a player with speed and quick reactions. No one covers more ground than the centerfielder. He moves with the crack of the bat. He covers lots of ground in a hurry to get to the ball.

"Whether it's a routine fly ball, a shoestring catch, or a base hit, the centerfielder must get to the ball and make the play. But even a mediocre centerfielder is quick and fast. A great centerfielder is that and more."

A fellow down the bar signaled for a refill.

"Hold that thought," Tom said.

Tom refilled the gent's glass and poured a pitcher of suds for a trio at a table. He settled up at the cash register with departing customers. After a few moments, he returned to our conversation.

"Go ahead," he said.

"A good centerfielder is moving before the crack of the bat," I said. "A good centerfielder reacts before the pitch reaches the plate. He knows where the ball is going to go before it's hit, and he breaks in that direction."

"You mean he gets a jump on the ball," Tom said. "Sure, I did that at second base. Every player does that if he has his head in the game."

"You're right," I said. "The centerfielder has an advantage, though. From centerfield you can watch the play develop, see it unfold. The centerfielder has the best vantage point. He's positioned behind the pitcher and looks directly at the catcher. He sees the catcher set up right behind the plate or off to one side.

"The centerfielder notices the batter's stance, whether the batter is trying to pull the ball or go to the opposite field. The centerfielder cheats a step or two in that direction. When the pitcher goes into his windup, the centerfielder is moving.

"The bat makes music when it connects with the ball, a pure tone when it catches the sweet spot, off-key when it gets only a piece. That crack of ash smacking horsehide lets the centerfielder know whether to come in or drop back. The fielder adjusts and makes the play. He's ahead of the game."

I lit a cigarette.

"I've been a lousy centerfielder these past few days," I said. "I've been slow to react, flat-footed. I haven't gotten a jump on the ball, haven't anticipated where the ball will be. I've gotten there too late to make the play."

"Bingo, I was right," Tom said. "You've been thinking about your case."

He had me there.

"Like I said. You're like reading a dime novel," he said.

Mabel came from the kitchen with a tray of food. One of the women met her halfway across the floor.

"Who are those gals?" I said.

"They're nursing students at Wichita Hospital," Tom said. "They were nursing students, anyway. They've recently graduated. Those gals took care of Mabel when she had her stroke. They're celebrating graduation and Mabel's recovery."

Tom poured a pitcher of beer for the ladies. Hightower's daughter came to mind, her bicycle accident when she was little. She'd lost a lot of blood. She'd survived, but something else happened at the hospital. Following her stay, Hightower wanted nothing to do with the girl or her mother.

"Let me get that beer, Tom. I'd like to chat with those nurses."

Tom raised an eyebrow.

"Come on. I'll introduce you," he said.

We walked to the booth together.

"Good evening, sweet angels," Tom said.

He placed the pitcher on the table. The angels got up and hugged Tom. Tom pointed toward me.

"The guy inside this rumpled suit goes by Pete Stone," Tom said. "He's a private detective and an old friend, old enough to be your father. He'd like a few words. If he tries to flirt, give me the high sign. I'll run the bum out."

The gals giggled. Tom went back to the bar. One of the nurses pointed.

"I remember you," she said. "You were there when Mabel was sick. You looked after Tom. That was sweet."

They made room in the booth, and I joined them.

"Do you mind fielding a few questions while you eat?" I said.

"Go ahead, ask away," one said.

"Tom tells me that you graduated from nursing school," I said. "Congratulations. What's next?"

They ate and talked with the animation of youth. One gal dropped a piece of sandwich into her lap. Mustard stained her smock. The others laughed. One bumped her glass and caught it before it tipped over. Suds sloshed over the rim onto the table. Tom arrived with a rag and pretended to scold the ladies. That triggered another round of giggles.

They'd each gotten employment offers from local hospitals. Two of the nurses would work at St. Francis. The other one was hired by Wesley.

"Will any of you be a surgical nurse?" I said.

"Maybe someday," one said. "We start as floor nurses until we get experience."

"During your training at Wichita Hospital, did any of you work in surgery?"

They all chimed in.

"Sure."

"We all worked surgery shifts."

"I loved surgery. It was fascinating."

"Did you work in the emergency room?" I said.

"Yes, of course."

"Suppose a patient has lost a lot of blood. What's the procedure?" I said.

People who enjoy their work enjoy talking about it. The newly -minted nurses loved medicine. The gals were fresh and eager to share their knowledge with an older guy who knew little about their field. I asked questions, and they answered. They spoke. I listened.

Friday

July 15, 1938

28

The previous day's cloud cover had burned off. Friday dawned sunny and bright. I woke up early, showered and shaved, and drank my breakfast from a coffee cup. I recalled Tom's rumpled suit comment from the night before and left my place on Lewellen decked out in a blue suit with sharply creased trousers, a starched white shirt, and a red silk tie trimmed in silver fleurs-de-lis. The porch steps didn't seem as steep that morning. My feet felt lighter.

I lowered the top on the roadster and took Thirteenth west to River Boulevard. The street hugged the river as it snaked its way south. A mother goose and her goslings waddled from a park to the right and crossed the road toward the river on my left. I braked to a stop and waited. Momma goose chastised me with a squawk.

A car from the opposite direction stopped, also. A woman behind the wheel looked over at me and shrugged. I flashed my pearly whites. The parade ended, and the lady and I waved at each other as we rolled by.

As I motored, I replayed a radio show in my mind. The night before KFH had broadcast "The Dream," narrated by Boris Karloff. I turned out the lights and listened in the dark, my only companion a glass of bourbon. The tale depicted an accused murderer sitting in a courtroom, awaiting the jury's decision on his fate. Karloff's deep voice with his distinctive lisp, groaned and quivered in all the right places. The narrator crawled into the mind of the accused and lured the listener to dwell in terror. Karloff was a master at his craft.

I considered the players in the Hightower case and heard Karloff's voice. Guilty? Not guilty? The jury deliberated. Haunting voices chanted, "guilty, not guilty, guilty, not guilty, guilty, not guilty." Which was it? Who was it? Who was guilty? Who was not guilty?

I crossed over the river and rolled through downtown. At Douglas and Emporia, I pulled over and parked in front of the Lawrence Block Building. I had my hand on the door and glanced at the reflection in the glass. The threads were sharp, but the mannequin underneath needed repair, a haircut and a shoeshine. I walked to the other end of the block.

The lobby at the Hotel Eaton was occupied but subdued. Deep carpets and high ceilings in tandem muffled voices and clatter. A gentleman in a wingback chair wore a tailored suit and a smug look. He lit a cigar and blew a cloud of smoke. Another gentleman near the window flipped through a magazine and sipped from a cup.

A man and a woman across the lobby sat next to each other on a sofa. The man leaned toward the woman and lectured nonstop. The woman sat rigid and gave no indication she was listening. She stared straight ahead and twisted the wedding ring on her finger.

I said good morning to the clerk at the desk as I walked by. The hotel dick approached from down the hallway. The dick was a retired cop, a good one. We exchanged greetings when we passed each other.

"Pete."

"Jeff."

The barber had a customer in his chair. I took a seat along the wall and picked up a newspaper.

"Good morning, Sam," I said.

"Hello, Pete. Just finishing up here," Sam said.

The copy of the *Eagle* was several days old. A column listed the teachers in the city's schools for the upcoming year. I scanned the list and tossed the paper aside. The article was as spellbinding as a telephone directory.

Sam removed the barber cape and ran a brush over his customer's shoulders. The gentleman rose, and Sam wiped off the chair. I moved into it while they settled up at the cash register. Sam thanked the man. He grabbed his clippers and comb and went to work.

"What's new in the world of crime?" he said.

He ran a comb through my hair and snipped.

"Murder and mayhem," I said. "I'm investigating the Hightower case."

He let out a low whistle.

"Say, I read about that. Hightower was a muckety-muck wasn't he, lots of dough?"

"He had money," I said "not that it helped him in the end. He bought a bullet cheap. Now he's dead. I don't suppose his coffin will be any bigger than the next guy's."

"How did you get involved?" he said. "Aren't the cops working that case?"

"The cops are on the case," I said, "but they try to stay out of my way."

Sam chuckled. We turned to baseball. Sam followed the Wichita Watermen. The local team was having a good year. We discussed their chances in the National Baseball Congress tournament scheduled to begin in a couple of weeks.

After he finished with the clippers, Sam daubed warm lather around my ears and ran his razor over the strop. He trimmed the edges with deft strokes and splashed on witch hazel with a flourish. I thanked the man and paid him.

"See you next time," he said.

My next stop was the shine stand near Sam's shop. Ellis Waldo stood up and thanked a man who climbed down from the chair, a high gloss on his shoes. I waited while they finished.

"Good morning to you, Mr. Stone," he said. "That's a fine looking haircut you're sporting. You look dapper in that suit and tie, too. Allow old Waldo to complete the package with a shoeshine. You'll be ready for the cover of *Apparel Arts* in no time."

"Sold, Waldo. Work your magic," I said.

Waldo went to work. He'd been reading William Butler Yeats, a favorite poet. He recited a few lines. Waldo was a walking talking library. The man read and retained volumes.

"Ralph had a case," I said. "Has he talked about it?"

"Yes, missing person," he said. "Wife ran off. Ralph found her right away, too soon it turned out. Her bruises hadn't even healed."

"I've seen that a lot," I said. "It's rotten."

"Ralph told the husband he'd found her," Waldo said. "He refused to tell him where she was, though. The husband didn't take that well. He took a swing at Ralph, and Ralph jabbed him on the jaw. Knocked him out. Case closed."

Waldo popped his rag.

"Ralph told me about Rum-Rum," Waldo said. "It left him upset."

"I barely knew Rum-Rum, and I feel like I've lost a friend," I said. "I'm trying to find the friend of a friend now, buddies during the war. They survived the war, but the war changed them. Men who survive wars are never the same."

> Waldo looked to the side and recited some lines.
> "I know that I shall meet my fate
> Somewhere among the clouds above;
> Those that I fight I do not hate
> Those that I guard I do not love."

"Yeats?" I said.

"From 'An Irish Airman Foresees His Death,'" he said. "Yeats crawls inside the young man's head and hears him speak. He comes to a grim conclusion.

> 'I balanced all, brought all to mind,
> The years to come seemed waste of breath,
> A waste of breath the years behind
> In balance with this life, this death.'"

"Death brings clarity," I said. "Two men have been murdered in the case I'm working. The suspects are at large. Those who are guilty must pay. The innocent must be cleared. Life is more than a waste of breath, Waldo. Those who are innocent, those who survive, deserve the years to come."

29

"Well, aren't you handsome?" Agnes said and smiled. "You're all clipped, shaved, and shined."

"You act like I never take a bath."

"You've done more than wash up," she said. "There's more. You've got that look."

"What look?"

"That nothing-is-going-to-stop-me look," she said.

I didn't tell Agnes that getting shot at does that to a man. Someone had tried to plug me. Someone had plugged Hightower. Bullets whizzing through the air affect a man's attitude.

"What's next?" she said.

"I'm going into my office to make a telephone call. Nothing is going to stop me," I said.

I dialed the telephone and listened to it ring. I waited. It rang some more. Ethan Alexander answered. He was out of breath.

"Give me a minute, Pete. I was down the hall."

"Take your time," I said. "I can call back."

"No, no. I'm okay," he said. "It takes time to wheel down the hall. I need another telephone. I put an extension in the bedroom. Maybe I should get one more for the bathroom."

"A man deserves privacy," I said. "Nix the bathroom telephone. Let it ring, and let the caller wait. Two telephones are one too many in my book."

"You're right. Nix the phone," he said. "I read the newspaper."

"Hightower's dead," I said.

"You didn't deliver the package?" he said.

"I have it for now," I said. "Listen, Ethan. Have you had contact, direct or indirect, with Bobby Lopez?"

"I haven't seen Bobby for weeks," he said. "Rum-Rum came to the door that night. Since then, I've only talked to you and the police. What's on your mind?"

"Lopez took that vase for a reason," I said. "He didn't want to keep it, but he had to take it. Hightower valued the vase. From the beginning, its return was his only concern. Lopez recognized its value. Hightower knew its value. That vase is still valuable to someone. Someone else will be looking for it."

"Who?" he said.

"I don't know," I said. "Even in death, Hightower remains a mystery. Where was Ava Hightower all those years, and why has she returned? The Hightower father-daughter relationship is a mystery, hidden in the shadows. Karl Weaver's murder and that fire in the studio happened because of events that took place prior to that night."

"Now what?" he said.

"Now I take a history lesson, professor. Now I look into Hightower's past."

We rang off. I dialed the operator and placed a call to Grant & Gray in Kansas City. Insurance agent Stu Kelly came on the line. I reintroduced myself.

"I remember you from your earlier call, Mr. Stone," he said. "I've just learned about Terrance Hightower's death. That's a tragedy. I assume that's why you're calling."

"Murder is tragic," I said. "Someone had a motive for taking out Hightower. Maybe it was the man I'm after. Maybe it was somebody else. I don't suppose you could tell me who stands to collect the insurance settlement, could you?"

"You know I can't discuss a client's personal information," he said.

"Not even if that information points to a murderer?" I said. "All I need is the name of the person who inherits the dough from the claim."

"Mr. Stone, I couldn't give you that information even if I knew it," he said.

That was a slip of the tongue. I pounced on it.

"How could you not know the name of the contingent beneficiary?" I said. "An art studio burned to the ground. You're looking at a hefty payout. I figured you'd know all the details."

"We do not insure art studios," Kelly said. "We insure art."

I let that hang while the wheels turned.

"Listen, I'm on your side," I said. "You have your rules, but I'm after a murderer. Your company insured the art lost in the fire, didn't it? You told me on my earlier call that Hightower was your client."

"That's correct. Grant & Gray covered the art that was lost," he said. "Mr. Hightower was our client."

A bee buzzed in my bonnet.

"And yet you don't know the name of your client's contingent beneficiary?" I said.

"You might want to examine your premise," Kelly said.

"Grant & Gray covered the art lost in the fire. Hightower was your client," I said.

The bee buzzed louder. It threatened to sting.

"Are you saying the art in the studio didn't belong to Hightower?" I said. "You said Hightower was your client. Did you mean you insured art for Hightower, but Hightower's art was located elsewhere, like in the gallery and in his home? You're telling me that the art you insured in the studio belonged to someone else? Is that what you're saying?"

"I'm not saying anything. Good day, Mr. Stone."

Kelly hung up the phone. The buzz in my ear was the dial tone. I hung up the phone, too.

Agnes batted her eyes and feigned a swoon. She acted like I never cleaned up. I placed my fedora atop my new haircut, blew her a kiss, and left the office.

Sedgwick County Courthouse was located at Central and Main. I pulled away from the curb on Douglas and turned left on St. Francis. At Central I made another left and drove west to Main.

Terrance Hightower told me at our first meeting that his father made his money in cattle and oil. They owned a ranch east of town. The words Hightower used were, "not far from this very spot." Sedgwick County extended a few miles beyond the city limits and abutted Butler County to the east. "Not far" could mean either one of the counties. I'd start with Sedgwick.

The Register of Deeds was located on the second floor. I climbed the stairs and opened the door on an office decorated in gray and gray in a variety of shades, all gray. I wondered if anyone in the place smiled. It was enough to make Pollyanna weep.

A counter in a lighter shade ran the width of the room. The counter separated customers from clerks at work on the other side. A half-dozen women sat at desks and thumbed ledgers or pecked at typewriters. Customer chairs in darker tones lined the wall. Nobody waited.

A woman appeared at the counter and brought color with her. She wore a yellow No. 2 pencil behind her ear, gold-rimmed glasses on a gold chain, and a grim look on her face. Her tight lips made a red slash that didn't commit to either a smile or a frown.

"May I help you?" she said.

The nametag on her dress read, Norma Norwood. I spotted a gold band on her ring finger.

"Thank you, Mrs. Norwood. I'm investigating a real estate transfer, land and oil rights," I said.

"When did this transfer take place?" she said.

I gave my information to Mrs. Norwood. What I had was vague and lacked detail. I gave her points when she didn't seem deterred by that. She removed the pencil from behind her ear and made notes on a pad of paper.

John Hightower sold his property twenty-eight or twenty-nine years earlier. The sale included a ranch of unknown acreage along with oil rights on the property. The sale may have also included oil wells not located on the ranch. Properties may have extended into Butler County. When I finished speaking, Mrs. Norwood read over her notes and "tsked."

"Is this all?" she said.

"That's it," I said.

"Hightower? This wouldn't be the Hightower that's in the news, would it?" she said.

"Terrance Hightower is the man in the news. John Hightower was the father. The father died not long after the property was sold."

"You said you were investigating the sale. Are you a detective?"

"Private," I said and handed her my card. She looked it over.

"This may take some time, Mr. Stone," she said. "Would you like to come back?"

"I'll wait," I said.

Mrs. Norwood seemed displeased by my decision. Her red lips betrayed her with a twitch. I took a chair along the wall and cracked the seal on a fresh pack of Chesterfields. She watched as I pulled an ashtray on a stand closer to my chair. I lit a cigarette, crossed my legs, and blew smoke toward a ceiling fan.

She turned and stepped over to one of the clerks. Mrs. Norwood gave instructions in a quiet voice. The woman at the desk rose from her chair and walked across the room where rows of gray metal shelves housed hundreds of gray-backed ledgers. She referred to her notes, retrieved several ledgers, and returned to her desk. While she thumbed the top ledger, I crushed out my cigarette and leaned back and waited.

Stu Kelly at Grant & Gray Insurance did not specifically say that the paintings that went up in flames weren't Hightower's. He let me say it, and he didn't deny it. Susie Donovan at the gallery told me many of the paintings were there on consignment. They belonged to the artists who created them. The gal who ran the art museum told me all of the art they had was on loan from other museums and private owners. That didn't explain the vase. Hightower was desperate for the vase. No one had claimed its loss to Grant & Gray.

I glanced around the waiting area. There was nothing to read, no newspaper or magazine. I tried to recall those lines of poetry Waldo had recited. My recollection did nothing to honor the poet, Yeats. I lit another cigarette and thought about baseball.

Time passed, and the woman at the desk handed a slip of paper to Mrs. Norwood. I stood up and met her at the counter.

"Here's what we've found," she said.

She handed over the paper. It noted the date of the sale and the name of the buyer. I didn't recognize the name.

"What do I owe you?" I said to Mrs. Norwood.

"Since this is part of your investigation, the county will waive its fee," she said.

"Well, this county resident appreciates you. Thank you, Mrs. Norwood. You've been very helpful. And thank you, too," I said to the woman sitting at the desk.

I left the county offices. At Second and Main I spotted a telephone booth on the corner and pulled over. I walked toward the booth and got distracted by sweet aromas from a bakery shop. I went inside. A woman with a smile and streaks of flour on her cheeks greeted me. She wore a snood, one of those mesh hairnets, and wiped her hands on a white apron.

"What can I get you?" she said.

"Is it too late for doughnuts?" I said.

"It's never too late for doughnuts," she said.

"I'd like a dozen doughnuts," I said. "Would you deliver them to the courthouse?"

"I can do that. My son is in back, pouting because his brother went fishing without him. He'll run them up there. It'll get him out of my hair. What kind of doughnuts would you like?"

"Anything, as long as they're pretty and colorful. Load them up with sprinkles and frosting, pink and blue," I said.

I wrote 'Norma Norwood, Register of Deeds' on the back of my card. The woman took my card and my money. I threw in an extra two bits for the down-in-the-mouth lad.

Outside, I went to the telephone booth and dialed the operator. When she answered, I gave her the name on the slip of paper.

"Patrick Fitzsimmons, operator. Do you have a listing?" I said.

She did, and she gave me the man's telephone number.

"Do you have an address?"

The operator had that, too. I wrote it down and thanked her. I slipped the paper into my pocket. I got in the roadster and started to pull away, then I slammed on the brake. I pulled the paper out of my pocket and studied the address. I'd never been to the house, but I could picture its location. I shifted into gear and headed east.

I didn't know Patrick Fitzsimmons by name, but I'd met the man who bought the Hightower ranch and the oil wells. I met him in an alley behind Hightower's place at Bluff and English.

When I'd asked for the man's name, he replied, "None of your business." He'd glared with his good eye, the one not covered with a patch. He bore a scar from the corner of his mouth to the cleft of his chin. The man who bought the goods from John Hightower all those years ago was the back-alley neighbor, the cyclops.

30

"**P**atrick Fitzsimmons," I said when he opened the door.

Fitzsimmons didn't speak. He rasped. He inhaled ragged breaths through a slightly open mouth and gray thatches lining his nostrils. The scar trailed vivid and white across his scarlet puss. He glared.

He wore wrinkled khaki slacks and a once-white undershirt. I'd interrupted lunch. Ketchup, or maybe it was tomato sauce, stained the shirt. When he spoke, he did so in a quiet, measured voice that masked his rage.

"I knew you were trouble from the first," he said.

He turned his back and walked away leaving the door standing open. I stepped in and closed the door. I followed him down the hall and into the kitchen. He sat down at the table and motioned to a chair.

"Sit," he said.

I sat.

"Do you drive a gray LaSalle, Fitzsimmons?" I said.

I looked for a car when I arrived and didn't see one. The door on the garage was closed. He looked at me like I was looney tunes.

"Do you always start a conversation like that?" he said.

"This is going to go better if you just answer my questions," I said.

"Call me Fitz," he said, "and I do not drive a LaSalle. I've been a Ford man all my life."

"Okay, Fitz," I said. "Do you want to tell me what happened or should I call the police?"

He mulled that over.

"Not that it's any of your business, but I was about to call the police myself," he said. "I thought I'd eat a little lunch first. I doubt I'll take to prison food."

A bit of spaghetti and a crust of bread remained on a plate.

"I'm in no hurry," I said. "Finish your lunch. We can talk while you eat."

He pushed the dirty dish aside and replaced it with an ashtray. He lit a Camel. I lit a Chesterfield. Then he reached across the table and fisted a bottle of bourbon.

"It's not my habit to drink this early in the day," he said. "I'll make an exception. It may be a while before I taste whiskey again. Care for a snort?"

I shook my head. He tipped the bottle and took a pull, then wiped his mouth with the back of his hand.

"Ask your questions," he said.

"Start at the beginning with you and the Hightowers," I said. "You go way back."

He ran his tongue over his lower lip.

"That we do," he said. "I worked cattle for John Hightower when he started ranching. I was his first cowboy, top hand."

He rubbed an open palm against the stubble on his cheek.

"Those were good days, the best. I was long on pluck and short on brains back then. I didn't give a whit for the morrow. I figured those days would never end. I'd be a cowboy until they shoveled dirt over me."

He tipped the bottle.

"I liked everything about being a cowboy," he said, "the roping, the riding, the smells, dirt and animals. Cattle are ignorant, ugly beasts, but I never held animosity toward them."

He crushed out his cigarette and looked me in the eye.

"You've got to understand this," he said. "Everything that's happened over the years hinges on this. Terrance hated ranching. Terrance hated hard work. And because he hated the work, I believe John Hightower grew to hate his son. Terrance wanted no part of horses and cattle and dirt and foul odors. He wasn't built for the outdoors. That didn't sit well with John."

"Hightower didn't say much about ranching," I said. "I understand they made their money in oil."

"Yes, John struck oil," Fitzsimmons said with a harsh laugh. "Terrance Hightower hated working in oil more than he hated cattle. It broke my heart when John sold off the cattle. I understood there was big money in oil. It broke my heart just the same. He sold the cattle and drilled for oil. Terrance stayed indoors. I stayed in the fields with John. I went from being top hand to roughneck."

"That's a hard life, roughneck," I said.

"It was hard work," he said, "but I was used to hard work. I earned every dime I made. The oil field wasn't like running cattle. An oil well reaps profits, but an oil well lacks a soul. I worked in the fields, but I moved into town."

"You bought out John Hightower," I said.

Fitzsimmons stared long and hard.

"You've been busy, shamus," he said.

I ignored that.

"You didn't buy out Hightower on a roughneck's pay," I said.

"Other men drew their pay on Friday," he said. "By Monday they were broke. I saved my wages and lived on little."

"That doesn't explain the money needed to buy the property," I said.

"You're right. I never saved enough money for that," he said. "It was John's idea. The man was nearing the end of his run, and he knew it. He knew Terrance would never have what it takes to run the business."

He tipped the bottle and lit another Camel.

"John didn't want his son to be destitute," he said. "He asked me to take over the business. He drew up a contract, monthly mortgage payments, a stipend for Terrance. Monthly payments over a twenty-five-year period. After that, I'd own everything free and clear. I signed the contract.

"I lived on a razor's edge those first years. After expenses and the mortgage payment, there wasn't much left, not more than a roughneck's pay. I struggled and paid my bills. John Hightower passed. I honored that contract. Terrance lived high on the hog. I didn't."

He pointed to his face.

"You see this patch? This scar? I was no leading man, but I was never the ugliest pumpkin in the patch either. Oil field work is dangerous. I did what I had to do. I paid Terrance every month.

"The oil business is as fickle as a prom queen," he said. "The El Dorado oil strike changed my fortunes. When the El Dorado field opened up, I jumped in. I hit it big."

"You made money," I said. "Terrance had money. What went wrong?"

"You tell me," he said. "I knew how to make money. I never learned how to spend it. All those years living on little made me who I am. I drive a Ford automobile and wear a working man's clothes and live alone. Terrance, the dandy fool, spent everything he had.

"My obligation ended a few years back. Twenty-five years of monthly payments ended. Terrance's art gallery didn't provide much income. He struggled, and my fortune continued to grow. Terrance felt I should continue paying him each month. He argued that his father never foresaw the money I would make. He was right about that, but a deal is a deal. I honored the contact. I paid every nickel I owed."

"What took place on Wednesday?" I said.

"Tempers flared," he said.

"That must have been later," I said. "What were you doing in Hightower's place earlier in the day, while he was away?"

He gave me that one-eyed glare again.

"You don't miss much, do you?" he said. "He threatened to get a lawyer; said he was going to sue me. He didn't have a legal leg to stand on. He wanted to annoy me."

"Is that why you broke into his home?" I said.

"I didn't break into his home," he said. "I've had a key to his place for years. When Terrance started showing his age, he gave me a key in case of an emergency."

He lit another Camel.

"I wanted to find out if he'd contacted a lawyer," he said. "I looked through his papers and didn't find a thing. So I left."

"You said tempers flared," I said. "You went back later. What happened?"

"We talked about money," he said. "I offered to lend him something to tide him over. The crazy coot was insulted. He screamed and ranted. He waved his cane in my face."

"How did the gun come into play?" I said.

"Terrance grabbed a pistol from that display over the mantel," he said. "He stuck the pistol in my face. I wrestled for it, and the gun went off."

Fitzsimmons looked down at the table.

"Terrance fell backward into his chair, dead."

I studied Patrick Fitzsimmons and said nothing. I wondered what the man's game was. "What then?" I said. "You didn't call the police."

"I was scared. I dropped the gun and ran out the backdoor to my place."

I lit a Chesterfield. The ashtray was full. Fitzsimmons didn't seem to mind.

"Let's talk about Ava Hightower," I said.

That caught him by surprise.

"How do you know about Ava?" he said.

"Her name came up. Tell me about her," I said.

"Ava is Terrance's daughter. She was his daughter," he said.

"Is, was. What does that mean?" I said. "Why did Terrance's wife and daughter leave home?"

Fitzsimmons gathered his thoughts.

"You never knew John Hightower," he said. "John was a hard man, especially with those closest to him. When Terrance got married, John let it be known he expected a grandchild.

"John's age began to show. The man was once robust and vital, but those last years he stayed indoors. Terrance and Marie visited every day. A year passed, then another. Terrance and Marie didn't conceive. John belittled Terrance. He made cruel remarks. He taunted his son publicly.

"John Hightower died as he lived, a bitter man, without a grandchild. Terrance was crushed by failing to father an heir."

Fitzsimmons looked up at the wall and drummed his fingers on the table.

"Eventually, Ava came along. Terrance strutted and crowed. He adored that little girl. He was a proud father."

Fitzsimmons paused, unable to continue.

"There was an accident," I said.

"There was an accident," he said, "Little Ava needed blood, a transfusion. The doctors suggested a parent be a donor. They ran tests to type their blood, mother and father. They didn't find a match. Mother and father both had blood type A. Ava's blood was type B."

I recalled my conversation with the nurses in Tom's Inn on surgical blood transfusions.

"Two parents with blood type A. A child with blood type B. That's an impossibility," I said.

"Marie loved her husband," Fitzsimmons said. "Before Ava came along, Terrance grew depressed, almost to the point of suicide. He wanted to father a child. Can you fathom the capacity of a woman's love, Stone? Can anyone?"

I crushed out my cigarette.

"Marie came to me for help," he said. "I helped her. Is that clear enough for you?"

A telephone sat amid the dirty dishes and clutter. Fitzsimmons picked it up and slammed it down in front of me.

"Make the call," he said. "I told you what happened."

"The police are looking for Ava," I said. "She's suspected of killing her father."

"I killed Terrance Hightower. Call the police," he said.

Fitzsimmons lifted the receiver. A scrap of paper fell loose and fluttered to the floor. A phone number was written on the paper. He retrieved it and stuffed it in his pocket.

I studied the man. He was lying about the murder. Patrick Fitzsimmons did not kill Terrance Hightower.

I put on my fedora and stood up.

"Make the call," he said.

"Maybe another time," I said.

I left Patrick Fitzsimmons sitting at the kitchen table.

31

Whoever shot Terrance Hightower was known to him, a visitor to the home who knew the layout. Patrick Fitzsimmons fit the profile, all right, but everything he told me smacked of a lie. Hightower didn't die in a fit of rage. His cold-blooded death was planned and premeditated.

As I'd told Lieutenant McCormick, the murderer knew the Colt .45s were showpieces, never loaded, never fired. Someone planned the murder and brought ammunition to kill his victim. The killer used a pair of bullets, not one as Fitzsimmons had claimed.

Lopez and his pal could have visited the home on occasion. If so, it was part of their job, not a social call. Hightower considered Lopez and Dunlap beneath his station. He would not have invited the men to drink lemonade in his great room. Neither man shot Hightower.

Ava remained a question mark. Ava had visited her father at the gallery where they had a heated conversation. Had Ava visited her father at home to continue that conversation? It was possible she had confronted her father. Had she shot the man?

The day dwindled. I sat at my desk. My morning vim and vigor waned with the late afternoon sunlight. Agnes leaned through the doorway with her hat on her head and her purse in her hand.

"May I leave a few minutes early?" she said. "My sister's coming into town."

"Give her my best," I said. "I'm going to make a telephone call and lock the door."

"I'm off then," she said. "I'll see you Monday."

Agnes scooted out the door. The telephone sat next to the late edition of the *Beacon*. I reached for the telephone, and it rang before I lifted the receiver. The caller was Lieutenant Thaddeus McCormick.

"Sit tight and don't leave. We need to talk," he said and hung up the phone.

I took my notebook out of my pocket. A piece of paper with a number on it had dropped from Fitzsimmons's telephone. I'd scratched the number in my book.

It could've belonged to a liquor store or a bookie or a cousin in Tuscaloosa for all I knew, but I had to dial the number. A detective would forfeit his decoder ring and secret handshake privileges if he didn't make the call.

The phone rang three times. A male voice answered.

"Hotel McClellan," he said.

That took me by surprise. I rolled the dice.

"I'd like to speak to a guest, Ava Hightower," I said.

The receiver thudded to the counter. A moment later the voice returned.

"Nobody by that name registered at the McClellan," he said.

"She might be using another name, Ava Argent," I said.

This time there was a sigh and a thud. I waited.

"No Ava Argent," he said. "Say, who is this?"

"Wrong number," I said and hung up the telephone.

I glanced at the clock and picked up the *Beacon*. The Yankees were leading the American League by a half-game over the Indians. The Pirates held the same lead over the Giants in the

National League. Tom's St. Louis Cardinals struggled to keep their heads above water. Only the lowly Phillies had a worse record.

An article on page twelve reported that Wichita would lay out fifty grand to add six buses to the city fleet. I tapped my finger on the newspaper. The bus depot was at the northeast corner of Broadway and William. The McClellan Hotel was on the southwest corner.

A hotel near the depot made a convenient oasis for travelers and transients, people who came and went, people who went unnoticed. A hotel near the bus depot would be a perfect hideaway for someone on the lam.

I heard the outer door open. Lieutenant Thaddeus McCormick appeared in the doorway. Mac didn't take off his hat.

"I'm taking you to dinner," he said.

"Nice to see you, too, Mac," I said.

He shook his head.

"C'mon, Stone. I have to be someplace, and we're going to talk," he said.

When we reached the sidewalk, Mac motioned to his car, a black sedan parked behind my roadster.

"I'll drive," he said.

We drove three blocks, Santa Fe to First, and First to Topeka. He pulled over and parked. End of the day traffic was steady. A guy on an Indian motorcycle wearing a leather helmet and goggles weaved around automobiles and gunned it through the intersection. He disappeared down First Street.

A crowd of people milled on the sidewalk and climbed the steps to an elegant, Romanesque building. The building shared the block with the Orpheum Theater to the west where a marquee sparkled. A sandwich board sign at the bottom of the steps read, "Scottish Rite Friends Dinner."

"You ever been inside?" Mac said.

"When it was the YMCA, years ago," I said. "I was a wee lad. Are you a member?"

"Yeah, there's been a McCormick on the rolls since the beginning," he said, "Granddad, Dad, uncles."

I'd been by the Scottish Rite Center hundreds of times, but I wasn't a member. The stone structure, wrought iron trim, leaded glass windows all lent class to the city. We went inside.

The dinner was an open house and fundraiser, a way of introducing the Scottish Rite to the community. Members and nonmembers alike filled the lobby. Mac huddled with a man in a burgundy blazer who carried a clipboard and consulted a list of names. While they huddled, I gaped at the pillars and chandeliers.

"Let's go," Mac said.

"This is quite a roost," I said.

We moved to a wide staircase carpeted in red and ascended to the second floor. A portrait of a founder towered on the wall. Another painting of another founder greeted us at the top of the landing.

The crowd flowed into a ballroom converted into a dining hall for the evening. Tables arranged for the banquet filled up with diners.

"You hungry?" Mac said.

"I hate to eat on an empty stomach," I said.

Mac grunted and headed for the bar. He returned with two glasses of bourbon on the rocks.

"Let's go up," he said.

On the way, Mac gave me the tour. Heavy, oaken doors led to rooms decorated with crystal chandeliers and leaded, stained glass windows. Rooms featured paintings by well-known artists. Another stairway took us to the top floor. We walked past a tapestry of the Last Supper on the wall.

The top floor was empty and quiet. Down the hall, a door to the chapel stood open. We entered the library. Relics and collectibles in glass cases lined a wall. I browsed the shelves and spotted first edition books.

Mac motioned toward overstuffed chairs in the corner. He reached for an ashtray on a pedestal. A booklet with a green cover, *Aunt Sammy's Radio Recipes,* lay atop a table. We placed our drinks on the table. Mac lit a cigar. I lit a Chesterfield.

Mac watched smoke curl to the ceiling and gathered his thoughts. Lieutenant McCormick didn't bring a private eye to the Scottish Rite Temple to ply him with drinks and buy him a meal.

"An odd thing happened this afternoon," he said. "I'd just come from a visit with the chief. The chief is not happy that we haven't solved these murders. He took me to the woodshed."

I tried to picture anyone taking Mac to the woodshed. I couldn't do it.

"I'm in my office licking my wounds," he said, "when a sergeant leans in the doorway and tells me they're booking the Hightower killer now. I'm intrigued by this development, so I investigate.

"The guy's sitting at the desk spilling his story. His mug looks like it's been through a meat grinder. He confesses to killing Hightower and takes the rap for the murder of the assistant, Karl Weaver, too. The man opens up like a morning glory at first light."

"Congratulations, Mac," I said. "Case closed."

Mac chewed on his cigar and looked at me.

"I take this man into an interrogation room, just the two of us," he said. "He gives me details, the how and the why. Then, he tells me he tried to surrender to a private dick earlier in the day. He says the dick refused to call the cops. I didn't bother asking for the dick's name. I added two and two and came up with Pete Stone."

"Patrick Fitzsimmons," I said.

"Patrick Fitzsimmons," he said. "Talk to me, Stone."

"Patrick Fitzsimmons didn't kill anybody," I said. "Don't tell me you bought his cockamamie line."

Mac reached for his glass and sipped bourbon.

"Of course Fitzsimmons didn't kill anybody," Mac said. "Nothing he said fits the crimes. The question is why would he confess to crimes he didn't commit?"

I sipped bourbon.

"What's your take on this man?" Mac said.

"Fitz is loaded with dough, nobody to spend it on," I said. "People who don't know him call him a curmudgeon. People who do know him don't call him at all."

"I didn't buy his story," he said. "His line was malarkey."

"Only a sap would buy what he was selling," I said.

"That doesn't explain why you didn't give us a call," Mac said. "A confession would clear Alexander's war buddy. You know something. Who's this guy covering for?"

A ceiling lamp highlighted a painting across the room. In the painting, field hands in dungarees and straw hats reaped wheat on a golden slope. Yellows and greens flowed beneath a blue and gray sky. The scene was captivating.

"That's Thomas Hart Benton," I said. "Is it the original?"

"Everything in the place is the original," Mac said.

I mentioned my recent visit to the Wichita Art Museum.

"Did you know that the art is on loan?" I said. "It takes time to collect art."

"That's fascinating," he said. "Answer my question. Who is Fitzsimmons covering for?"

"Your guess is as good as mine," I said. "Hightower owned art at his gallery, not all of it. It must have taken a pile of dough to collect the art that went up in flames. That studio belonged to Hightower. Maybe he didn't own the contents."

"Where are you going with this?" he said.

"Fitzsimmons told me Hightower had money problems," I said. I told Mac about Fitz's mortgage arrangement with the senior Hightower. "Fitz paid off the mortgage, and for the first time in his life, Terrance didn't have a goose to lay the golden eggs."

"He must have made money with his gallery," Mac said.

"According to Fitzsimmons, whatever Hightower made he spent," I said. "That gallery strikes me as high overhead, low profit. Then there's the fat man."

"The vase," Mac said.

"Hightower was mad to recover the vase," I said. "He told me his father bought the vase years ago. That doesn't add up. Terrance was the art collector, not the old man."

"None of this explains why Fitzsimmons confessed," Mac said. "Who is Fitzsimmons trying to protect?"

"Maybe it's the daughter, Ava Hightower," I said. "He'd have no reason to cover for Lopez or Dunlap."

"Why would he cover for the daughter?" Mac said.

"That's a question for Fitzsimmons," I said.

I wasn't going to tell Mac what I'd learned about the daughter's parentage. Mac looked at me for a long moment.

"We're going to find them," he said. "All of them, Ava, Lopez, and Dunlap."

"What about fingerprints at the residence?" I said.

"We found prints," he said, "nothing on the pistol or the ammunition. Hightower was the only one who touched his lemonade. The other glass was clean."

"Fitzsimmons has a key to the place," I said. "His prints wouldn't tell you anything. They'd be all over. He claimed that tempers flared that night. Hightower didn't die in a fit of temper. His murder was planned and executed with a cool head in cold blood."

Mac crossed the floor and opened a cabinet. He retrieved a bottle of Four Roses bourbon. He poured the amber liquid, and we drank it neat. We sipped and talked and forgot the time.

By the time we stopped drinking, the banquet was over. The Scottish Rite Center was empty. The streets outside were quiet. Mac's sedan was the only car on the block. We climbed in and pulled away from the curb. Mac turned the corner at Broadway.

A familiar looking car approached us and went by. Street lights cast too dim a glow to make out the color. One thing was clear. The car was a LaSalle.

Saturday

July 16, 1938

32

The neighborhood was quiet on Saturday morning. I woke early and breakfasted on coffee and tobacco. I bathed and shaved and got dressed. I wound the clocks, the Black Forest cuckoo, the Seth Tomas grandfather, the Austrian Zappler Animated, and all the others.

I closed the door to my place and walked down the steps to my roadster. I carried a thermos bottle filled with black coffee in one hand and an empty jar in the other. Kitchen noises came through the window of the home next door. A dog barked behind another house. Lewellen Street had no traffic on my block.

I pulled from the curb and turned right on Eleventh. I circled the block, Jefferson to Twelfth and back to Lewellen. I didn't spot a gray LaSalle coupe. I headed to Waco and dropped south toward midtown. Traffic was light. I kept my eye on the mirror to be sure I wasn't followed.

I replayed my previous evening's discussion with Mac. It had been two weeks since July 2, the day Karl Weaver died and the art burned. I met with Ethan Alexander in his kitchen on Independence Day.

Money motivated the Hightower crimes. Money connected the paintings that burned, the fat man vase, and the calculated murders. Who stood to gain?

Downtown, I turned east toward Broadway and dropped south to William. I pulled over and parked on the northwest corner in front of the Innes Department Store. The department store hadn't opened yet. The spot gave me a clear view of the intersection. The McClellan Hotel lay straight ahead. The bus depot was to my left.

My watch read ten minutes before seven. I poured coffee into the thermos cup and lit a Chesterfield. My stakeout was a hunch. Sometimes my hunches paid off. Sometimes they didn't. Ava Hightower was not registered at the hotel under her real name. She wouldn't use her real name. My hunch said she registered under an alias. If she did, she had Lopez and Dunlap stashed there, too.

The hotel was perfect for someone wanting to go unnoticed. A guest who stays quiet doesn't draw attention. Why else would Fitzsimmons keep the hotel's phone number handy?

The stakeout played with my mind. The clock ticked. My hunch weakened. Ava could be anywhere. Lopez and Dunlap could be anywhere. How could a detective fall for a blind woman's story about a silver bird? I watched and waited. I drank coffee and smoked cigarettes. The thermos ran dry. I used the jar.

Traffic picked up, on the streets and on the sidewalk. Airbrakes hissed. A Trailways bus pulled into the depot. Families filed in and out of the Innes Department Store. Guests at the McClellan exited with luggage. Some crossed to the bus depot. Others left in taxi cabs or personal vehicles.

I grew discouraged, the ninth inning and down a run. I looked at my watch. Then, I looked at the McClellan. There she was. She came out of the hotel and stopped at the corner. The lady looked side to side and jaywalked to the bus depot.

That day the lady was a brunette, not a blond. The wig didn't mask the wearer. I studied the face I'd seen at Green Gables and the Blue Moon. The face belonged to Ava Hightower. Under the brunette wig was a platinum blonde.

Ava went into the bus depot. A few minutes later, she came out. She carried a cardboard tray of food wrapped in paper. I counted three paper cups. She watched for traffic and jaywalked back the way she came. I got out of the roadster and tailed her.

Inside the hotel, she bypassed the elevator and climbed the stairs. I grabbed a newspaper off a table as I walked by and followed her, pretending to read as I walked. On the second floor, she went down the hall and tapped on a door. The door opened, and she went in.

I strolled down the hall with my newspaper and noted the number on the door, 205. I continued to the end of the hallway. Another set of stairs led to the ground floor. I took the stairs and left the hotel. I returned to my parked roadster.

I tapped a finger on the steering wheel and considered my options. I could go back to Room 205 and knock on the door. I didn't want to spook them. If anyone was armed, I wanted to avoid gunplay.

I had an obligation to Ethan Alexander. I wouldn't call the police. Ethan deserved a chance to help Lopez turn himself in. I decided Ethan needed to talk to Lopez. The people holed up in Room 205 at the McClellan weren't leaving anytime soon.

I was only a few blocks from my office. I took William east to Emporia and went north a block to my office on Douglas. The Lawrence Block Building was usually quiet on Saturday. An attorney or an accountant sometimes put in a few hours on the weekend.

The front door was unlocked that morning. I spotted an open door to one of the offices on the ground floor. I took the stairs to the third floor. The hall was unlit, but even in the dim lighting I could tell something was wrong. My office door had been jimmied.

I entered quietly, not knowing who or what I would find. I was unarmed. My Smith & Wesson .38 was under the dash of my roadster. The office lights were off. I stood in the shadows and listened for sounds from my inner office. I heard nothing, so I crossed the floor and looked in.

My office was empty, but someone had been there. A desk drawer was slightly open. The lock on the bottom drawer had been sprung with a lever. Contents had been picked through, but nothing was missing. I returned to the outer office and turned on the lights. Agnes's desk looked intact.

The door to the closet was ajar. I looked inside. Office supplies and one of Agnes's wraps lay on the floor. I reached for the paper bag. Good old Agnes. The contents of the paper bag looked undisturbed.

I removed the vase from the bag and took it into my office. I unwrapped the vase and inspected it to be sure. Then, I wrapped it in the towel again.

The telephone rang, and I answered it.

"Pete, this is Ethan," he said.

"I was just going to call you. I've found Lopez," I said.

Ethan didn't react to that remark.

"Pete, I'd like you to bring the vase to my place," he said. "I'd like to have another look at it."

That was an odd reply to news he'd been waiting for days to hear. Something was wrong. I played along.

"Sure, Ethan, I'll do that," I said. "I'll have to get it first. It'll take some time. Shall I come by in an hour?"

"An hour will be fine," Ethan said. "Sooner if you can. I'll be waiting."

"See you soon," I said. "So long."

"Stielhandgranate," he said and hung up the telephone.

Ethan's sendoff sealed my suspicions. Instead of saying goodbye, he closed our telephone call with the German term for hand grenade, the potato masher that sailed into the trench years ago and put him in a wheelchair. Ethan was in trouble.

I grabbed the vase and left the office. I'd bought an hour. I'd do reconnaissance at Ethan's place. At Hillside I turned north.

The murder suspects were hiding in a room at the McClellan. Neither Ava nor her companions had broken into my office. Fitzsimmons had tried to play the bad guy, but the role didn't fit. Fitzsimmons was innocent. Hightower was the only person who'd shown an interest in the vase. Hightower was dead. That left one card in the deck, Hightower's accomplice who'd been there all along.

I turned off Hillside and idled around the perimeter of the university campus. I found what I was looking for. The gray LaSalle was parked two blocks down the street from Ethan's place.

I took my ankle holster out of the glove compartment and strapped it on. I reached under the dashboard and freed my Smith & Wesson .38. I slipped it into the holster. I pulled up at Ethan's place and killed the engine. With the fat man under my arm I got out of the roadster.

I was a mouse reaching for the cheese, but I had no choice. Ethan likely had a gun pointed to his head. I had to help him. I knocked on the door and braced myself for the trap to spring. The door remained closed. Ethan's deep voice invited me in.

I opened the door and walked in. I was greeted by the sharp jab of a gun barrel in my spine.

"Hold it right there," a voice said.

"Take it easy, Mr. James," I said. "You wouldn't want me to drop this priceless relic, would you?"

Henry James uttered a harsh laugh and ordered me to turn around. He kept his gun leveled at my midsection. Ethan Alexander watched our exchange from his wheelchair across the room.

"Open your jacket," James said.

I had the vase under my left arm. I unbuttoned my jacket with my right hand and gave him a look.

"I don't bring a gun to visit a friend," I said.

"So, you figured it was me," James said.

"It came to me," I said. "Your gray LaSalle tipped me off. It fit the picture. It matches the gray suit you wore when I called on you in Kansas City. You're a gray man, Henry James."

"It also matches this gun aimed at your guts," he said.

"You have a gold lighter, too. Terrance Hightower used it to light his cigar," I said. "The initial H is embossed on one side, J on the other. Hightower acted flustered when I complimented him on it. He said it had belonged to his father, John Hightower. The lighter belonged to you—Henry James."

"So I have a gold lighter," he said.

"You left it the night you killed Karl Weaver and burned down the art studio," I said.

"You framed Bobby Lopez," Ethan said.

"You left it behind when you hightailed it into the night," I said. "I might've forgotten about it if the lighter hadn't gone missing when you killed Terrance Hightower. You plugged the man and pocketed the lighter. You're a rotten specimen, James."

"You're breaking my heart," he said. "You'll take this to your grave."

"You'll be right behind me," I said.

"What's that mean? Who have you talked to?" he said.

"I talk to lots of people," I said.

"You've got three minutes," he said. "Tell me what you know."

"Tell me why that vase is worth taking lives," Ethan said.

"The vase is worthless," I said.

Ethan gasped. "Worthless?"

"The vase is as phony as a three-dollar bill," I said. "That's why it had to be recovered."

"Keep talking, gumshoe," James said. "The clock is ticking."

"The art that died in the fire was worthless," I said. "Bobby Lopez knew that. That's why he blew the whistle that night. Lopez grabbed the phony vase as proof."

James removed a handkerchief from his pocket and wiped his lips.

"You concocted an insurance scam, James. You planned on burning the art from the beginning. You insured the art with Grant & Gray. You sold the originals on the sly at your business in Kansas City, then you burned the copies."

"All of the art was worth nothing?" Ethan said.

"Karl Weaver painted copies of the originals," I said to James. "You sent Weaver to Wichita. You wanted to keep the dirty work out of your backyard. Hightower played along because he needed the dough. Hightower allowed Weaver to paint in the studio. Your plan might have worked if Weaver hadn't hired Bobby Lopez."

"Karl Weaver was a stupid man," James said.

"Weaver thought he hired a couple of bums to do the heavy lifting," I said. "He didn't know that one of those men had studied art with the best. Bobby Lopez recognized the fakes."

"Weaver never should have hired Lopez," James said.

"Maybe that's why you shot him," I said. "Weaver had outlived his usefulness, just as Hightower did. I may have missed a few of the details, but you can dot the i's and cross the t's when you talk to the police."

"Time's up," James said. "Hand over the vase."

I held out the package and kept a grip on the towel. James held his gun in his right hand and reached with his left. I yanked on the towel. James tried to balance the vase. It teetered in his hand. The vase fell, and I went down with it. James flinched when it splintered into pieces on the bare floor. I pulled my .38 from my ankle holster and fired.

33

I was off balance when I squeezed the trigger, but James was only a few feet away. I didn't miss. He squealed like a pig when the bullet pierced his shoulder. He fell to the floor and cried. I pocketed his pistol and stood over him.

"You'll live," I said and pressed the towel to his wound.

It took several minutes for the desk sergeant to track down Lieutenant Thaddeus McCormick on a Saturday. Mac came on the line and told me he was on the way.

I gave Ethan the number at the McClellan Hotel. Ethan made the call, and after a wait, he spoke to Lopez.

The ambulance and a patrol car arrived just ahead of Mac's black sedan. Mac gave the boys in blue instructions to stay with Henry James. The ambulance and the patrol car left with sirens blaring.

"This is the weapon that took out Karl Weaver," I said and handed James's .38 to Mac.

Mac slipped the gun into his pocket. I gave him a *Reader's Digest* version of what went down.

"I'll need a full report," Mac said.

"Monday morning," I said. "I'll give you everything I've got."

Mac stuck out a bony paw. I shook it.

Ava Hightower arrived with her companions. She was a blonde again. Bobby leaned over Ethan. They spoke quietly.

Ethan hugged Bobby and slapped him on the back. Dunlap stood to the side and looked uncomfortable.

"So, this is the gang every cop in the city has been looking for," Mac said. "Stone here delivered the guilty culprit a few moments ago. You're off the hook for the crime, but don't disappear. I need statements from each of you."

"We'll come to the station," Bobby said.

Mac was satisfied, so he left. Ethan and Bobby made introductions. Bobby squeezed my hand and thanked me. The crowd moved toward the kitchen. I pulled Ava aside.

"Do you remember your childhood neighbors?" I said.

"There was Miss Devlin," she said, "and Uncle Fitz."

"I've spoken to them. They'd love to see you," I said.

The group sat around the table. Ethan and Bobby chattered like magpies. Dunlap listened and laughed. Ava smiled. I walked in and stood next to Ethan.

"Pete, I—"

"I know, Ethan," I said. "We'll talk soon."

I left and drove over to Hillside. Adrenaline drained away and left me exhausted. I needed to heal. I needed Lucille.

I had one thing left to do. I made a couple of stops and bought two items. I mulled over senseless deaths. Most people lived and died, mourned by those they left behind. Others never left a mark and were forgotten when they were gone. Some people lived in the shadows. Those lives counted, too.

I pulled in at the cemetery south of the Baptist church. I made my way to the unmarked plot Ralph Waldo had described. The dirt hadn't settled. I stood over the mound of earth and found myself at a loss for words. I'd never spoken more than a few words to the man when he was alive. Rum-Rum wouldn't have stood still for it.

I leaned over and laid a wreath atop the fresh earth.

"Thanks, pal," I said. "I won't forget you."

In the center of the wreath, I placed a bottle of rum.

THE END

Acknowledgments

Pete Stone and his Jones Six roadster have taken me along on another *Shadow* adventure. As always, I'm grateful to those who've helped smooth the way.

I'm proud of my long association with Meadowlark Press. We've been together since the beginning. I can't imagine better running mates. Thank you, Tracy Million Simmons and 2023 Emporia State University intern, Emilie Moll, for your friendship and support.

Dave Leiker created the cover art for this book, just as he has for each *Shadow* story. Thanks, Dave, for waving your wand and working your magic once again.

I'm grateful to Tracy Million Simmons, Cheryl Unruh, and Monica Graves who read early drafts of the manuscript. Each one made suggestions that improved the story. Thank you all.

Finally, Dear Readers, thank you for your continued loyalty to Pete Stone and the *Shadow* series. Your comments and encouragement keep the ideas coming and the ink flowing. I appreciate you.

About the Author

ichael D. Graves created the character of Pete Stone as a memorial to his grandfather. The first and the third in the series were selected as Kansas Notable Books: *To Leave a Shadow* (2016) and *All Hallows' Shadows* (2021). *All Hallows' Shadows* was also the J. Donald Coffin Memorial Book Award winner by the Kansas Authors Club in 2020 and a silver medalist in the Midwest Book Awards in 2021.

Mike's writing has appeared in *Cheap Detective Stories, Thorny Locust, Flint Hills Review,* and elsewhere. He is an author of *Green Bike, a group novel,* along with Kevin Rabas and Tracy Million Simmons. He lives with his wife in Emporia, Kansas. They are both members of the Kansas Authors Club.

When life conjures its riddles, Mike turns to back roads and baseball for answers.

Meadowlark

FICTION

Books are a way to explore, connect, and discover. Reading gives us the gift of living lives and gaining experiences beyond our own. Publishing books is our way of saying—

We love these words,
we want to play a role in preserving them,
and we want to help share them with the world.

PETE STONE
— Private Investigator —

serving Wichita since 1937

To Leave a Shadow

Shadow of Death

All Hallows' Shadows

Shadows and Sorrows

by Michael D. Graves

Meadowlark Press
— since 2014 —
meadowlarkbookstore.com